Lost In Red Mist

Sandeep Dahiya

Invincible Publishers

First published in India in 2016 by Invincible Publishers

ISBN: 978-93-86148-26-1

Invincible Publishers
F-55, Sushant Lok II, Hong Kong Bazar Lane Sector 57, Gurgaon-122003

Opposite Kasturba Ashram, Radaur Distt Yamuna Nagar, Haryana- 135133

For

Ma and Pa, Uncle Satbir, Manju and Pardeep, Sudesh and Uttam,
Amit, Saifiya, and Nevaan
Special thanks to Jeena Majumdar for editing the manuscript

O Mother,
My first footstep lies in thy womb,
From such a start,
How can I go wrong?

...and finally the sun has to smile to drive away the particles of darkness clinging to the twilight mist, for life, for love, for happiness...

Foreword

* * *

Ordinary beings possess extraordinary potential to win against odds, to jump over hurdles, to smile over tears, and, most importantly, to be happy when there aren't enough reasons to be. They are the faceless constituents of a massive commonality. They are surrounded by a swiping generality. They are coloured in the monochromes of mundane reality. Still they are special. We have to acknowledge and celebrate the extraordinary in the ordinary people. I see heroes and heroines in my simple characters. They fight, and oftentimes fail, but write a little passage in the infinite book of life: an ordinary life that was lived substantially. On the small stage of life, they live very intensely. Somehow, the world would not be the world that is still beautiful without their contribution. They heave humanity onwards in its march to some better destination.

She is a courtesan fighting for a respectable identity in the quagmire of degenerated nobility, wars, intrigues, debauchery, lust, and, last but not the least, love.

She is a foreign tourist in India—raped—picking up the fragments of her violated self, walking with bruised honour, her innate goodness intact, to reach the house of justice to salvage her identity, to redeem her pride.

A circumstantial pawn in the checker-work of sex trade, she passes much of her youth in the muck of lust and flesh trade, to finally redeem herself, to free herself in her forties, to begin a new life.

Kashmir is burning and in the bigger fire are smouldering little worlds of common hopes, mundane dreams, routine aspirations and regular cravings.

He is huge and lifts unthinkable weights for a living, goes on living and lifting weights only to be crushed by circumstances.

On a badly stomped platform, he gathers the nameless pieces of his dusted identity to have a name, a face, an identity of a common person belonging to the normal world.

In the Tsunami ravaged Andaman, she, an Australian

anthropologist, survives and looks with hope at the remnants including the sole surviving Shompen tribal.

On the devastated eastern coast of India, he, a mere kid, takes the onerous task of caring for his still smaller sister, while the world around seethes in chaos.

He dreams big from his small village, only realizing later that the dreams which grow in disproportion to one's circumstances are as good as nightmares.

He, an old man staying alone with a cat, patches up the holes in his present through tales of the past, to survive, expecting a painless end in the future.

She, a Western tourist at Rishikesh, opens her spirits, while a whole world drags around her feet.

The Shadows of Love

* * *

These were languid days somewhere in the last decade of the eighteenth century. Time and its trappings seemed eager to shed old feathers for a new plume. A new century was beckoning with amorous pout. In April Lord Wellesley, busting with fiery pragmatism, had arrived at Madras. During the century just about to bid adieu, the firm foundation of British conquest of India had been laid. The enigmatic checkerboard was full of ploys and pulls. Internecine struggles among the successor states after the Mughal break-up had created a dangerous and fatal mist of intrigues in which late Mughals, Afghans, Marathas, Rohilla Chiefs, Jats, Rajputs, and Nawabs of Oudh battled for supremacy in north India. Power, the seductive songstress, was calling shots. The ensnaring temptress was attracting human passions to grab land, power, and prestige with malicious excitement.

In the south meanwhile, Mysoreans, Marathas, and the Nizams provided ample scope to the East India Company to further set its political designs on firmer grounds. The Portuguese had been left innocuous by this time. In their amicably shrewd manner, the Dutch and the French for some time made the scene even murkier pulsating with political ambitions. In a nutshell, mother India had been impregnated with the semen of colonialism. The favourite child was to grow in its full reformative and exploitative form.

Exponential sequence of British control over Indian Princes took firm foot-hole under Lord Wellesley. Robert Clive, Warren Hastings, and Cornwallis had done enough spadework for Wellesley to start a subsidiary alliance system on an aggressive scale. The imperialistic Governor General's hot-headedness found Tipu Sultan bowing out forever on May 4, 1799. Nizam, the ever-swinging pendulum among Marathas, Mysore and the English, was offered some territories from the vanquished empire of Tipu Sultan.

In this mild winter of coastal southern India, English supremacy was taking energetic yawns to welcome the new century. But these bright sunny days interlaced with gentle and sometimes torrential showers of N-E Monsoons tried to allay all intrigues at the crossroads of empire-building adventures and misadventures. This fine weather had to be utilized for the propagation of the Governor General's imperialist designs.

The company had started by lending troops to friendly princes; then they took to field-sharing for common interests with the native states; still later, the native princes provided money for training and maintenance of wholly British army units. Now the Governor General wanted the protected Indian states to abandon all foreign relations to them allowing subsidiary British force in the heart of their territories. For their upkeep, some territory had to be provided to the British whose revenue would be used for operating the company.

Nizam-ul-Mulk had died in 1746 and his son Nawab Nizam Ali of Hyderabad had witnessed almost half-a-century's ascension to sovereignty by the trading company that was now becoming a great political power. The French had intrigued with the Nizam, Marathas, Scindhias, and rulers of Mysore and the Carnatic region to upstage the surging British supremacy. In between had been the hot-beds of court intrigues with the Marathas and Mysore. Pax-Britannica-lorn Company was playing cat and mouse with the rulers to extend its dominion from sea to sea across the peninsula. Old, helpless, and wizened Nawab knew that he himself and his fellow native rulers were mere incompetent cogs in the whole scheme. For 50 years he had explored every possible alliance with every possible survival technique—betraying others before they could betray him. His illustrious father, the kingdom maker on the ruins of the Mughal Empire, had settled deep in the south to escape the horrific degeneration among the later Mughal nobility that split royal blood limitlessly while the crown of Hindustan waited for the next winner to grab it.

Nizam Ali knew that the European bayonet fighting techniques supported with field guns were sure to prevail over the traditional fighting techniques of the native rulers. The Presidency towns were progressing rapidly and developing military fortifications supported by an almost free-wheeling and dealing navy. Lord Herbert, Madras Governor since 1794, and his Madras council were doing things that made it look like the sun was rising fresh over the dusky sun-setting ruins amidst chaos across the peninsula.

Way back in 1766 the Nizam had entered into an offensive defensive alliance with the Madras Council. For the next 20 years he was almost an innocuous player in the game among the Englishmen, Marathas, and Mysoreans, being kicked from one court to another. Weak enough by 1788, he surrendered Guntur to the English—his only outlet to the sea—that connected their northern and southern possessions on the Coromandal coast. However, the ever-greedy Madras Government let him down in March 1795 when they watched from a distance while he was humbled by the Marathas carrying their flag with lofty impetuosity. As the Maratha storm was building up to hold him by the throat, he had run to meet Sir John Shore to bring him to action. But the latter was firm-footed with his prudent policy of conspiring only through passivity as more and more intrigues among the native rulers unfolded in the south.

Drenched in pleasure and luxury, Muhammad Ali (died on Oct 13, 1795), the Nawab of the Carnatic, played host to the duo's meeting at his magnificent palace at Chepauk, a tiny fishing hamlet in the suburbs of Madras. Having abandoned Arcot, he was fattening his vanity through blatant show of extravagance and lavishness by borrowing from the company officials at exorbitant rates of interest. More *pagodas* he wasted, lower sank his existence, and still greater became the company's hold over the revenue and administration of his dominion. The old Nawab's motto in life appeared to be: What is the use of loitering knee-deep in the shallow brook of one's passion; go deeper and deeper, throat deep or even drown yourself in the depthless sea of your desires. Omdut-ul-Umara, no longer young and energetic, was almost a mute spectator to his father's pathetic fall to debauchery.

Mir Alam, the Nizam's minister, was almost dying of an urge to have an alliance with the English. He looked at the faces of sahibs like a dog does at its mater. His each pore was taut with goose-bumps to become a cringing lackey of the white men. But Ali Jah, the Nizam's son, appeared to smell the prospects somewhere else. At that time, 'somewhere else' could be easily interpreted as the French, who were ever ready to take up the cause of any native ruler against the British. So the Prince was putting up his nose in air to smell some prospects from the Isle of France, modern-day Mauritius.

Caught in the ironical drone of times it had been a grand and gala affair. It appeared as though before dying in October later that year the Nawab wanted to give a quick summary of his gluttonous festivities. There was amazing amiability in the air. However, there was an undercurrent of frightful expectancy—strong tobacco smouldering in the clay bowls of smoking pipes, oriental nymphs wearing bodice with sleeves and crests embroidered with gold, Company soldiers in red doublets and leather cross-belts; company officials in their ceremonial uniforms and ornamental cloaks, their shoulder seams tight with excitement and pride; stockings, breeches, and doublets of the Company standing in stark contrast to the jewelled fineries and gemmed headgears of the natives. The stout phrases of colonial modernity appeared pulling the creases and folds of silk, satin, and gossamer of the oriental robes of the Nawab, Nizam, their sons, and important ministers.

A special company attired in particularly designed canvas jackets gave the Governor General the Sword of Honour as he came—parading his promptitude—barging in, smelling sovereignty from the sickening smoke of depraved, debilitated oriental air. His jewelled sword-scabbard glinted under the noon sun and stamped the doctrinal emphasis of his plans in the East. Impenetrable self-possession loomed over his features. His jet black boots gave musical screeches as they majestically trampled over the velvety carpet rolled out for him. Scampering and pioneering through the shower of choicest flowers from the Nawab's garden, his triumphant march met a flowery obstacle as a rose got entangled in his shoe buckles. The flowery shackle chimed with scared intonation. His Excellency's jaunty dignity halted to catch the fleeting moment. The silver-laced buckles coiled the rose like a mating snake. The beautiful hand, the gentle thrower with honeyed poise, was still hung in air. It was a landmark time carrying harmonious subtleties. The fleeting moments stopped to pause in amazement.

A flower at his feet! Fascinating exactitude of the incidental happening sashayed an intimated silence on the onlookers' faces.

The cocky, shrewd professionalism drawn stiffly around the Englishman's mouth turned to an appeased curve and then changed to a smile. There was a languid dissipation of stony protocols. Abandoning his majesty, the Governor General was just about to stoop down for it if not for the aide-de-camp in his staff holding a colonel's rank who beat the top boss in agility and got tiny stem off its silvery noose and proffered it to His Majesty. The latter even more surprisingly held it against his nose and had a full glance at the beautiful thrower as he crossed her. Her image stabbed him like an enchanting female does to a male. It was beyond ranks, race, and religion. Plain instincts! Taking out the ostrich feather—gifted to him by a seafaring Knight friend whose overblown spirit and energies had found him waddling in African and oriental deserts—he braced its tip against her scarlet red blushed cheek. Her face lit up with a beatific smile of feminine triumph over masculinity irrespective of race, colour, ethnicity, and rank.

The Governor General was a very shrewdly tailored warrior-politician. He took every step with utmost care and caution. Somehow the swift horses of his polished tongue became uncontrolled and exclamation went giddy. It was uncharacteristic of his persona. After all, it is perpetually feasible for the savoury soup of female beauty to put cardinal regularity at a backseat for some moments at least.

The luxurious refinement over her features proclaimed her panoramic presence. Her eyes were mocking, consenting, defying, and proud as if seeking a pleasant punishment.

From the European finery of a tall, strapping blonde with glistening blue eyes, a staffer's wife whose beauty had aroused the basic instinct in him while he was furtively engaged in empire-building, came a jealous rustle of her gown. Looking into her eyes, he promptly declared:

"Whoever gets the flower gets her kiss!" His Excellence threw the flower with guttural pronunciation.

It was incredulous. He betrayed a dazzling spendthrift air—an exceptional easy-aired moment. Many hands were raised for the grab even at such a short notice (mostly European) because among the natives only the translators understood what had been proposed.

Robertson, the young lieutenant of the company manning the fort batteries at Madras had not raised his hand to grab the petalous trophy. His handsome face appeared lost somewhere far. He had not seen his lover for two years and during this period his pining love for her had increased exponentially. With perfumed, honeyed breaths his soul gasped for his lady love's touch. He carried her well-drawn and safely framed little palm-sized portrait in his pocket. Quite incidentally, the flower hit his pocket having his lady's portrait and instinctive suppleness of his hand cupped to prevent it from falling. It was like His Majesty had thrown something for him to catch and he just followed the instinct to grab it and make him happy. Immediately it was followed by a long round of applause. Meanwhile, Muhammad Ali's translator told him about His Majesty's little jaunt with tongue. Defying all decorum, the Nawab's pathetically over-sized portly figure hit the diwan's soft gravity-defying plane as if it waited for this very opportunity. In heightened disdain with ranted and cascading breathing, his puffed up eyes threw silent, impotent obscenities at the foreigner. But he had to maintain the decorum of unfading smile on his lips. His heart was almost stabbed. And why not! After all, Swapnasundri was the most prized possession of the Arcot court. The crest jewel of the royal dancing troupe, she was an unparalleled picture of beauty and poise in her lithe movements, features, and body contours. A mere look at her was sufficient to satiate many passion-aroused souls. The spirited sunshine and facetious charm of her body and movements suffused the court with continual bouts of amusement. Her masterly tact and regally swift swirls literally fanned away death and despondency from the old Nawab.

"His Highness has no right to tatter our *ijjat* like this!" the debt-driven Nawab blabbered to his interpreter.

At this age, his feet dangling in the grave, he made love to her through his eyes and his lusty touch gratified him more than anyone else even during the heyday of his youth. After all, sex is in the mind and its gratification takes convenient shapes as one grows old. His consumed, decimated body came back to life as this rejuvenating spring of youth sprayed its watery mist on the dried desert of his physique. Her smoothly gyrating curves sent jitters down his bent spine, making him tauter and upright for more debauchery to follow. He was addicted to her visage and it was only due to this type of addictive liking that her honour was almost safe in comparison to other girls in the royal dancing party. Her strictly guarded luxuriant chamber had enough defence to thwart any wavering eyes of any courtier of any designation. Only prince Omdut-ul-Umara had succeeded in penetrating the silky veils of her bedstead and make love to her almost once in a fortnight. Just this frequency was manageable given the Nawab's all-round efforts to keep his flower safe from all prying black-bees. She allowed him to fall over her without giving much in return because her heart beat for someone else. Still apparently she tried to do her best to appease him because she knew that what happened to her just fortnightly could normally happen many times a day by different scions of nobility like it happened to many other courtesans surrounded by barbarous debauchees. So she had to maintain her exclusivity and did it well. The definition of saving your honour varies, given ones position and standing in life. Among the freely available courtesans, it was her sense of honour that earned her respect and safety not available to other girls.

However, apart from the body, the heart also craves to make someone the sovereign of his or her soul. In her case it was a young cavalryman in the select body of Nawab's guards. It was a love of sight, sighing, and cravings—its gurgling impulsiveness chained by their circumstances.

Coming to know what the matter was, Swapnasundri's precariously hanging pride got a furious storm-shake. She felt like any other cheap, commodious, flesh of utility to be sexually devoured by anybody in the court. Tragically pursing her lips, she left the scene. Looking at her unease and sense of dignity wounded, the Englishmen around heaved a pleasant sigh of some relief as if they had already taken an upper hand in cutting down the native blackies to their real size.

Out of sheer courtesy, the Nawab had arranged for the Governor General to sit on the royal, precious-stone-embellished golden chair. More than courtesy it appeared a still potent mortgage in future. His Majesty's thick hairy hands proudly spread over the filigreed arm-supports of the chair. After a few drams of Highland Whiskey, His Majesty turned merrier.

"Nawab sahib, by the quirk of time's sudden ordinance that flower from your garden now belongs to this lieutenant!"

"She represents our court's honour, culture, and tradition," the Nawab tried to put it emphatically but managed to bleat like a helpless lamb.

"He will give her due respect," the top Englishman gave a long, drawling laugh.

"Your Majesty, can we talk about more urgent matters?" Nizam Ali blubbered through his interpreter trying to subdue the glare from his garrulous, sly looks. "The Marathas are baying for my blood. I hope as the Company promised I will receive armed help without any delay," the old ruler already appeared to have surrendered to the ferocious Marathas plundering his territories.

"O yes...Nizam Sahib's case deserves more seriousness than discussion about just courtesans," His Majesty seemed to have come to administrative matters all at once. "I hope the young lieutenant won't take to his heart if we agree not to force down the providence's verdict of drawing her out of the rotting harem and put her in an orderly attic for some civilized lovemaking," he again gave into the tease of light moments puffed by the whiskey and laughed garrulously patting his thighs.

Deep in the secret recesses of his old debauched self, Muhammad Ali used choicest foul words, but kept a well-meaning smile on his haggard features. He needed to raise more loans from the Company so had to grin condescendingly at whatever His Majesty chose to say at this moment.

When it was time for the treat of the affair, the exotic dance by the royal troupe, the most splendorous feather, Swapnasundri, was missing. However, not having much clue about the traditional Indian dances, the half-drunk British enjoyed this gathering of oriental women sashaying their curves and movements of limbs to the tunes of sitar, drums, and *shehnai*. While the prominent Company officers, members of the Madras Council, Governor of Madras Lord Hobart imbibed their spirits in wine, Swapnasundri, considering her pride tattered by a foreigner, had taken a decision to leave the Nawab's court. She called for the prince of Hyderabad, Ali Jah, and put forward her proposal to become the crest jewel of his harem. Before they left the place stealthily on horsebacks, she left a message with one of her maidens for the dashing cavalryman who made her heart beat many times whenever she came to face him. So, while ribbons and sashes of various ranks lost away their distinction in the drunken merrymaking back at the place of meeting, Swapnasundri was heading to a new palace and court to shower the celestial charms of her movements. Prince Ali Jah, so far sulking morosely in the debauched shadow of his father, was very much enjoying this enlivening adventure in his life. More than her looks, he was enchanted by foul words escaping her beautiful rosy pouting lips against the Europeans. The uncontrolled rapidity of her sweet voice made her appear the carrier of bewitching majesty. With gallant, gay gallops his heart was beating with tantalising excitement. Many a time he adjusted his gold and silver embroidered gown. She was looking at the new prospects with imperturbable ease. The way she held herself appeared to subdue the poetic enfoldment of her softer sex; instead some majestic tact oozed mysteriously from her hardened expression.

All tired and mired in feminine sweat, from a distance she looked with fresh vanity at the ramparts of the Hyderabad palace. When the palace gate's locking bar was raised to welcome this new addition to splendour and luxury, even the armed guards around the gate could not help being mesmerised by this new ray. She was exquisite. Just from the mere first look one could sense the class and contours of her exclusivity. The prince's middle-aged overblown physique shook under a thunderous wave of lust, love, and excitement for this new diamond of his harem. His hand slid around her waist. But she was no ordinary concubine. Swapnasundri was different. She was witty and she knew how to manage the lust-blinded males around her. She knew that the exclusiveness around her blew from direct inaccessibility and rare exquisiteness—the uncommon instinct to spare herself from becoming a commoditised courtesan. She could very well access the value of her favours and knew exactly what she had to be given in lieu of these apart from respect and dignity. She proudly drew away his hand as the strong tortoise-shell embellished wood and iron-work was bolted again behind them. Helplessly the prince could only caress the precious ruby on his sword hilt. Sensing suppliant lust in the prince's demeanour, she flatly refused to be lodged in the harem quarters reeking with the odour of unchecked sex and orgy.

"Very well, you deserve a better place surely!! Indeed, eh!" she had already taken a firm grip on his senses with her furtive, fleecing, escaping manoeuvres.

She was led to the section where there were ivory-panelled doorways leading to a spacious chamber exquisitely decorated with colourful draperies, silk curtains, and marvellously carpeted floor. All worn out of tiresome journey with a sigh of relief, she threw her feminine weight on the divan inlaid with precious stones. In tumultuous enthusiasm the prince rolled his multi-ringed fingers over his paunch bulging under gold-worked and intricately embroidered ceremonial cloak.

In the days to come, the prince's lust-smitten concrete steps to impregnate the soft, wily, pleasantly contriving curtain of her feminine refrain were thwarted by the increased threats of Maratha attack and the Britishers' lukewarm response to the pleading of their partner. Meanwhile, after getting her message through the court maiden, the real prince of her heart deserted his armed unit and reached Hyderabad. The feminine secrecy in her apparently innocuous physique was sufficient to get him inducted in the royal cavalry guards stationed inside the palace. She had played her cards very smartly and hence could very well avoid invoking the prince's jealousy on account of this favour of hers to the deserter.

Nothing substantial changed for the nobility. There was the very same interminable indulgence in pleasures defined by riotous debauchery and wincing orgies. Very soon the Maratha menace was at their doorstep. In the battle of Kharda (1795), the still left respect and dignity was tattered to dust due to the Englishmen's neutrality. Swapnasundri's real prince's valour did not go unnoticed. He fought bravely. Pushed to the brink of survival, the Nizam called for French help and under a fearful secret arrangement with them paid for the maintenance and training of 14,000 men under French commander Francois Raymond. As astute in court intrigues as in warfare the French commander was consolidating a pro-Tipu, pro-French, and anti-British party at the court. Minister Mir Ali, the main English pawn in the court, was the chief stumbling block in his scheme.

While whole of the Hyderabad court was mired in these intrigues, Swapnasundri became the sole strain of sanity and relaxation as she carried the mighty task on her slanderous shoulders with finesse and surprising dexterity mixing her artful dance and coquettish manners with sound scheming logic of her brain. Much to the forgetful delight of the dispirited nobility and debauched royalty, her dances in the Rang Mahal took them to a world of oblivion where they could for solacing moments forget the tattering realities biting the very existence of the state. Once in a month, the mighty balconies of the amusement hall were thrown open for the common masses to sip the nectar of her gracious movements and eyes moving to express uncountable expressions. Her beatific, rapturous smile drove away gloom from thousands of eyes.

As the queen of courtesans and dancer beyond any skill known to anyone else in the state, she knew how and where to spend her favours and extract the advantages almost as per her will. She allowed Prince Ali Jah to make love to her only in lieu of most special purposes and motives. He was almost her puppet. She knew exactly well how to pull the cords. The strong female in her had the out-worldly nymph-like dexterity to ensure a smooth ascension into the arms of the real prince of her heart without arousing Ali Jah's suspicion and jealousy. She knew she was playing with fire. But the heart's cravings are unstoppable and she very well took the risk. She had enough contrivance in her kitty to keep their love-making sessions unknown even to the closest of her female attendants.

Under Francois Raymond's clever leadership and training her lover rose smoothly through the ranks. His capabilities had tremendous prospects and these were polished rapidly by the Frenchman. Fortification of the capital was going on. Recruitment and discipline in the army showed satisfactory trends. The prince of her heart became the main stay of Hyderabad weaponry in subjugating and punishing the refractory tributaries and chieftains.

Although she was leading very much of a public life, she appeared majestically inaccessible. Powerful resonance of her seductive charms and vibrant audacity of self-respecting will power created a halo around her persona. Exponentially fuelled by her hate for the Britishers, Swapnasundri became the ringleader in the pro-French party at the court. Mir Alam was their main foe. He was ever coiled around the Nizam and sang him lullabies of British prudence and competence. Like a child sometimes the Nizam rolled in her lap and she like a firm mother in all control ranted out her overflowing condemnations of the Britishers, the old ruler just meekly ogling at the movement of her bewitching lips. Her monumental charisma assured his ruffled and scared soul during such moments.

Her prince charming was now an officer leading a trained and disciplined company of musketeers. The sight of him leading his company of 90 infantrymen in a parading and saluting position in front of the Nizam gave her the happiest and proudest moments of her life at the court. The Frenchmen too, almost all of them voracious guzzlers of champagne and terrible eaters of roasted ducks, admired her beauty and dancing skills. To them she stood out as somebody worth taking seriously amidst all that appeared inexpressibly ridiculous.

There was clandestine communication with the injured lion of Mysore, Tipu Sultan, with the prince of the Carnatic and with the French General, Perron, who maintained Daulat Rao Scindhia's 40,000 army under his well-meaning, disciplined command. Apart from these court intrigues, French privateers, pirates, cannon-laden merchant ships with ruffian crew members, as well as those carrying legitimate company ensigns were also in touch and part of the French scheme ably directed by the Governor of the Isle of France in the Indian Ocean. Their combined effect had become a menace to the Britishers in the Indian Ocean. Revolutionary wars back home had given a storm push to the French fight against the Englishmen in the East.

The Captain-General of the French in India was furtively trying to win over as many Indian allies as possible. Under his initiative a secret meeting was arranged in the wild tracts of Central India in Scindhia's domains. It was the area once occupied by the Gondwana kings during old times. The campsite was chosen in a grove of teakwood. Nature showered its bounties through small rain-fed rivers, lakes, and sambar, cheetal, and neelgais frolicked freely, barking deer galloped, hyenas hooted, jungle cat walked stealthily, sloth bear slumbered contended, and tiger, leopards, and cobras roamed menacingly. Through utmost secrecy, the French Captain-General invited Daulat Rao Scindhia, Perron, Raymonds, Prince of Hyderabad, and Swapnasundri. They hoped to hatch a concrete plan for the British expulsion from India. Time seemed appropriate to exploit John Shore's relative neutrality in Indian affairs. Further, a plan for the overthrow of the old Nizam by his son was also taken up. The old Nizam had this incurable malady of licking English boots despite their numerous let-downs. When it became apparent that the pro-British party led by the minster Mir Alam had reached the brink of success, the prince and Swapnasundri decided in finality to ease the old ruler's fragile shoulders from further carrying the burden on this treacherous path.

It was 1797. The pro-French party fought well. The prince of her heart would have definitely beaten the sagging and dispirited loyalists of the old ruler if not for the Britishers who suddenly arrived on the scene. Tormented by love-pangs for his fiancé back in England, dashing lieutenant Robertson fought with extreme ferocity. While Rahim Khan, the Muslim lover of the fairy of Hyderabad court, was led by the love-promptings of his lover's celestial charms. He led the charge against the Englishmen with equal vengeance. In this war of swords, spears, axes, cannons, pistols, and muskets, dangerous, heterogenic, and chaotic meanderings of a shocked and bleeding time brought Robertson and Rahim Khan face to face in a life-to-death sword duel. Blood in their eyes told each other that it had to be necessarily a fight till finish. Rahim khan was a classic sword fighter. Just as he was about to finish his fallen rival, a musket ball ripped through his bubbly heart. The valiant fighter collapsed on his back. Bruised and lacerated, Robertson saw his enemy dying. The handsome dying soldier kissed the precious ring on his finger and when the last breath was forced out of his collapsed body he gasped aloud "Swapnasundri".

This name had become a thorn in the English flesh. Her angst and hate for Britishers had become an issue of helplessness, sarcasm, bubbling intrigues in the English camp. After that incident even Robertson had become the butt of many jokes about her. The repertoire of these jokes increased over time as did her role in the French intrigue machine. On the impulse of a vague instinct he freed the ring from the dead soldier's finger and wore it as a war trophy. He just wore it; a simple impulse without any greed or malice. He knew that only providence had saved his life, so in the heart of his hearts he was aware that it was no winner's take-away. It was indeed the dead heart's symbol of love for the famed dancer. She had herself put it on his finger as the undying token of her ever-existing love for him. This token carried many dreamy descriptions of their secret love-making sessions. Looking at it through the corridors of his war-numb senses, the image of his lady love surfaced sending down sweet-sour pining pangs through his war-battered body. His blood-drenched fingers braced his doublet pocket carrying the portrait of the queen of his heart.

Now when the most valiant fighter had fallen, the pendulum swung and the revolting army was systematically routed by the combined forces of the Nizam and the Britishers.

Before she could be arrested by the victorious party, Swapnasundri escaped into the forests. Not able to accept this blot on their victory, Mir Ali launched an all-out search to capture the famed lady. He seemed crazily drawn to suppress her regal flamboyance. Very much eager to have a relook at the face of this charming foe, Robertson led a party to arrest the coveted lady. He had not forgotten that look of feminine pride almost two years back. With much reinvigorated self he carried his red-doublet attired soldiers through the thick green foliage.

Swapnasundri, the nimble footed dancer of unparalleled classic grace, exotic postures, and scintillating persona, was now on the run. Her gold-encrusted leather sandals with gold studs along the sides firmly locked into the metal straps of the saddle belt. A precious-stones-studded locket was bumping against her heaving bosom as her horse galloped carrying her mythical weight. Then one of her attendants in a linen night shirt and cap—probably a French Infantryman's cast off—fell headlong from his horse as a musket ball hit him around ear. Her soft curvaceous body safely hidden beneath the silky folds of her flamboyant oriental finery shivered at the bloody scene.

Robertson, the tall young lieutenant with piercing blue eyes was on the scene. What a tough career he was pursuing here in the forests of

Asia! Away in his native land he grew up on a culturally rich diet of school choir, festive finery on Christmas, and Scottish and Polka dances in his school. He was fairly talented and suitable to fall deeply in love with a lady of fair morals in a circus troupe who sang Greek songs of love to him. However, his was a conservative upper-class family where the baton of maintaining the legacy of courage and conviction was handed down the generation; where the historical—but tragically unfulfilled—ambition had been to win Earldom and coveted titles like OBE (Officer of the Order of British Empire). The spreading tentacles of colonialism were opening new vistas for such talent. So instead of becoming petty, secure personnel in the Company like the desk clerk, they preferred arm-bearing.

The peak point of their lineage had been achieved by his great grandfather who rose to a prestigious position at Bombay fortification. During nights his eyes were awake like the keenly burning watch-fires ever eager to spot the gleam of Portuguese sails in the Arabian Sea; while his fort batteries ever eager to catapult cannon balls on any naval frigate sneaking into the Bay where the Company ships were docked. He had a strong knack for recognising the incongruities of colours on gun-ports, hulls and the consequent mismatching of crown flag and Company ensign thus marking out Dutch East India Company vessels, Portuguese privateers, and pirates. He had honed his skills to give prompt orders with the precision measuring to a fraction of a second to his gunners. He dined with prestigious native families under chandeliers on tables glittering with oriental crystal. The handsome Englishman had plum shades of sensuousness over his battle-hardened features. In the breezy, warm, and moist weather he had a raging affair with a young Parsi female from an upper-class business family in Bombay. She would arrive in her stately carriage. His grandfather was a ship commander in the Company's naval squadron at that time. A real seafarer his galleon had laid anchorage at so many different points that the hull of his ship boasted of planking made of different wood ranging from pine, oak, teak, sal to any type capable of breaking sea ravages. He had become an important instrument in the British scheme of sea intrigues. In the skirmishes off the coast of Diu—little Portuguese island off Kathiawar—all his sea acumen came to be tested. The Portuguese won the loyalty of their neighbours, the Siddhis of Janzira. It was a maritime warrior tribe of African origin. Their culture and music were distinctly shaped by their seafaring instincts. Just when the British thought they had defeated the Portuguese, from a little island hidden by lagoon reeds came a long volley of musketry. Lead and iron balls and grape shots came all too sudden without any prior hint. Most of the British party was gutted to blood and bones. His great grandfather was the only one who survived. His blood-soaked appearance won the sympathy of Maldharis, the local herdsmen in Girnar stretch of dry deciduous forest and grasslands. They gave him special treatment because of the colour of his skin. He convinced them to take him to the state of Junagarh. Using his experience and cleverness he caught a lion and a leopard to present to the Maharaja. Meanwhile, he drew the images of a cheetah, peacock, and boar on the parchment paper he carried in his canvas bag. In spirit-easing solitude he secretly made love to Maldhari women at nights while jackals hooted around mischievously. But then his frisky horseplay was stalled. From the tumultuous cusp of his orgasm he was pulled into the faulty shades of death. Just a day's journey away from the Maharaja's palace he was brutally murdered by an envious young man whose girl he was enjoying that night.

His fate unknown, his son and then grandson tried to build the family prestige on land right there in England. But this safe anchorage in the safe waters of headland's lee bored the latter and he sent his son to the oriental lands before the young man would have wasted his life on a petty circus girl but not before the revolting young man got engaged to her in secret. When he set on sails he promised never to forget her till his safe and earliest return; when he would just lay his sword and shield to rest and enjoy the lovely loneliness of their marital bliss. It was a summer-scented day and melodious wind was whispering in his ears egging him to eat the forbidden fruits. However, the marvellous myth of chastity was written too emphatically in terms of norms. Furtively fluid gush of passion was checkmated and the ominously smouldering lust changed to an ethereal kiss. They parted with fragmented dreams of a happy future after his return.

Swapnasundri, the fair-hipped maiden, who rested under the feminine whiffs of air born of shiny flywhisks, was now under dark, masculine gusts of enemy seize. They had heard so much about her. More than anything else their eyes were full of curiosity, wonder, and amazement at this female who had become almost mythical on account of her beauty and talents.

Realising that her small band of armguards would be easily decimated by the Englishmen, Swapnasundri forbade them from falling into any foolish bravado. One of her guards was wearing a blue French doublet. A young sergeant in Robertson's company spat an obscenity and shot him in the head. He did it without even sparing a look at the company leader's face. Robertson thundered to discipline him. She was arrested and taken to Madras fort. Meantime, with extremely impartial look at the offender, he handed a roll of wax-sealed parchment paper to a native footman. He untied the red ribbon and read out the charges against the famed damsel of the Hyderabad court. The Nizam, now totally under British control, had promptly issued a death warrant against her. There was an air of extreme defiance over the misty strains of her exquisite features. Their eyes met. She looked at Robertson with strange pride. Her look still seemed to chase away the looming strains of subjection, servitude, and submission. Her dark eyes explored the bluish depth of her captor's. In the sepulchral silence of that moment she caught that flashing moment when his hands had grasped that flower. That was the breaking moment from the former court. The declaration had stabbed her ego. A faint smile seeped from the corner of her luscious lips. It was as though she airily proposed something. A strange serenity was spread around her persona. He could feel the power of her charms. In discomfort he just looked the other way when they arrested her.

Manacled like a criminal and lying in her dark stone cellar she heard the military band of victory and arms of honour for the young lieutenant. Massive stone walls and redoubts made of masonry hewn from the rocks of plateau made her soul cringe with pain at the realisation how much the foreigners had strengthened themselves at the cost of local resources and traitors' support. Inside the slave-like cubicle in the basement of the massive fort she was pushed against cold stony walls with shackles screwed almost to her womanly bones.

Robertson had a good grasp of Latin and apart from that he knew some common sayings and smattering phrases in Dutch and French. His two years of stay in India had added dozens of more native words, so that he could understand some, made others understand as well through his keen linguistic skills accompanied with frantic gestures. The beautiful conspirator who had been imprisoned in a slave cellar haunted his conscience. Such had been the force of mocking defiance on her exquisite features that he could not help going to see her. He was driven more by curiosity to see this interesting persona. She was totally unlike what she was supposed to be. Her beauty was bewitching. She was supposed to be satisfied with seducing men around. But she carried untraditional sense of respect for a lady of the court. More importantly, her motives reached beyond the world of dancing and carousal. She appeared like a bright ray of guiding light in the darkness devilishly dispersed around. When they had arrested her she was solemnly composed and sedate resignation in those big dark eyes pulled his being with a strange magnetic force. That look of utter free will and independence even made her holding onto some mysterious egotistical whim. It was completely unlike other natives who psychologically deprived themselves of self-respect and confidence to get scared of Englishmen, hate them in secrecy, or cringe before them to draw favours. He felt she was above all this. He could very well sense that steadfast demeanour amidst the wild revelry. Her spirit appeared ultimately pristine. He knew that she had recognised him as the flower catcher. At that time the narcissistic strains oozing out from her curvaceous body seemed to declare to this world that her sense of self-respect could not be touched even by the superior coloured race. He himself carried the traces of a white man's burden to evangelise the less-cultured oriental world. He had been victorious in that battle. His ego murmured with complain. After the victory, his ego had exponentially expanded. With her exuberantly feminine grace she seemed to subdue his sense of victory. However, in chains she wasn't defeated in the conventional sense of the term. He felt an irresistible urge to overpower her sense of pride. He reached her cellar with a vague sense of punishing attitude. The battle and the related happenings and mishaps had laid bare the secret of her love affair open by this time. He knew he possessed the ring of her lover.

"This butterfly will find herself on flames as soon as she sees the ring of her lover!" he had a strange convulsion in his body to somehow see her cowering down like a broken female pleading for mercy, seeking favours for life.

"Swapnasundri, that cowardly lover of yours, was killed by me in straight man-to-man fight," he declared flaunting the war trophy on his finger. He didn't look her in the eyes. These were too proud. Moreover, his soul wasn't that incorrigible enough to speak a lie to torment somebody and still look into the eyes with cold-blooded muse.

What remained still unbroken inside the crystal palace of her heart came crashing down under the force of this utterance. Tears welled up in her fiery oval big eyes. The unhindered splendour of her majestic persona still shining in chains appeared to melt and flow down to mix in dust around her feet. "More than his death I weep over the fact that he got killed at the hands of a poor English soldier like you!" her native tongue lashed him like a sword cut.

"Calm down my lady! I had stronger claim over you than him. Do you still remember that flower thrown to decide your fate by His Majesty?" Robertson's repertoire of native words and fervently amused gestures conveyed the message.

Through tears she stared at him like a wounded tigress. In the snail-like silence the dreary undertones of her captor's declaration filled her heart with inexpressible sorrow. Of all the fragments of lust-driven love that nobility threw around her, she had secretly gathered a love nest in her heart. It had been broken now. She really loved her soldier. She had to take revenge. In order to sustain her hate for the Britishers she had to play her cards again. The blow was crushing. Struggling against the chains and crying over her lover's death she decided to live afresh and die in a different manner so as to assuage her wounded soul. No blow was sufficient to decapitate and throw her into the pathos of passivity where there was no hope, no reason to live. The wall of this man's character looked breachable to her fuming femininity. Heavily manacled, her rosy weight sagging under iron chains jewelling her coarse-clothed homespun cotton sari she moved towards the cellar bars. Her bare feet took little steps of some vague determination. Her eyes stared at his white face with a mysterious smile lurking around the corner of her lips. Holding the bars she protruded her juicy dry lips. He was almost jutted against the bars. He wanted to move away but a strange magic held him back. She took out her hand and held him by neck to draw him closer. He just helplessly gave in. It was outrageous. It was totally unexpected. He was shocked. Before he could even react in any way, she kissed him. Face to face. A full kiss. It was the lethal kiss of a vindictive hissing female snake. Full of danger and unprohibited pleasure. Its relentlessly cascading effect rippled each and every pore of his skin. Its jolting strike numbed all his senses.

"Swapnasundri settles all dues. Doesn't keep anything due either good or bad. The chance fall of that flower entitled you for the charm of my lips," she had always used her seductive charms to her advantage. "The men in you is more impotent and helpless inside this slave red dress than the female is in me in these thick iron chains," her fragrant breath hit him hard in the face and the tremors went deep into the chambers of his ego, his distinct self, his identity.

There was an uncontrollable surge of feminine power in her eyes. Delightfully vague vistas of her consent would make it impossible for anybody interested in maintenance of morality. He was standing stonily. She looked deep into his eyes. "Swapnasundri chooses to live even in the face of death!" she raised her chin and her lips parted as the gateways of unheard pleasure and sensuality.

"Within a week the tribunal will decide which type of death suits the anti-British tigress in you," he tried to hold onto the ramparts of rigidity, his duty, his status of a winner.

"Eh, liberating death. That would be freedom. How much I myself wish for it than rot in the prison of these rot English people. Do it tomorrow. Why take a week? You will be doing a great honour to be a soldier," her nostrils in a shapely nose were drawn as she hissed out her resentment.

Perturbed by the incalculable hate hovering around her limitless beauty, Robertson walked along the stony corridor. The man in him continued to be mischievously tickled by the robust pull of her sensuality all this while. She had irresistible charm. For sure the battle hard soldier in him had been shaken. It was a sleepless night. Her image was nightmarishly striking at his senses. Her persona was too powerful and on top of that her act had been even stronger. The experience was strangely exhilarating and uplifting beyond imagination. Next day too he could not help going to her cellar.

"Trying to fleece that stone-hearted beauty in chains, eh!" his senior jested.

He just winked in return and said, "I have legitimate claim over her. His Majesty's flower fell in my hands. So I can very well try for the remaining few days of her life," he just laughed it off as a casual remark.

Our basic instincts are much stronger than any logical scheme driven by rules, conventions, and duty. Definitely some changes were rapidly forming up in the young lieutenant's rationality. His line of thinking and emotions had been misaligned from the normal course. Of course the event had thrown an episode beyond all expectations. She had acted totally opposite to her fabled persona during that moment. The firebrand and proud antagonistic nymph had shed her stony inhibitions and touched his love-deprived physical self with the pining warmth and softness of her flowery lips. Whenever he came out of Fort St. George's secret underground chambers reeking with slavish, damp air, he felt the warm tropical fresh air of an open free world slapping his being with contradictory glaring visions. In the mysterious underground corridors the Madras government was spreading its strength by clobbering down all the wrong players coming as rock beds in its sledge-hammering movement on the path of intrigues, wars, and trade. Passing along one of the damp corridors he had crossed the storage vault of ice blocks. Ice had been imprisoned to entertain company officials, convenient free merchants and hobnobbing dealers. The coldness in the air brought him back from the footloose fantasies. It was like the air back home. His lady love's face rose in his conscience and tugged at the moralistic cords. He paused and recalled the parting kiss. It was however too far both in terms of time and distance. The present beckoned him with full force. He walked out into the open tropical air, his conscience in a benumbed slumberous state, and a new experience beckoning him with ecstatic coquettish charms.

His strangely shaken love-cords found him musing, "Charm of East lies in the free air of warm and humid panorama! Alas, ice and flower have been caged!" It was his heart's own-decided outpour, beyond the chains and reach of his reality and calculated judgement.

His love appeared to cast off its old skin and get a new shining one. The surroundings seemed bathed in paradisiacal delight. This experience was beyond all cultural nuances. Today's talk and the look on her face were tormenting his soul. She was smiling resignedly and fiddling with the inscribed bracelet on her wrist. But all the harsh realities had not been successful in subduing the proud vanity of her strong persona. She appeared divine and too cheap side by side. He could not assess why he was continuously thinking about her. And that kiss!? It defied all logical senses. Was there some motivation in it? Was it just a joke, an emotional outpour of a broken heart on the verge of death? What it was, he just could not make it out. Her helpless pulls at the merciless grasp of iron chains made him recall some long forgotten song about a chained flower. Yes, he was continuously thinking about her now. To make it worse, it was more than just thinking. He was feeling for her. He feared the massive wooden rafters, stones, and iron grates would crush the oriental flower any time. He was in this world outside, alive and free. She was there in a dead world, more dead than alive and this flicker would be blown off by predetermined hand of justice in the Fort. Anxiously he looked at the roughly plastered stone walls of the premises and officially authoritative brick masonry of the building where the formalities of her case would be completed leading to the inevitable judgement. He felt a painful shiver serpenting across his spine. Had the fangs of her fake, poisonous love bitten deep enough to intoxicate him, killing his reason and paralysing his senses? He felt alone in the victorious crowd of Company officials, soldiers, free merchants, dealers, and recuperating ship commanders and crew members scampering with ease and joviality. Beneath the place where he stood was the safety vault for gold and bullion—the fruits of colonialism. The little cubicle situated at the end of a long corridor divided into multiple security tiers. Here the Governor let loose a guffaw of ecstasy while he inspected the gold and bullion stacked to the ceilings.

The verve and vigour of these new love-blooms had taken him in its flowery grasp. Walking forlornly he reached the Madras Bank building. The newly constructed building galore with fresh-found financial optimism. The offices and warehouses on the lower floor were echoing with excited voices of traders and merchants. Above them were the halls of free public exchange buzzing with official and unofficial prospects of money outflow through trade, barter, exchange in spice, gold-starred pagodas, gold bars, and bullion. Out on the first-floor balcony facing the Broker's office somebody hollered at the man on the ground:

"Now that the day's lighthouse is all blazing which way does thy ship sail to?"

"No, last night that thing was nicer in inviting me into her harbour than this one," the onlooker yelped from below as the tropical sunrays hit his seafaring face. "So I prefer to stay for cosy anchorage here," he dismissively waved at the lighthouse hovering 90 feet above sea level at the building top.

A man was loudly reading some names from the second storey balcony of the managers' committee room. Robertson raised his eyes in the direction, but instead of the man his attention was caught by the big sign board hanging from the end of the timber beam. "London Coffee-room" it read. Many times he had beaten his homesickness there. But today the malady of his heart was totally different, not to be assuaged by any coffee served there.

Again the chained figure loomed large in his memory. The rebellious undertones oozing from her wounded self were creating ripples in his disturbed self. Today when he had approached her cellar he found her coming out of the tiny wooden cabinet erected in the grooves across the floor masonry. Adjusting the folds of her rumpled sari with chained hands she looked at him from the corner of her eyes. She knew how to pass a message just through eyes. It was a look of crisp summation. It sent the message that time could be infinitely ecstatic, happy, and long with this body if somebody cared to free it, otherwise it will just carelessly run into oblivion. In her solemn grandeur she appeared a queen of silence ruling over men's hearts just through eyes. His heart was beating fast. He was all alone in the crowd. Despite best of his efforts he just couldn't free himself from the tentacles of her charm.

Warmed by fervent coffee an enterprising European big landholder was gesticulating, "If that seditious French-hobnobbing Tipu is obliterated, I'll turn Mysore's tropical slopes into international hub of coffee!"

In fact in the coffee-room more alcohol did rounds than coffee. Coffee, however, was the prominent point of discussion from the traders' viewpoint. Robert Massey, a free merchant, drew out a blazing gold leaf from his breast pocket.

"The Italian harlot liked my love-making so much that at parting she tearfully gave me this present," he thumped his chest.

"Well, here in life, love and loss complement each other," Peter Hughes, a ship commander, philosophically poured out jangling handful of star pagodas to ensure they were still in his pocket. He had the medallion and citation to prove his seaworthiness and efficiency. Many privateers sitting on adjoining tables looked at him carefully, giving him due respect.

Mr. Cassin, a notorious outlaw back home but wayfaring in the East as if on parole to further the Empire's strength, slapped the ebony table; his other hand busy in the unknown chambers of his leather jacket. He took out an ivory case inlaid with flashing gemstones, garnets, and turquoise. Others were dazzled by its costly look. The Governor had given it to his lady love but he stole it from her during last night's banquet. He considered everything fair in love and breaking a law for some profit. Before he could brag something about it, he saw Mr. Nelson, a member of the Exchange Committee, about to enter coffee-room. The well-meaning gentleman stood in the doorway, but moved away as if realising some more urgent matter.

Peter Hughes, the efficient, shrewd commander dealing in spices, oriental fineries, gold, silver, topazes, emeralds, and olivine was lost in the blurred vision of some paradisiacal rich island. As a commissioned privateer he had enough skill to bear the storms of pirates and naval frigates of rival companies in the gloomy waters of unchartered seas. The keel, ribbing frame, and planking of his galleon-cum-frigate had woods from as many destinations as his seafaring spirits allowed him to spread his wings. So pine, oak, sal, and teak—a profitable mixture of Eastern and Western lands—studded his hull and bulkheads. Even now when his ship was standing low in the harbour—indicating heavy cargo—its anchor cable without much strain as the ship was safely docked in the safe waters of the headland's lea. As the light dimly penetrated through the hatches to reach the lower decks, it could barely see the faces of slaves and prisoners in leg-irons in the slave deck. A fortnight back he had plundered a French privateer ship. Cassin had performed remarkably well in this favourite outing. Since their meeting the commander's cargo had been increasing in the holds.

From the tone of their conversation Robertson knew that they could help him. He had already reached a conclusion after hearing their adventurous conversation.

"Would you help if somebody's love is in need?" he addressed the commander.

"Why should we if it does not fetch us any profit apart from the union of two hearts?" his aide, the outlaw, threw back.

"Not even if it comes with plenty of gold and silver?"

Some ears were definitely raised. Promptly the outlaw closed the matter. "We will talk in our skiff at sea."

The commander waved towards two of his boatswains and off they went to the dock and then into the sea to discuss the finer points of the deal. While passing the ship, Robertson read the ship's name on the transom. The man on the anchor watch saluted the commander.

"She is a princess. Her people will pay enough for her release," he tried to befool them.

He could not reveal her identity to them fearing punishment by the Admiralty Law. They will flatly refuse, he knew. So he just discussed the possibility of boarding their ship to reach homeland. Not smelling something too fishy, and taking him love-dazed to the extent of paying any cost in money, the ship commander quipped, "We'll be leaving next week."

Cassin had broken every law of the land back home and the world outside. He had miraculously escaped death many times both in the hands of those authorised to protect law and the people like him ever eager to tear it to shreds. Robertson baited him. They went sightseeing the budding colonial town. Moderately elegant Governor's palace loomed over their head with a vague warning as they walked plotting by its stone and brick walls. An old gentleman, a multilingual interpreter, greeted Cassin as he passed with a European and a native. Standing at the quaint and sleepy market square, they decided to enter a broad dusty side street. After passing a few stores, Robertson confided in him the plan with such friendly audacity and openness that even the outlaw was taken by surprise and did not say much except being drawn into the plan degree by degree, his instinctively law-breaking self-pandering him all along. A rattling carriage went by and the horse taps on the dusty street were swallowed by the disciplined notes of the Drums Corps marching on the Fort premises for a patriotic parade. Robertson knew that the farce and tragedy of her trial had begun that afternoon.

Robertson had proved his mettle for the cause of the Company. Add to it, his demeanour was too disciplined. So nobody suspected anything when he took Cassin with him to meet Swapnasundri. She had been condemned to death on the fifth day from the verdict. Much to their strategy-forming minds it was a day after the scheduled departure of the ship to England.

"The flower deserves all risk for setting her free!" Cassin was itching with excitement. They greeted a medical missionary as the holy man tired in charity in the East crossed them.

Their plan was to take her into the ship just before its sail-off around midnight, for it was a peculiar custom and convention with the idiosyncratic commander to draw off her anchor cable about zero hour to go with her rigging and sails flirting with a night song. Nobody except for them was to know the secret. The jewel was to be hidden in the holds even without knowledge of the commander.

Cassin's options came to a satisfactory stop at a certain Reverent, a famed medical missionary who had the propensity to avert death and pain to any limit if the compensation came to be the acceptance of Christianity by the to-be-relieved being. Cassin, the all-out plunderer, had workable knowledge of Latin, Dutch, French, and Spanish—all the required tools in the mouth of an over-ambitious outlaw eager to spread wings internationally.

For a decade, France was boiling in revolutionary wars. However, the front against the Britishers was left untouched; only its form and character changed. The Ministry of Marine and Colonies was sending military adventurers and nobles at seafront. The merchants, privateers, pirates, and company officials were all acceptable and accommodated as long as they served as the cogs of expansionist designs. Port Luis was being used by the French privateers to disturb English shipping in the Indian Ocean. Hardly a fortnight passed when the rival vessels were not engaged in skirmishes. The Captain-General of the French in India was furtively contriving against the spreading tentacles of Englishmen in India. A good chunk of French nobility had taken to the sea. Back home, the Revolution saw peasants burning their luxurious chateaux. While the last sinews of monarchist France were being uprooted, the surviving nobility was taking to a new form, status, and function.

Cassin had a French confidante named Madec—a vestige of the royal past—a baroque musician who performed in front of the royalty on extravagant sets in the royal halls. But the famed Versailles operas looked unfathomably distant after the blood-soaked revolutionary decade. His patron noble and Madec were at sea when the revolution broke out, so they decided to be seafarers till the storms on the land subsided. Their private vessel very easily became an agent of sea war against the Britishers managed from Port Luis. Just for the sake of old days Madec was training the crew in baroque music, just to have some leisure days to beat boredom on board while their ship rolled in the doldrums. One night when under the spell of moderate champagne his small group was performing under moonlight on the open deck an ugly shape of a galleon approached. Britishers Peter Hughes and Cassin had arrived on the scene. The French vessel was nastily overpowered. Many died and many were taken slaves. The survivors' fate was chained to ringbolts in the bulkheads of the slave deck. Humming his classical music, the musician was the only one who came alive after a month-long journey to the African coast during which the day's only meaning had been tiny gravel in the middle of stew bowl. Before getting off, the survivor was ordered to man the deck pump. Standing in the poop-deck, Cassin saw the surprising effort of those hands. The former musician worked lost in some old tune that he had played to thunderous applause back home. Cassin laughed at the character. Then after a month, while they were enjoying hospitality at a tiny British settlement, the Company slaves revolted and what Madec did then was sufficient to make him a life-long confidante and upkeeper-cum-friend of the famed outlaw.

Reverend Father Alfred Barker was an old ritualistic character. The medical missionary carried enough reputation to force greetings from anybody coming across from the highest to the lowest. He had played an important role in the colonisation of Indian elites. His missionary customerage ranged from the Indian merchant princes to ordinary millworkers. To do something by breaking the systemising fencing was something Cassin's soul ever craved for. Moreover, the last journey had been a nondescript one. Lounging dispiritedly on the deck while the unfilled sails of the ship hung lifelessly in the desperately calm and eerie doldrums, in a mood of criminal boredom he had shouted at Madec manning the whip staff; and handed out an old battered violin ordering to play something more sorrowful than the berating doldrums. To keep his spirits alive, the outlaw was fabulously clothed in period clothing and appeared an archetypical colonial icon. Perhaps he hated to set foot on ground. Whenever they stepped onto any Company settlement, he taught walking on stilts to the children. He was a man of great whims and fancies.

The famous medical missionary got a new ray of life in his old eyes after coming to know about the prospects of converting a rebel native woman. Cassin knew exactly well how to convince Father Alfred, the garrison chief, and the Governor that her belated baptisation should take place in the twilight of the day before her execution. Standing in the stable-yards and hatching the final sinews of the conspiracy, he looked anxiously at the stony ramparts where the watchfires would burn to easily show the big wooden ship cradled, its larboard side facing the coast. He had told the commander that on the evening prior to the ship's departure he would go into the sea in a longboat to catch some fish and would join the ship a few kilometres down the coast. Three storm lanterns burning in the ship's stern galleries were easily spottable. The commander as usual was aware of his useful man's idiosyncrasies and consented as long as the rascal outlaw helped him in their plundering seafaring moves.

The word in the Fort was that the legendary British-hater had fallen for the handsome lieutenant. Before death she was Christening herself to marry him and be his wife for a night. It had satisfied many a British ego. This submission to their faith was even more satisfying than the scenario where she would have fallen at their feet pleading for life. The church was situated north of the Fort. Cassin ordered three of his trusted boatswains to wait by the shore at the nearest point. Much to his excitement he saw a British naval frigate moving up the coast. Its differently painted gunports in the hull seemed to prompt and instigate the lawbreaker in him.

The rebel female warrior was put in light chains for the occasion. In the twilight the horses carrying the prisoner carriage swiftly moved on the dusty road. Robertson, Madec, and Cassin waited with bated breath to strike. Swapnasundri was sitting impassively, her eyes downcast. Whenever she lifted her big eyes she looked only at Robertson. Swaying raylets from the lantern dangling from the carriage roof added a mystic aura to her oriental beauty. Robertson's eyes were continuously set on her. It was sufficient to obliterate the last vestiges of his fiancé back home from his heart. A shudder of horror sauntered across his spine at the thought of the executioner in his dirty canvas apron working the noose around her wheatish neck that one time wore costliest of necklaces and pendants. He was so much lost in the thoughts that he was totally unaware of Cassin's crude jokes about the beauty in the cage.

Tracing the last signs of the day through the barbed little window, he harked the two sepoys inside to stop the carriage. "Why?" they chorused while the one outside sitting by the side of the coachman had a careful view of the coconut grove by the roadside.

"The lady wants to ease herself," Robertson said.

"But we did not hear her saying anything," they intoned a bit irritated.

"She indicated to me through a gesture."

"Haa haa so much in love with each other," they drew out their share of fun in the jokes that were spreading about the two of them.

One of them moved to the tiny hatchet behind the coachman's seat. Opening the wooden slit he let out instructions.

As she sneaked into the coconut grove, the notorious seafarer and his accomplice jumped at the sepoys while the helpless native coachman looked meekly at this strange turn of events among the foreigners. He just sat there obediently holding the bridles. It was not a bloody battle. It turned out to be just a scuffle as the Company sepoys had been caught unawares from such a breath-feeling short distance. There was no chance of using weapons, just jostling and pushing was involved. The three rescuers easily overpowered them. They tied their hands and feet and gagged them. Doing this Cassin thumped the powder flask flanking his left side dangling from a flap in his broad waist belt. Then drawing out his sword from the right hip he moved towards the cowering coachman. The man quietly surrendered and fell at his feet. Prodding his chin with sword end he made him stand up. He never lost an opportunity to miss one more loyal, obedient fellow in his tow. One look at Robertson was enough to pass the message.

"Do you swear by all your Gods to serve this man faithfully as long as you live?" Robertson jabbered in his thickly accented native wordings and disjointed phrases.

Immediately the man started swearing in the names of as many Gods he could recall in those fearful moments. To add to his superstition, Cassin drew gunpowder from the flask and put a bit in the muzzle and asked the man to take a pinchful from it and lick it. He did it without losing time, all this serving to save his life.

"Now I have control over your death!" he guffawed.

It turned out to be the oath of poor native's service to the superior being in front of him.

Tying the horse reins to a roadside tree, they dumped the three men in the grove and moved up the coast to look for the skiff. It was a bright starry night by now. From the bag of his trickeries the outlaw quickly brought out a plucker and set her free. He handed out a man's wear to her and she took it with a new meaning in life. Within fifteen minutes of his blowing a signal whistle his men came running.

Sitting on the oak planking of the skiff she stared at the stars with a strange detachedness. They devoured fish, bread, and bacon while she sat demurely.

"You old fart, you have plucked tons of skin off people's backs with that braided knotted leather whip of yours!" Cassin was joking with the ship's whiplasher.

Looking at the star position, Cassin assessed that it might be the time when the mooring lines of the ship were being removed and her mizzen sails unfurled. So keeping a safe distance from the coast they rowed down the coast. To give a clearer signal, the ship had two extra lanterns on the larboard and starboard allowing the skiff to see it from up or down the coast as the big ship made straight into the sea for supporting fathoms and then move to its right down the coast on its journey around the peninsula.

As they intercepted the ship, Cassin hollered, "Put down the side lights! I want to enter like a thief, for I am a class thief and super outlaw in reality!" He started singing in a bawdy, rowdy tone. Rope ladders were cast down from the ship's entry-port.

"Do as he wants, the bastard is drunk. Otherwise he will create a scene and we will be delayed by an hour!" the ship commander ordered the burly coxswain just about to throw the rope steps and the boatswain chain overboard. Cassin slumped into the hauling chair while Robertson and Swapnasundri gingerly made their way upwards. All their confidantes from the boat were on board by this time and were manning the ropes from above. Under the starlight Madec led Robertson and the disguised fugitive across the deck. He stepped down the open deck hatches to lead them into the stern cabin of the outlaw.

While on the deck, the commander embraced his most useful crewman-cum-colleague. "Feasting in the sea after christening the bride of a night! Hope they are enjoying their sole wedding night in all majesty!" surprisingly there were some traces of irony in the commander's rough tone.

The word in the Fort and the city had been that Robertson would marry the freshly christened prisoner and would next day hand her over to the noose of justice. It had created a strange excitement across all ranks and classes. People were simply curious about the situation. After all, it was such an odd occurrence.

"It was a nice ceremony. Christening and the wedding. Both of them did not seem gloomy. Appeared rather starry eyed for the prospects of a night. Each and every moment of their once-in-life night will be sucked by them with infinite greed and grandeur!" the lewd character in Cassin appeared a bit toned down under the gravity of the ironical incident.

Her beauty shone even more vigorously on Robertson's dazed face. Hiding in the holds she and the deserter talked hesitatingly. But their looks told more than any talk could ever have done. They had a light intake of biscuits and bread. She but had eaten a bigger morsel of freedom. But was it really freedom? She had her doubts. She felt uprooted from all her past. A new life was beckoning. It takes some time to come to terms with your redefined self. All this was unreal like a dream to her. She was gripped by contradictory emotions. The proud female in her knew that her charms had seduced a white man to the extent of turning him a traitor to his people. But here was the man who had killed her lover in a duel. This though would create a stifling admance in her demeanour. She felt like she had cheated her former lover by eloping with his slayer. But wasn't it revenge to uproot him from his identity and take him on an unknown course. He had lost his identity for her. Too big a sacrifice she thought. Despite best of her efforts she couldn't hate him from the core of her heart. In eloping with her he had literally accepted a death sentence if ever caught in the path of law. She hated him—the one who had killed her lover—less than any other Englishmen. She tried to convince herself to hate him and take revenge upon him whenever a suitable chance arrived. But hadn't he killed him in a fight, an instrument where the deed escapes the categorisation of evil or good deed. The warrior in her knew that he was no sinner in killing somebody in a straight fight.

Like the beautiful flower sipping few sips of dew and few quantum of sunlight to shine brightly for the world, she was catching at the slightest straws of hope, of real freedom, of dignity, of respect. She hated the Englishmen. She even hated Robertson for being one of them. But he had cast away literally his whole identity, his British self, to get her freedom, to elope with her. She wanted to love him for this sacrifice. But all this had been too quick, nightmarishly beyond her belief. So she was too shocked to have a logical sense of her position.

Robertson knew that by eloping with her he had opened all avenues of the unsparing law of his land. "I will marry her and raise my family at some nondescript colony in Africa under a new identity," his brain was now settling down to a scheme for the future.

As a court dancer she knew the rules of etiquette and courtesy. And when she sat impassively these just oozed out of her in all their silent majesty. Robertson's shaken and turbulent mind suddenly flashed a vivid image of her fiancé. The image went crackling like a thunderbolt across his being. He remembered how she had sat sewing by the window and he hovered around blowing love kisses. But only love knows its real cooings; its criteria of right and wrong; its choice of one over the other. His aching heart knew that he loved Swapnasundri more than anything and anybody in the world now. Some hidden instinct vaguely settles the predicament regarding any judgemental thought regarding the morality of right or wrong. When you know your truth, you stand by it, and it supports you in return despite all the apparent proofs of your wrongdoing. If not for this, he would not have had the courage and heart to cut all his past, all his identity in one single stroke with a single soulful stroke of love-sabre.

Both of them carried bigger storms inside them than the sea outside. The heaving events had shaken them to the core of their basic values. They remained numb for almost two days. Life but is too impulsive and slowly takes us back in its exciting folds. She was looking at his handsome features. Here was a man who had forsaken his identity for her. More importantly he hadn't tried to win her over physically in lieu of all the losses he had accrued. She could see that it was real love from his side.

He had been so caring, so respectful, and so decent in his manners. Still unsure about her feelings she moved to him and surrendered her much coveted body out of her free will. The fury of all her contradictory pathos oozed out from her rosy lips. She kissed him so forcefully as if to subdue any voice stopping her from moving ahead. He melted under the heat of her passion. She showered all her warrior self in making love. She wanted to forget her past. He reciprocated with equal fury of flesh. Deep in the whirlpools of her oriental sensuality he forgot all fear and apprehensions. After the storm was over their perspiring faces and dreamy eyes said much more than what could be expressed through words. In the sleepy grandeur and after-glow of love-making he whispered in his broken native language to explain the real cause of her former lover's death. She sobbed on his chest. He caringly grasped her wheatish back and kissed her dark hair to assure that he really loved her.

It was the seventh day of their journey. There on the bosom of the Indian Ocean the ever unfolding naval intrigues between the Britishers and the French were far more treacherous than the strongest storm the sea could let loose.

It was the brightest of a noon. The ship's fate came in the compass of a notorious French Privateer. His fathomless character of sea adventure could not stop him from an attempt at piracy in broad daylight. That was how privateers, pirates, and commission holders on both sides functioned in multiple roles ranging from waging wars, committing piracy and trading, all depending on the most suitable chance. Even before the man with telescope perched on the watch-ring at the top mast could shout warning instructions the attacker came hurtling dangerously. It was a wooden behemoth; a type of modified *carack* for long and lugubrious warfare; to wear and tear the enemy through stamina rather than swiftness. It was lethal as this large ship of burden approached furtively from the front. They tried their best to escape. But the wind was such that their escape was thwarted and the enemy's approach was aided. The seaman at the capstan got panicked at the sight of the Hercules wooden monster which through false display of colours and flags had sneaked so close without raising too much alarm.

Battened down deck hatches were thrown open to coordinate the warring parties on the upper deck and the lower ones handling guns. The engineer who was working on pawl and pintle ran and got busy in loading his musket. The efficiency of the attacked ship can be gauzed from the fact that it was the first one to catapult all armoury stored behind its gunports. Tallow candles in the lovers' chamber shook at the ship's recoil.

It was poetic justice as lead balls struck the false flag in the first salvo. After the deafening thunder of guns a pall of smoke, silence, and gloom descended on the scene. It was broken by cries of the maimed and shouts of still intact bodies. However, they had missed the opportunity of first strike. They had aimed too high. The hull and decks were almost safe except for inconsequential markings born of grape shots. Then hell was let loose by the enemy ship. It was astute marksmanship. Hawsers and sails went to pieces. Kegs, casks, and barrels on the upper deck were blown into the sea.

Robertson's reverie was broken. Instinctively his hand touched the ornate pommel of his sword. Rising in a valiant soldierly manner he stepped out. His sword in hand, he moved to his lady love and kissed her lips—a long and passionate kiss. It held them like a magnet and then gasping for breath she had to push his heaving chest to break the floodwaters of his torrential gushing love. Saluting her like she was a queen he ran upstairs. There on the upper deck, despite the havoc wreaked by the enemy's first strike, the crewmembers and the fighting party all had an iron-willed expression to last till the end of their strength. The steely resolve had been apprenticed in years of being together and having borne agonies and enjoyed ecstasies together. Claymores, swords, sabres, muskets, and pistols appeared livelier than the humans wielding these. The game of death and destruction glared through agonised cries, shouted orders, bursts of volleys, challenging swords, puffs of smoke, and angry volleys of filthiest words. Then the planking under their feet shook as the reloaded muzzles spewed vengeance. Most of it was absorbed into the hull of the enemy ship. But their cheers were short-lived as they saw almost a dozen of skiffs being lowered into the sea with the help of thickest hemp ropes and cables. Now the enemy was diversifying, a clear advantage in naval warfare. The second strike from the enemy went into the hull at the level of water-level holds. Water gushed in as the scattered travelling trunks, oak chests and teak tables came flooding with water. Like an afraid gazelle she too laid her nimble hands on a light sword showcased against the bulkhead and came out of her hiding hole. Moving through knee deep waters she found the seamen furtively manning the pump-handles to siphon out the flooding waters. Her beauty struck them like a hallucinating daydream, but the urgency of the task at hand was such that they had to go back to their work in all attention. The cowering figure of a British lawyer in his bow-tie and winged collar almost dropped on her as he ran downwards from the scene of battle. It was the nasty world of illogical injustices above where his jurisprudence had little relevance. Looking at the sword in her hand, he dropped his eyes, trying to hide his cowardly shame.

With her gazelle-eyed mocking look she seemed to urge him to pick up weapons and fight. She had been in contact with many males, hated majority of them and at the most respected some, but had not loved anybody except for the valiant soldier, the prince of her heart. It was a strange new feeling about Robertson. There was a mysterious sense of goodness about him. She respected him for that. More than her own life she was scared for any danger to him. Possibly she could see her love for him through the deadly gunsmoke. A feeble smile surfaced on her dry lips. It was the most passionate kiss she had ever received in her life. It was lifefully given by somebody almost on the brink of fatality after having negated the very life that defined him. Its effect was seeping into her bosom and heart. Out of wartime excitement her sensuous lips started quivering.

An Italian merchant brig, a small sailing vessel, was fleeting from the scene of war. A couple of nautical miles away, the English captain of a schooner hailed the Italian:

"Witnessed piracy fellow! I suppose the French have drawn one more nail in the coffin of our shipping."

Pursing his lips into the announcement cone, the Italian hollered back, "Very soon it might be two if you do not take to your heels! It's again the very same square-rigged three-masted monster! Wonder when will you Englishmen construct something to beat it in strength?!"

The ship mentioned was the crown of French piracy in the Indian Ocean. Without losing any time in commenting on the Italian feedback, the English Captain immediately ordered to change the course of his ship so as to pretend all along his life that he never was near the incident. However, the takeover this time had broken all records of efforts by the French ship. The opponent was a nastily tough nut to crack. Monstrous hull of the attacking ship was tightly secured to the English vessel. Almost the whole of the enemy ship's fighting crew was now baying for blood on the attacked ship's deck. The imposing bulk of the notorious French privateer shone in the bow. His splendid seaman's livery was far more attractive than his coarse features.

His blood-smeared sword that had sliced through many English coats, medallions, and breeches shone triumphantly in the sun. Wearing a black leather eye-path on his decimated eye-socket, he would spare quick side glances with his sole eye, even while his sword cut the enemy's breast. He relished bloodletting as much as he enjoyed his animalistic forays in the sleazy nightclubs with waitresses, dancers, and harlots. Coffee shops and ale houses in the port cities shook at the news of his arrival like he was some ghastly typhoon.

With the swiftness of a tigress, she finished two opponents. For a moment her resplendent aura brought the fight to a standstill as the bright star off her beauty beat even the sun in dazzling the scene. Lowering her head, the sword held tightly by her nimble fingers, ready to take on any attack from any side, she came fighting in Robertson's direction. Then hell broke loose again as the enemy fought with reinvigorated strength as if to grab her as the most coveted diamond in the plunder. Of course this living diamond was far more precious than any form of wealth hidden in walnut chests in the holds below.

The more she fought the more she realised her love for him. She wanted to stay with him as his wife and mother of his children. She had forgotten her past. A new life was beckoning her through all this bloodshed. Their eyes met whenever the moments allowed. Her looks gave him all the strength to fight till the last ounce of his strength. He knew that she was fighting for him only. This mere thought gave goosebumps on his wounded body. Winning her heart was even more satisfying than the prospects of making love to her in the lee of rocky outcrops with all her consenting self under him. However, the inevitable that had been delayed for too long happened at last. The English resistance broke as Cassin fell as dramatically as he had lived. Peter Hughes lay half dead at the point where formerly he used to watch his helmsman struggling on the whipstaff. Robert Massey, the free merchant, who had amassed a mound of star pagodas in South India, was babbling his proposals of showering gold on the one-eyed pirate if his life was spared and he was set free at the next halt. Cassin's French orderly, his hands tied behind, was crying over his master's body. The big one-eyed hawk was foolishly ogling at the oriental aura clinging to her injured occidental lover. Robertson had been stabbed. Fatally for sure. His face heaving with mortal pain had the cushion support of her soft bosom. Blood was tickling down her slender arm. The Englishman looked deep into her teary eyes and all his pain appeared to subside as a faint smile surfaced on his lips. Her sorrows gushed out through streams of tears. She had been a very strong woman and could decide and choose what happened to her body even though surrounded by unchecked orgies around. But the sight of her dying lover shattered her. She had at last loved him like a woman without any scheme or motivation. She had made love to him just as a prompting of the flesh emotionally guided by overpowering emotions. She had dreamt of spending her life with him without any splendour or luxury.

"Such diamonds are beyond the laws of piracy," the pirate thundered in French. "In all illegal honesty and respect for her beauty I make a bid for her favours," he announced in broken English, hoping she would understand smattering of this language. "If anybody can beat me in price he is welcome to come with the offer," he threw challenging glances around.

People seemed to take back steps as if to avoid the scorching fury emanating from his eyes. His hand touched the drawstring of the purse hanging by his powder horn. His thick fingers jingled the gold coins. Money for her! Just like any other sellable female would have attracted the lot! The ever-burning lamp of pride in her flared up at the gutsy filthy whiffs of this announcement. Having a deep look into the eyes of her lover she laid him against the deck railing and stood up with full dignity for herself. Nodding to Cassin's French orderly to follow her she drew her majestic steps, completely undaunted and fiercely feminine, towards the auctioneer.

"How much you can pay for me?" she calmly whispered without any outward sign of rage inside her. Cassin's orderly, the multilingual artistic French, translated it for the pirate.

"Ho ho my whole ship is at your disposal my queen!" she got the message as he swiped the length of his ship with a movement of his spread out hands.

"This is for my body?" the rage in the depths of her heart was now surfacing through her beautiful eyes.

"Most of it for your body, and some sail bits can be spared for your heart," he put the end of his sword against her bosom just above where her enraged heart was thumping rapidly.

"But there lies someone who has given all just for this heart," she tightened her grip around the sword. "My heart is now completely satisfied with the favours it has got. As for the body, you can pay for my corpse!"

She drew all the power stored in her lithe frame and lunged forward, allowing the cold steel to sneak into her real womanly heart. Turning around she had a long look at Robertson now fatally unconscious and slumped on the deck.

She was in death as she had been in life. From beginning to end. Judged either good or bad. Such people who are true to their self, who know their truth, are real characters. She always held her feminine majesty in highest esteem. Even when she deviated from the path, it again was just to maintain the identity of her real self. She never had the slightest doubt about the narcissistic pride and self-respect for herself and lived and died for it.

Fragments of a Full Smile

* * *

Jenny was an adventure photographer. She had this knack for clicking the button at the fractional precision of time. Adventures, misadventures, happenings, and mishaps do happen in the flash of a moment. Very rarely did she miss her date with such flashy, fleeting moments. Unsurprisingly, her portfolio consisted of publications in many reputed magazines, newspapers, and illustrious periodicals. A string of rewards in the field ignited her to cross an extra mile in search of hair-raising moments. A hunter with a camera she was thus on predatory prowl after the shy, exquisitely rare, and unique natural and social phenomena.

Convincing herself of India's status mired in such moments she decided to tour India. The chain of events drew the lot in her favour. A welcoming mishap arrived. Monsoon was at its full fury over Bombay as her ever-helpful boyfriend Michael held the umbrella above her head while she zoomed the lenses around the rain-soaked taxi-stand outside the airport terminal. Suddenly the invisible shutterbug clicked and a dazzling flash of lightening made the grey day lit up with a blinding spasm. Lighting had struck. Even in that fleeting fraction of a second, the artist in her knew that her index finger had clicked at the right moment. In the next moment, the earth shook from the rumbling bowls of the sky and a large burst of water eased out on the ground. A few dozen yards from them, two porters lay lynched and a third one was struggling onto his feet. A drenched crowd gathered around the little stage of nature's fury like tiny dots on a frizzled screen. It was a moment of victory for the photographer. But for the human in her, it was a moment of pitiful sigh and shudder. Unable to react more she looked into Michael's eyes. He, the national rafting champion, was dazed beyond wordings. He was a man who made love to the water's spate of fury and really liked the unrestricted brushstrokes of her photography.

Bombay to Delhi, they decided to go by train. After all the true charm of India lies in its bustling, teeming transports chugging across huge swathes of tiresome humanity lost in a self-eating mad race of survival. It was a long and tedious journey, but hugely exciting nonetheless. It was early morning. Sitting by the window she was sipping train tea to get a real feel of Indian passengership. The train had halted at a nondescript station: a couple of platforms with iron-sheet shelters with hawkers, vendors, and little stalls. Coal smoke made the small crowd appear all lethargic and sleepy. There were just four railway lines to facilitate crossings. To her right the platform at the other end ended with yellow-walled godowns. A goods train was being loaded on the track. Its dark purple bogies full of coal bustled with labourers. Just in front of her a separated bogie was being unloaded. Two labourers were standing in the gap chatting merrily in oblivion putting their life into the conviction that the bogie would not be shunted without their knowledge. But then human fallacies and mistakes are as many as there are stars. The engine driver started shunting with a pernicious jerk. It happened before her eyes. She saw the first jerk. The plastic tea cup slipped out of her hands. Instead of her finger tip on the camera button her tongue clicked. There was just a meter and half gap between the metal rumps of the bogies. Her shrill cry ran to intervene. The labourer's startled eyes moved in her direction and from the corner of his eye he perceived the mortal jerk of the carriage and ducked right beneath the connect shaft. But the other one was not as lucky and was almost jaffed like a fish between the thick cylindrical protruding. It was horrible beyond imagination. For a moment her hand moved to camera, but then she slumped back in her seat.

"India is a land bustling with such tragedies," Michael embraced her consolingly.

For the rest of her journey she could not put the horrific scene out of her mind. This tragic misadventure had left an almost indelible image. A forlorn day in New Delhi followed this. She found it busy, boring and filthy, a caricature of a European settlement. From a distance of 300 kilometres the great Himalayan range was calling with basketful of pleasant adventures. They set up their itinerary. A rafting expedition in the upper reaches of Himachal Pradesh. The monsoonal spate of Sutlej in its upper valley seemed winking mystically in a photograph in their travel guide.

Deeply dissected topography and varied geological structure of the Himalayas assuaged her feelings as the toy train moved into gorgeous mystery of the mighty mountain after starting its journey from Kalka situated at the base Himalayan foothills. Rain was continuously falling as the toy train chugged into the temperate, magically plentiful flora of these tropical latitudes. Breath-taking sceneries, stripped agricultural fields on the slopes, tiny rural settlements, rivulets gurgling in little waterfalls, all this soaked in monsoonal haze found her taking copious snaps of leisure photography from the train window. She felt her quirky, pin-pointing, concentrating self was spreading unhindered without any focus. It was on the rare occasion that Michael was watching the unrestricted, unrefined beauty of her features.

"Dear, forget about adventure, let us visit this place," she twisted her tongue to pronounce Kharjiar, her finger on Chamba district. "It's called mini Switzerland because of its remarkable similarity to the European paradise."

But how could the champion rafter miss this opportunity to victoriously foam over the mighty Indian river originating in the Tibetan highlands to enter Himachal Pradesh from the eastern side. "Look at the continuous rain, even the tiny channels sparkle with a rafting invitation. Just wonder how spiteful the big river would be!" his enthusiasm prevailed over her cooing request.

Reaching Kalpa, Kinnaur district headquarters—the district through which Sutlej unleashes its full spiteful fury after gushing into from the Tibetan side—they hired rafting equipment and support crew from a rafting club. The dark-grey veil of clouds hung over the valley like an unflickering shadow as they moved eastwards into the rugged terrain to start rafting from the upper reaches.

Their rafting crew comprised four battle hard locals. Their brownish faces glowed with adventurous expectation in the company of these elite travellers. Water was gushing at such a speed that it splashed and splattered foam in air. A soaring, scary euphoria hung in air buzzing with exciting fresh water drills. A pulverising, incising Sutlej was eating into the V-shaped gorge with a killing effect. Its muddled grey waters rumbled ahead noisily carrying huge boulders at the bed. Some adventurous spirit seemed to be riotously ricocheting off to the nook and corners of the valley.

"Please be warned of the danger. It's raining continuously for the last few days. Sometimes lakes on the Chinese side burst unleashing death and destruction in the valley on the Indian side!" the club manager had amply warned the couple.

But where Indians stopped, Westerners started, so Michael's overblown spirit would only listen to the river's rigorously rolling watery growl. So he just laughed off the premonition, while Jenny's hand tightened around her camera in gleeful anticipation of capturing nature's catapults at its rowdiest best.

Before letting themselves to the gay abundance of the furious waters, Suresh, whose knowledge of ramshackle English naturally made him a leader among the local crew, led a short religious ceremony to inaugurate the venture. Finding a niche at the base of a big boulder he sought out a piece of canvas and held it before the tiny hole like a tent entrance. Securing the upper end of the protective flap with thick glue tape he put pebbles at the lower end leaving only a little opening by the boulder side through which a hand could just grope in. The foreigners were lost in the spectacular assemblage of multilayered reality carrying best and the worst side by side, literally life and death arm in arms. In deep attunement with this unifying facet of nature their eerie was broken as incense smoke reached their nostrils. With folded hands all four hill people were muttering some prayer to a local goddess. The little oil lamp and the incense stick spread a cosy religious aroma inside the makeshift shrine. Finishing their prayers, Suresh looked into their inquisitive eyes and before they could put any query he reeled off his explanation.

"It's worship to the river Goddess. We believe it will save us from the flooding waters," he saw a glint of non-believing rationality in the white man's eyes, while his girlfriend did her best to look understanding and believing in their faith.

Once the raft was launched into the waters and their hands started working in full dexterity and professionalism, it was swiftly carried into the lolloping folds of greedy waters. She gave an excited cry born of suave enthusiasm caught in the blurring boundaries of fear and enjoyment. It was a feeling that seemed to break through all existential dilemmas.

"Up to now it was yours, now onwards it shall be mine!" the river seemed to chuckle with muddy mirth as it sucked the boat into its swirling swathes.

The danger, fury and risks were enough to test the all-out skills of the national champion and the local crew. While they rowed and manoeuvred for life, she—almost glued to the gunwale—tried to meet the most fearsome moments of watery delight running down slope in unbridled ecstasy. The moments flew in sparkling rapidity. It was adventurous beyond imagination.

What a journey! Those great lakes situated like ancient puddles on the roof of the world, Tibetan plateau, saw their outpours winning across the majestic ranges. Lake Rakas, connected to Lake Mansarovar by a stream, is the watery womb of the Sutlej. It sneaks into India through a pass called Shipki La. Its majestic gorge incised on the bulging breast of Nainadevi Dhar ranges. Old sedimentary and granite rocks—the highly folded, faulted, fossilised *karmabhoomi* of this mighty stream—of the Greater Himalayan range bear enough testimony to the fact that even the rise of Himalayas could not beat the river's erosive power. The river being antecedent in nature, as the Himalayas evolved slowly, the chasm kept on deepening. Geological upheavals could not defeat its march. Sediments embedded deep down the plains in Punjab bear testimony to the fact. Large blocks of rock have been dragged over thousands of kilometres. The mighty torrent has toyed with boulder debris; writing its signature on this mountainscape in the form of numerous lines, faults, plateaus, rugged northern slopes of ranges and forested southern slopes. All this has just been silently carved over centuries. On the steep valley-sides, river decimated archaen rocks like granite, gneiss and schist gaped like famished old ladies as Jenny captured their curious wild looks. Somewhere high in the misty hilltops Alpine forest degenerated into low evergreen scrub and dry xerophytes. Massively forested hillsides smirked with dark green carpet of mixed foliage of deodar, juniper, pine, birch and rhododendron.

Cutting through the flooded music came the jocose cries of armymen. The Indian army is famous for its discipline and belief in core values of democracy and humanism. The group seemed to be enjoying in full spirit beyond the pale of the heavy wagon of discipline and risky duties. All of us sometimes unyoke the institutional burden to shout with joy and excitement. With an exciting fury their raft approached from behind. Four military uniformed crew members manoeuvred their raft to beat the flooded watery snares. Moving from one detachment may be they were carrying some provisions. There were two agile young soldiers—drawn from the tough north Indian peasantry class—more of energy and less of caution. While the Naib Subedar and Havaldar in their fifties appeared the stabilising forces in the raft that seemed to prevent it from capsizing. Looking back, she apprehensively watched the coming raft's cascading fury. Mint-fresh junior officer blew her a kiss as their rubbery platform was thrown in air. She but appeared lost in the fruitful moment for having captured exactly the way she might have wanted to her full photographic satisfaction. The light had flashed against the background of pine, cedar, silver fir, cedar, deodar, oak, laurel, and bamboo.

The young soldiers seemed to have forgotten the seductive fury of the flooded river. What a harsh life they had led during the past couple of years. Earlier in Kashmir, where every fearful step into the night on reconnaissance patrols was heavily laden with possible death. During the days, cold staring eyes of the locals—especially women—spitted almost in their faces. They were like aliens where everything seemed affiliated to Pakistan. "We are with terrorists!" the local people's eyes glared openly and defiantly. Deadly rounds of night patrols, search operations, encounters, and ambushes were indelibly etched on their fatigued psyches. They drowned their sorrows and grudges most often in wine and sometimes—when it was most suitable and secure—by their frustrated manhood on available Kashmiri women turning half consents to full and changing unwillingness to careless surrender. Now in these rugged detachments along Sutlej, nature's unblemished charm deprived them—for they were no poets and artists—of all the sweet charms of human frailties and basic instincts. There was no immediate enemy here. Only the pining loneliness of the basic instinct in them had to be fought against to curb it to decency. So within six months of their arrival, one had his sweetheart at Kharo village, while the other had his at a place called Tangling.

As the military rafters passed them, one of the young soldiers gave her a flying kiss. However, she was struck by the cold, lusty melancholy in the other's eyes. He appeared more lethal.

"Having a good time in Sutlej's piss sir!" he shouted with a great effort at English without removing his eyes from Jenny.

She felt a cold shiver, but like an empowered Westerner stared back boldly. Right from her school days she always had this stomping competitiveness against the opposite gender that found her rubbing shoulders against the boys' attitude and superiority complex. The carefully constructed contours of her feminine notions and convictions made her stand out as a deeply self-respecting and confident young woman. But then it was the East. She was very well aware of the swarming cynicism of the patriarchy here. As a woman she could very well catch the discomforting vibes and tedious shades of grey born of overheated passion. She was even scared by the eccentric look in the soldier's eyes. That invasive stare put her in a state where a woman gets guarded instinctively in the face of any unwelcome advancement against her physical self. Her deeply expressive eyes clearly showed that she was scared after being literally buffeted under the impact of that acrimoniously impassioned stare.

The one having more lethality in his eyes was taller than the relatively jocose one. The shorter one slapped the tall one's shoulder strap and winked. Who cares about rule books and discipline during such rare, flirtatious moments! The hardened leaves of their challenging existence brushed against the soft petals of this chance for soul-stroking moments.

"I've had experience of bigger pisses. Just take care, Mister, this little one might find you upside down!" Michael retorted with mild irritation plainly reading their minds and having a clue to the object of their lusty eyes.

The taller soldier was named Rakesh, but nicknamed Raka on account of his daredevilry and fondness regarding the topic on women.

The other was Sukhwinder and was called Shaka for being pally with Raka's overenthusiastic self regarding many sensitive topics. They had served in differed units in Kashmir, but here chance had thrown them in the same basket for synchronised sojourns in the relaxed wilderness in this part of the Himalayas. So Raka-Shaka the duo was on fun and frolic prowl in these imperilled waters.

"Have a nice time and safe rafting young lady and sir!" Naib Subedar's condescending thickly dialect-accented baritone English sailed over the gushing torrential surge of the river.

Such a long period in the army and a senior's fluent reprimands are enough to make the semi-educated rustic native tongues twist and turn along the sophisticated syllables and phrases of the international language. Among his nondescript, simple features, his eyes shone with simplicity, understanding, and openness. She acknowledged the elderly soldier's good wish with a smile. With that smile she appeared like an Empress of Sweetness. The corpulent Havaldar's glassy eyes stared with stony neutrality. But then they could not match the champion rafter's skills, so after a few minutes they could only see the beautiful lady's back from behind and the distance increasing in surges.

"She is a queen in beauty!" Shaka gasped at her tresses mystically engulfed in foam and watery frills as he slackened his moral reins to enter the den of gluttony and plain physical hunger.

After some time they could just discern the back of her vivid green life jacket. Raka's expression was grotesquely profound as he was caught by the virile humming of the basic instinct in him. Forgetting rank, files, and age he helplessly gave coarse, weird exclamations. The two elder soldiers appeared shame-faced against this helpless surrender of the young man to the wildly adventurous call of lust.

Then with a snorting flourish something sneaked into the waters. The river below them felt a massive tsunami shove. Even before they could think of some rescue strategy they found water level had gone several feet up the narrow valley. The flood had suddenly acquired intimidating, formidable, and disorienting parameters even in relation to the most critical category of severe danger in rafting. Furrows of worry surfaced on Michael's brow. It was dangerous to anybody in the art of rafting. His face told the nasty realisation. They saw a whole village being eaten by the watery deluge. Just by its side a military installation had been ambushed by the gushing waters. A bailey bridge a couple of hundred meters downstream collapsed and water tossed the wreckage as its wanton weapons of war. They saw army personnel and villagers being washed away like helpless, lifeless twigs, and branches. Watery power was such that an army truck rolled along the boulders.

The champion rafter in Michael was furtively drawing every bit of skill and strength from the book of his experience to save some lives. But running and bumping through this fleeting macabre they could draw only two almost decimated lives—an army Naik and an old woman. The latter had been miraculously thrown into the raft. Gushing waters ate away all other cries.

The tragedy was unfolding in screeching circles. The watery onslaught was contemptuously screwing up anything coming its way. Some big lake falling in the river's course in Tibet had burst...suddenly... somehow...unleashing watery assault in the Indian territory. Within an hour so much of life and property (both civilian and military) had been destroyed as would put months-long war (manmade) statistics to shame.

Violent waters tossed the raft with such demonic tumultuous force that it now became only a foregone conclusion when'll it capsize. And then it happened! After half an hour's gut-wrenching struggle, Michael's hands showed that momentary lapse, that fatal mistake like when walking on the tight rope, and the muddy, greedy waters grasped its chance. At the most crucial moment, the champion rafter's hand tightly gripped the wrist of the most beautiful hand in the world, as they were tossed into the fearsomely spiteful waters. Even during these deathful moments her other hand held her camera sling around her neck. After all, this digital piece had captured so many hair-raising moments for which no human eye would dare to bear testimony.

First the swirling eddy just pinched them down with such deadly force that their bodies hit the boulders beneath. She would have been fatally injured hadn't it been for the rafting helmet over her dark-brown hair. During such moments, like a chanceful draw of lots ones chances of survival are totally decided by some inexplicable throw of dice. They struggled as one would in the face of death but the result was totally out of their control. And as chance would have it, one sudden spurt, which could have very easily taken their lives, quite incidentally, became a saviour and threw them against a firm rock valiantly jutting out a few feet above the highest water mark. Like decimated insects they clung to it. Between their hold-out and the life beyond water was billowing with such fury that any attempt to even touch it would have surely undone that lucky chance's work. The wreckage sped by. They took shelter in the lee of this mighty motherly rock.

"Will have to wait till the waters go down," Michael's teeth chattered.

"Or till something comes smashing into the gap to the slope."

It was now completely a question of faith. Sticking to the rock, their fingers clawed around the sharp rock edges, teeth chattering, rocky hardness eating into their shrivelled finger skin, they cooed little words of support to each other. Desperate forehead bumps saw a couple of hours pass with unusually drawn-out slowness. It was raining with even more fury now. Though it was just afternoon, the whole surroundings were lost in twilight grey. Just a couple of hundred paces up dangerously lolloping tongues of water were eating the muddy slopes. A massive old deodar dangerously tilted into the waters as water cut into it foothold few feet below. The increasing angle of tilt brought invigorating glint in their eyes as they helplessly peeked around the corner. Then their prayers were heeded. A big chunk of land slid beneath the huge tree's root-hold and headlong it crashed into the water. It massive, long trunk laid like the arm of a clock as water lashed against its foliage. There were still enough roots left to keep the upturned lower end still pinned down to the root-hold. With life-giving succour the top branches of the foliage softly came to brush against the hard rock.

The leaves appeared to muse, "We the lower forms of life sacrifice to save you the higher ones!"

With many cuts, gashes, and bruises they managed to crawl along the tree to reach the slope beyond the inroads of water. They had seen settlements along the river course. So surely there will be footpaths and goat tracks or even road (for they remembered military installations). Going into the forested upslope was the only choice. Life meant to be away from the water as much as possible. Believing it to be a journey for the better (for they already felt lucky due to that providential escape) they moved ahead. Detouring around the rugged mountain slope their resultant direction of movement was to go upstream. But you just cannot choose your best path in mountainscape. One can choose only a rough direction to move into and the zig-zagging path is decided by the mountain itself. Within an hour of their purported upstream journey they were a good kilometre away from the flooded river bed.

Soaked to their bones now, life appeared mired in an unconquerable watery deluge. They clung to each other as the light faded fast. Very soon the rainy mistiness changed to irrevocable gloom over the forested hillside. They had almost nothing with them. Clad in shirt and shorts (they were still wearing their life jackets) they felt the rhythmic rustling of life beating through their hearts. She had her camera and he just a packet of biscuits and a chocolate bar in his belt purse apart from some local currency and credit card. The night brought only one solace: rain stopped. But even from it they could not draw any consolation for the foliage would continue to drip almost like a light drizzle. Sharing half of their emergency ration, they gave each other life by embracing lovingly. They held each other to assure themselves that all will be well. Removing all of their clothing they wrung out water and then touching each other's body with mischievous love-making finger touches they started that primordially old pleasant game of male and female which for ages has found the species rolling in oblivion far away in a world deprived of all anxieties.

Their tired and worn out bodies clung to each other to reciprocally sneak into each other's zone of warmth. They knew all the nightlong hardships could be trivialised this way. Their caressing hands stroked away all tough moments. There was not anything hurried about this love blossom. Their breathing mixed to form an airy cocktail of cosmic forgetfulness. Snail-like movements of paired lips had no hunger, but just licked into each other's privacy with marvellous contentment, just giving life to each other, not taking anything in return. A majestic calmness spread around. A causeless mirth gripped their bodies responding to each other's touch. The cheerless monotony was shooed away by the rapidly rhythmical motion of their bodies. The peerless virginity of the surroundings was impregnated with love strokes. The soft sedateness of this spectacle appeared to assuage the monsoon-lynched ridges around. The clouds parted and a full moon gaped through the foliage to sprinkle its soft, milky whiteness over them. It was an eloquent picture of peace and tranquillity drawn by the ultimate connoisseur lost in dreamy drowsiness. Her enchanting submissiveness seeped into his masculine being creating dazzling chaos. The swelling tide of his dominance generated unsurpassed blooms of ecstasy in the niche of her desires. Above, the juniper, pine, and birch stood as spellbound spectators to this silently, mystically, noiselessly flowing stream of river on the gentle, plain surface of their bodies. And the night passed as beautifully as it could. The forest just stood in jealous loyalty. A grand despondency hung in the air. The love storm was too strong for any further worries to disturb their contended, fatigued bodies.

On the previous day, the other inflatable raft that had been left behind by Michael's dexterous oar strokes had, as can very well be expected, also capsized. All its four occupants were flung into the greedily lolloping mirth of water as the raft hit the wreckage of the broken bridge. The elderly Subedar was hit on the head and his unconscious body was washed away. His fate was unknown in the flooded pell-mell. Badly shaken up and bruised, the two young soldiers, Raka and Shaka, had a providential escape. Thrown ashore by some unknown hand of providence and fortune, the rugged terrain of a few hundred yards separating them, they crawled to console each other's death-scared and shocked bodies. Shaka's backpack, bigger than Raka's, contained emergency first aid and ration. They nursed themselves as best as they could. Then the dreary, desultory and aching night somehow lumbered in the foliage above them.

A full hour before twilight they decided to struggle towards the destroyed army encampment site. The rain had stopped completely. There was a pinkish grey slit behind the ridge through which the day peeped to ask permission to call its turn. The twilight was soaked and saturated with water. In the distance, the river's rumble had abated considerably. Through the chink in the sky's cloudy fabric a yawning sun glittered on the rain-washed glory of the greenery. But then all their broken muscles and fatigued limbs came to life suddenly. Two embracing naked white bodies—their statuesque curves jutted against each other for warmth—lay asleep. Their clothing spread under them on the grass. The dawn lit up their primordially complementary curves. Afterglow of that unison of bodies, minds, and spirits during the mystically slow and silently spread moments of life still blanketed around them.

The onlookers' breathing was strangulated. Gasping instincts hammered their almost numb senses. For a long couple of minutes they just stared at the female half of the love-lost unit—the other half almost hidden from their view. Lying side by side, her partner's head was lost in the cushion support of her pinkish-white breasts. He lay on his left side; lower hand stretched as a cushion to support her rosy cheeks while the upper right hand was resting in the marvellously arching hollow of the side of her back. Her left hand going under his right armpit was spread around his shoulder blade. Her lower hand was buried under her breasts and her long slanderous fingers were lost in his hair. His upper leg was bent in a protecting right angle over her thighs. His masculine independence safely anchored in the slumbering feminine bay of her receptivity. It appeared as if those surrendering moments were still sonorously lingering in the morning fresh air.

The sweet long-lasting after-glow was suddenly shoved by the lusty fury. Hovering with their hypnotised selves they were helpless before the attack of their basic instincts. The moral and ethical compass had stopped to function. These are blinding moments when one shuts off reason to enter the domain of outright, rapacious illegality. The lust-driven criminality is blind to any notion of sin and its consequences. There is always a beast inside that secretly continues worshipping devilish desires. And when its collective illusions beat the giddy optimism of goodness it strikes to gather plum plunders. One can feel the murmuring undertones of its incendiary restlessness deep within the self. In the so-called law breakers it becomes ruthlessly authoritative and strikes to create some toxic moments. With profound agility the soldiers tore them apart, and before the afterglow left their eyes and heart, they found two wolfish predators holding their revolvers against their heads. A fearsome cry escaped her lips. These feminine notes of distress and horror went sailing in all directions for help.

"One more word and ants will eat your brain!" Shaka gnashed to convey his intentions through a great effort at English.

Noticing defiance in Michael's eyes, Raka forewarned, "No rafting... it's a game of death and life...so no heroism!" he appeared helpless and gasping before the criminal urge.

"Look, if you commit this folly your future is surely lost," Michael tried to bring sanity to their devilish desire.

They but had been blinded—totally helpless before the sexual monster that had puffed inside them like a volcanic eruption. Raka, following the rules of his seniority in rascality, raped her first. Her boyfriend tied with their clothing and some cords from their backpacks cried, shouted, and closed his eyes. Impotent rage lynched him leaving him tossing in agony. Before the wounded emotion could force him to do something almost futile his eyes met the muzzle staring into his face. Shaka was holding both weapons to him. She resisted to all her strength. But since she was already naked, half of her struggle was already over before it even started. The rapist was naked below waist. She bit him; her fingers clawed into his face; pushed him away; her soft fist beat against his strong body. Finally he pinned her down on her back and successfully struggled to break open the defensive gates of her tightly squeezed legs. How long will a woman resist the criminality? She gave into the sinner. Her tightly squeezed hands opened and palms lay like a corpse. She just put her face away to one side to be away from the evil puffs of her offender's heaving self, trying to keep away her soul, her heart, the flower of her modesty, the buds of virtues and the purity of the womanly emotions in her, as far away as possible from his rapacious lips. Her eyes tightly shut with the pain of soul and body as she tried to free her spirit and take her to a distance and sobbingly watch this unpardonable sin. Her body was in revolt. Each cell of her physical self was buzzing with silent defiance. Not even a single molecule anywhere in her violated self had the least bit of condescending trace for this brutal act of sexual criminality. The tiniest sinews in her being cried in silence for this violation of her body. It was an endlessly long trauma. She never felt so near to death. She could feel her spirit had left her body and the sinner was just raping a corpse.

Leaving the stains of sin on her flesh and still graver ones on her soul, he moved with lassitudinous ambers of his once fiercely burning desire. His flushed smart young face already mired in worries about the consequences. Like a stone he took the position of his companion and nodded him to become an equal partner in crime. He had felt it, the eternal aloofness in her. She had been successful in not feeling him inside her. The crime and any of its evil fruits were his own. She was beyond the gloomy pal of his crime. That judgement of hers about his crime was mocking. Whole hundred percent of the crime in his share; she the victorious had slapped his sin hard in his face. He had raped women a few times in Kashmir. Lust-blinded male chauvinism in him drew solace from deep, mysterious, painful feel in the victim's body. And this agonised, agitatedly condescending miniscule portion of the deed from the body whose ramparts he had breached saved him from any moral pricking later and swooning over mugs of alcohol he would smirk:

"Oh, just to prove that she was not a slut, she feigned resistance initially. But later I know she enjoyed it...I could feel that!"

Allowed to go scot-free by the wispy invisible court of conscience he need not fear anything else for things had been muddled from all sides and particularly around the time when there had been Kargil War between India and Pakistan putting armymen, civilians, and terrorists and secessionists all in a burning cauldron.

Shaka was but oblivious to such subtle nuances of the sinful game. He was taking much time. Then his flesh could no longer run as fast as his desire and he gave in collapsing on the ground. His desire but still kept beckoning and after a couple of minute's passive, stony, lifeless tugs at his flesh it once again got onto its feet and run a bit longer on the track of crime.

Desperation, despondency, envy, fear, and boredom were creeping into Raka as he stood watching over Michael. Though he held the weapons as firmly as his training and experience allowed him, a vague defeat lurked around his face and he avoided the hostage's eyes. Almost all his reflexes had gone impassive to the surroundings. His colleague was naturally blind to any light around for he was deep in the dark cavernous pit of his deed.

Suddenly there was a painful mutter from behind. The first sinner looked behind. The perspiring face of the first sinner flushed purple and still remaining upstanding sinews of his conscience went flabbergasted. Scornful, desperate and mocking gaze of the Subedar pierced through him.

Yesterday, tossed by water and lashed by angry waves he had slammed backside into an underwater boulder. But his moderately corpulent body had enough cushion support around his bones to save these from a fatal breakage. Though his teeth chattered with almost mortal fear and head spun, he still was alive. Much to his good luck, his helplessly floating semi-conscious body was carried through a lean and safe stretch. Here the bottom and sides were free of those monstrous hindrances to the gurgling river. He not only regained his consciousness, but successfully planned his escape from the watery war and ambush. Firm determinations of renovating his house, getting his daughter married, providing good education to his son to make him a commissioned officer in the army, all these and many wise thoughts kindled his spirits through the lonely night. He was moving lugubriously along a hollow separated by a low ridge from the scene of crime. The early morning air had swiftly carried her cry over the ridge to reach his ears. After that he had used all his knowledge to follow its course.

"O God, what the hell...and the government thinks..." the elderly soldier put an effort to speak out his English words, "the country's honour is safe in your hands!"

Shaking with rage, seeing this grossest, meanest form of human misdeed, the burly Subedar spat on the ground and moved with firm steps of justice.

"Subedar Sahib just do not move!" Raka hollered more out of fear than aggression. Desperation dawned upon him, "You know me well, I won't hesitate in firing the shot!"

He brandished one of his weapons in his direction. But the meanest of the mean have to promptly—almost on the spot—repay for the misdeed. His sin had sapped into his courage and alertness. His finger twitching around the trigger, he fidgeted and shook like a lynched beast.

"Shoot his legs! What are you waiting for?" muffled, panting, and gasping sound escaped the second sinner's throat.

But Raka's eyes went blind with fear, shame and regret as the firm-footed elderly soldier moved forward, his eyes staring hypnotically into the offender's. The Subedar knew any action on the trigger will be preceded by the same standard twitch in the eyes. Life and death depend on this threadbare separation between the eye twitch and the shot. As the thread of desperation was broken, with the mighty effort of a bull's heave he swung his upper body to one side. The shot echoed in the surrounding vales. His left side moved in greater proportion to the effort he had put in. If not for this perfectly executed manoeuvre, the bullet would have surely hit him.

It now just grazed past his left arm. Raka's whole strength seemed to have gone with the shot, and before he could think of anything else the Subedar's hairy fist struck him and he went rolling in the damp, muddy grass. Pinning him down, the elder soldier locked his knees into the pits of the culprit's stomach. The latter groaned with pain. Like a pernicious predatory animal, athletically built and lithe Shaka was gnawing at Subedar's back, his arm trying to strangulate the big man. Realising its futility, he lunged forward to grab revolver from his friend's hand that had been pinned down to the ground. But as the chill of success in getting this harbinger of death and injury ran down his spine, a shudder of fear rumbled along his taut spine. The latter one frantically rode over the earlier fleeting sense of victory for a nanosecond. The opponent too had succeeded in snatching the other weapon. Marking each other they stared at each other above the helplessly lying body of Raka between them. Their cold, steely eyes struck like arrows. The elder soldier knew that the rapist won't hesitate to shoot him, so slipping on his heels utilising the muddy earth below, he let loose another manoeuvre as he fell backwards. The shot rattled above his head. It seemed as if the younger soldier's advantage had been nullified by the gory deed. A second shot rang. Just at the moment his broad back hit earth his stubby fingers had done the task. Shaka had been hit on his right flank, above the armpit, near the collar bone. Convulsing with pain he staggered, fired very high above the mark and fell onto the ground.

O Justice, how fervidly we crave for you! The woman with her modesty ravaged, dragged herself to life from the stony slumber and deadly impassivity. Jumping like a wounded tigress she snatched the weapon from the injured man's hand. Utterly dazed, almost paralysed with strange forebodings, Raka was still lying on ground. Her face distorted with raging revenge, hair dishevelled, in the depths of her eyes a boiling sea of sorrow and pain, all this and much more gripped her in its typhoon swirl. A teary blink preceded the shot. The second rapist grunted and leapt to the other side. Clawing at his thigh he rolled in muddy water. Before the full fury of her vengeance could match the lethal metal in the magazine, the elderly soldier came between her and the two wretched lives that were mortally indebted to her for their crime. For rape is no particular crime but a mammoth universal sin whose limitless contours define how half of humanity can be abused, exploited, thrown into mud, mortally injured (all soul, spirit, and the body) by another chauvinistic half of humanity. Torrentially abused her eyes were red with rage. Every pore of her body seemed to instigate her to empty all bullets into the sinners' bodies. She was greeting her teeth with unthinkable anger. Meanwhile, Michael fought to free himself of the unsystematic and hurried tidings, and his naked body writhing with the fury of an injured leopard fell upon one of the injured soldiers.

"Ma'am I...I know, they must be killed, but..." all thoughts blanked out of the elderly soldier's head as he pleaded with the woman to hand over the weapon.

Michael was crying and fiercely slapping Shaka's face.

"Please, please...ma'am!" he pleaded as if seeking forgiveness from the side of all men, the wrongdoing species, from the side of Indian military, India the dirty country as a whole, whole world, whole universe. Failing to voice his agony, he pleaded with teary eyes and folded hands.

In silent fury a wave of sorrow again rose to its crest inside her. Her face contorted in consequence to it. The writing pain of her soul surfaced on her pursed lips. She had been robbed of her identity, her pride, her belief in the beauty of this world and this feeling cut deep into her soul. Oh, the fearsome face of an offended woman! There was such sea storm of emotions that the old soldier was completely lost in her facial fury. In devastating desperation, unable to rein in the grape-shot of revenge, she even brandished the weapon at the belated helper.

"They...they deserve...worst punishment," he muttered. "But if you colour your hands with their dirty blood...it will lessen the woman in you. They are dogs. They don't deserve to die at your hands. They have raped their own human selves. Law will see them into the den of their sin," he folded his hands in true Indian fashion of entreaty, pleading, and request.

Michael had turned their faces into almost bloody pulp. She the sufferer of their ravenous onslaught stood shaking with infinite pain and rage. She could have very easily spent all the metal into their sinning bodies and stay contended in her conscience throughout her life. Their killing was justified on all grounds. Possibly even law would have ultimately absolved her of the deed. Their offense was even worse than killing a human being. But then killing a human being is no simple task however justified the killing might be. She the catcher of agonising and ecstatic moments from the endless stream of time for a better world possessed more of a human inside her than the instinctive urge to take revenge on spot. She vented out rest of her injury and ravage into the foliage. Holding the revolver in both her hands above her head she shot one bullet after another; pitch and notes of pain rising exponentially with each rebound of the catapulter. Throwing away the weapon she realised her nakedness and moved towards the knotted heal of their clothing. Back into the modesty of their torn and muddied clothing they fell into each other's arms; their respective sobs going like painful waves into each other's body. Instantly his caresses felt like succouring balm on the invisible scars in her soul and the gashes and bruises on her body.

"As per the one and first form of justice they should be shot right here on the spot by the sinned person," staring on ground, his hands hanging dejectedly, the elder armyman bespoke forgiveness and apologies from the side of his land. "But we are long past that age of eye for an eye. Even revenge is also taken as a crime. In order to move over to higher, more sophisticated form of wrong and sin, we notify the previous ones in gilded letters," he was speaking sensibly, intelligently in despondent tone. God knows how much effort he was putting on his tongue to sound intelligent and overcome the whirlpool of strange emotions.

"It is so easy to preach...but do you even have an idea of the brutality of their crime and what she has undergone...will she ever be able to feel safe in life?" Michael cried, clenching his fist. "See the deeds of the so called protectors of law in your country and you speak and sermonise about law and justice!"

Before he could speak further, Jenny tartly pressed her lips against his mouth as if to dive into the sea of love leaving behind all traces of the gory act and forgetting all memories of the crime against her. The veteran soldier, who was rising in the ranks of thought and ideas through reading a lot many books these days to kill the boredom in barracks, was heard saying in a warm, moist, sighing, and suffering tone—"Second form of justice is to leave then here on their fate and wait for God to do justice. But in that case it will mean like pretending to take ourselves out of the sin and leave it to the wheels of natural uncertainties. But then we will in that case carry the dirty baggage of their devilish act on our back singlehandedly into uncertain future."

He was now sitting on the ground. On the same ground where the rapists were groaning with pain. His personage was solacing and understanding. The couple now moved towards this suffering, fat figure that out of shame for the deed of his countrymen was even hesitant to look into their eyes. As she came closer, she saw tears of shame and repentance rolling down his chubby cheeks. Slowly, she was taking control of herself; gathering the sinews of her senses after the devastating earthquake had shaken her physical self. They sat in front of him. He raised his teary eyes to them. Her eyes welled up with massive emotions. Here was a man who was soulfully crying and repenting for the crime against her. He wept like he would have done had it been his own daughter in place of her. She could feel the genuineness and purity of this stranger's tears. She felt a strange succour to her wounded soul. Sloth and slovenliness in human hearts can break us. But purity of hearts can make us as well. His tears of repentance appeared to wash the blots of their sin from her skin.

"As we stealthily devise higher forms of wrong, we make a public show of openly, constitutionally punish and penalise the lower forms of wrongs. The suitable form of punishment left out is to take these swine to the doors of justice and put shame of public filth on their faces...to get their story published...to tell to everybody whoever hold them in slightest esteem...to get the Indian army rub off its name from their epaulettes and condemn them like petty criminals...to leave them to face their mothers and sisters," his refined, calculated courage and books-ignited convictions got tired under the force of overpowering emotions and he stopped.

"You know ma'am what I'm asking you is one of the most merciless requests I have ever made in life," his plump hand was fatherly resting on her heaving shoulder.

She saw thick clots of blood trickling down his sleeve. For the pain of a fellow human being this man was totally ignorant of his own injury. He knew the ravaged modesty of a woman any time surpasses the deepest cut on anybody's body. She felt it. She felt supported and more importantly respected. He was talking in terms of contemporary justice; in exact definition and terms of the law of her own land.

"Without your help...oh, it is shameless to ask you...to ask you... to..." he could not complete his sentence.

"I will not allow my rapists to die here without getting them publicly raped in the eyes of their employer and their families, friends, and society at large. I know the way to get them punished in the severest manner. To get them branded rapists for their whole wretched life!" she yelled with fearsome determination tightly tying their wounds.

A long and tough ordeal waited ahead. Shaka was carried by the armyman on his shoulder in the military fashion of fetching a casualty from the battlefield of honour. The only difference was that he was carrying a casualty from the field of chaotic, filthy, muddy passions. Moderately tall and averagely build body of Raka hit in the thigh was carried by the couple, holding his sinned hands across their shoulders and dragging him in between. There was very little strength in his legs, so they had to literally drag him along. Shaka's shorter, lithe body contained some traces of consciousness. They struggled along the ravaged valley, the victims carrying the culprits' bodies cautiously, carefully stepping along treacherous precipices and muddy slopes in the hope of getting justice; to drag them into the public cage of condemnation, to throw light on their dark crime, to highlight their sin and throw it into the face of society and justice dispensation machinery. Humankind's eternal quest for justice... pure...unstinted...fulfilling the contemporary needs.

Justice!

In a local English daily she read about the spating valley:

"No telephone working...bridges collapse...people die at Tangling and Kharo...army under stress...casualties referred to command hospital, Chandimandir..."

She hadn't the courage to go through the main page key item about a raped foreigner whose sense of justice had prevailed over the sense of revenge to publicly rape the rapists.

The Frozen Smile

* * *

1974, Mahuwa township in Rajasthan's Dausa district. Sandy summers bear-hugged the desolate landscape. The desert around the district lay sun-baked. Scattered thorn trees and bushes stood in pools of hot eddy. Prickly branches arrayed in battle-march column guarding their stony ramparts of leaves against unrelenting sunrays ever eager to bring out more evaporation and thus more life out of the desert vegetation. A lovely flower blossomed in a dusty alley in a lower-middle-class locality. It was, however, a doomed flower. The social and the caste soil under its soft, innocent stem did not blend, although its roots tried its flowery best to gather around a fistful of the two constituents.

The young couple's sin was laid in the open under the scorching scrutiny and hateful sandy sighs. The boy belonged to a relatively lower Bairwa caste; the girl to a relatively higher one—Gujjar. They were minors. They knew the consequences. From skirmishes and slaps inside their own respective walls, it could flare up to engulf the two communities involved. Sarla was particularly scared. Couple of years ago, there had been an honour killing for the same crime as hers.

Caste panchayats pleasantly smirked at such on-the-spot judgments. During those days media hardly existed. There were no women's organisations, social activists, and human rights groups as are safely patronised by the Women's Commission during present times. Whatever we can imagine as a semblance of women's rights and their protection must have been in embryonic form. Reactions against such inter-caste affairs were taken as acts of unavoidable desperation to keep the social fabric intact. So even police preferred to ignore such cases; sometimes they even covered up if it involved influential local families. So the scorching sands contained the unknown sand grains of those unfortunate lovers—mostly girls because the stigma was bigger on their faces—who, somehow, suddenly died during nights and hurriedly cremated during the late hours of a mutely, conniving night. Hence, eloping was the only escape option. Thus one night, Ramesh, his life stuck in his throat, eloped to save his and his flower's life.

"My widow aunt Saraswati, who is a domestic help in a big house in Delhi will help us," he tried to calm Sarla as she shook with fear and wept.

Reaching Delhi was the longest journey of their lives. "We will somehow hide in this crowd and eke out a living," they sighed with relief looking at the capital crowd.

Saraswati lived in a filthy shanty neighbourhood. Ramesh's uncle had died five years ago after a struggling matrimony lasting the same number of years. Just after his marriage, the adventurous labourer in him had prompted him to seek greener pastures away from the barren land. These five years saw drunkenness, domestic violence, arrival of a bony girl, bone-breaking toil, loneliness and uprootedness in the merciless, uncaring crowd. Then from the path of misery he was swiftly plucked by death as he fell from some few-storey high scaffolding and died on the spot.

A young widow mother, and on top of it appearing exquisite in her Rajasthani rustic charms, she was very easily preyed upon by Imarti Lal. A pock-marked wretch, and an acquaintance of the diseased man, he hurriedly sneaked in with natural ease taking advantage of her helplessness. He arrived as a selfless sympathiser to begin with; got her the job of a domestic help; brought gifts for the sickly baby girl; raped her after a month feigning almost innocence and helplessness all the while; and proposed marriage after another month. She reflected over this and found no other way out. There was no past or future to do calculations about. The sands of Rajasthan appeared too far and uninviting, even scornful. She thus consented, or rather gave in.

Then the real drama of villainy started. Addicted to visiting brothels he led the parallel life of a pimp, slowly acquiring mastership in his modus operandi. He arrived late, accompanied by hollow, consumed drunkards whom he introduced as his friends and partners in trade. After some days, she too was leading the gutted parallel life of a domestic help during the day and a paid woman during the night. Soon afterwards the sickly girl child died. She too would have died of grief, if not for Rizwan, a young and handsome pimp under whose swarthy muscular body her wheatish sweat-soaked body writhed in love, pleasure, and painful groaning. He had sex with her not as a customer, but as a lover. She could feel it. From among the many men who were intimate with her, she felt only Rizwan inside her, rest of them just extracted their money's worth from the impassive dummy. They even complained to her husband that she did not open the full treasure trove of her body to them and Imarti Lal had whacked her many times for this. But now she felt far less insulted, for she herself let out long chains of unbearable foul words, firstly with a bit of momentary hesitant tongue, and later with perfect ease—a thorough-bred sex-worker in the making.

Having served as a field worker in the industry, gaining valuable experience in striking deals, fixing up rooms in guest houses and hotels, her husband now thought of moving further in running a more lucrative prostitution racket. Saraswati helped him under the garb of many pretexts which continuously, invisibly kept on sending subtle sexual advertisements that were easily smelled by the brothel birds.

Ramesh was struck by the change in her manners. His first memory of hers stretched back to that diminutive, cowering, almost child-bride ten years back. He was seven then and thought she was only as old as him. The little bride was casting curious looks around. Next time he saw her five years back when they were in the hometown for a relative's marriage. Despite the trials and tribulations of the gripping urban struggle, she then appeared a fully blossomed female, who at least had the consolation of a husband and a child, if nothing more.

But now the change was striking. Once all the inhibitions are cast out, sex-workers take life head-on, without caring a damn about any social expectations based on norms and beliefs. Flesh trade is such an overpowering system that centuries-old female inhibitions and shyness are blown into society's hypocrite eyes. Words, behaviour, and gestures acquire such grotesque, pugnacious tidings that it strikes the so-called cleaner society, shaking them up from their so-called better claims to status. Dress, make-up, hair do's, and language make them super-females who can beat any man in wanton display of aggression and domination.

Once she started carrying that typical air around her, she had to quit her job meant for a more decent society. She carried her identity too strongly now, so entry in the so-called good houses was not welcome. It happened just a month before the eloped couple landed there. Rizwan, Imarti Lal, and Saraswati were on the threshold of a more enterprising trade. Their eyes said that they were more than happy in receiving the fleeing couple.

Ramesh was confused and surprised when a wealthy-looking gentleman addressed his aunt as Sarkia and she responded in an unheard of coquettish way, in a peculiarly flattering manner overarched with Rajasthani-accented Hindi. It was her new brand name. Her over-coloured and over-done lipstick and bright silky red *salwar kameez* appeared to tell him many stories on the very evening of their arrival, but then greenish traditional tattoos on her wheatish forearms and around the corner of her eyes dispelled the uneasy thoughts and the minor couple fell into a fatigued sleep.

Asharfi Lal, a notorious pimp from Mumbai's red light district visited them after a couple of days. Surely, some significant upswing in the hosts' business was in the air. His middle-aged decimated, tobacco chewing face spent in illegal trappings of helpless, fleeced, ignorant, sold, and cheated females across India, glowed as he saw the wild, fair, sharp-featured, glowing with the peak of youth countryside beauty.

Sarla looked really beautiful. Her supple body galore with abundance of fresh youth. A fountain of fresh water in the land muddled with impure rivulets carrying social sewage. In the obnoxious, dimly lit corridors of flesh trade, the people involved took pride in counting 'the buds violated for the first time'. Though the male in him was almost satiated—or it had been broken like a criminally overworked pack mule—it still hissed in its full hunger when it saw the opportunity to register a fresh name in the dark book of prostitution. In the lewd language of the trade he conveyed his dirty intention to his beetle-nut-chewing hostess, her lips smiling with coquetry to appease this important cog who could help them in rising further in the illicit trade. The trade was rapidly growing in the areas along the highways. The booming transport industry with its over-strained, overworked, frustrated, tired, and fatigued truck drivers, helpers, cleaners, hotel and restaurant servants were being swiftly sucked into the momentary dives of forgetfulness in the pool of paid sex.

Taking a full bright rose from the hair knot at the back of her head, Sarkia threw it at his greedy lips watching the girl passing out of the tiny door of her dingy best room. He in turn took the gold chain off his neck and gently held the bait before her greedy eyes.

"Full purchase! She will serve better than here," he gloated and explored the possibility of striking a deal.

"You want to open the cork, drink the wine, and sell the bottle to cheap fucksters! For this pittance I'll just allow you to open the bottle, have a few hasty swigs and leave the rest with me," she mocked at the uncontrollable urge in the greying pimp.

The deal was struck. The fate of this new entrant was sealed. At night Rizwan took Ramesh out on the pretext of attending a marriage function. "It'll ease your spirits," he slapped his shoulder in a friendly manner. Immediately after they departed, Sarika laid snare. First she cajoled, used all fleecing tricks to get her consent, but when the dumbfounded girl did not budge, she and the old pimp dragged her into the dark, dimly lit cellar where her helpless screams had no effect on the crowded, noisy, unconcerned world outside. Old Asharfi Lal was drunk and raped her with the fury of a young body.

She and Ramesh had made love during their minor courtship back at the home place. They had taken the risk of their lives to satiate the love–lust-born storm clouded with infatuation of the age. These were the moments they had stolen from the unforgiving society around. The ratty society has a special knack to smell out such lovers' rendezvous moments and their natural, innocent curiosity into each other's anatomy entailed a painful rumble in the bowls of the social cloud unleashing a storm. They somehow saved themselves from the torrential fury but landed here into a bigger trouble. The world is never sufficient to accommodate the love cooing of hearts in conservative societies. She was just fifteen.

It was a night of nasty parallels for the couple. Rizwan got Ramesh drunk. When his suspicions, hesitancy, fears, and cautions were untied by the fuming spools of alcohol, he introduced two semi-naked middle-aged whores (who were not left with much of business) in the sphere of his boozed up spirits and closed the door behind him. Even tipsy to the core, Ramesh resisted, as a love-bound man, committedly tethered to the peg of faithfulness. "What will Sarla say?!" it flashed in his mind as the expert sex-worker tore through his clothing. The huntresses were too insistent. The prey was just left with a portion of his physical and mental strength. They succeeded in raping him. He vented out the full fury of his youth in wrathful convulsions as a punishment to them as well as himself.

Next day, the couple's dead cast eyes stared at each other. Without speaking they sulked indoors for a couple of days, almost in mourning. They had lost a significant part of their respective identities and were well aware of the gravity of their loss. One is most often forced to accept the circumstances. The rarest of the rare have the strength of breaking the circumstantial shackles. Like a game of dice we accept the favourable throw as well as the worst one in utter humility. We might shout with both joy and sorrows. We might sulk. But we accept and reconcile nonetheless.

Once initiated into the tribe, the love and affection of those around doubled. During this period of reconciliation and coming to terms with reality, they shut themselves in the cellar she had been raped, first wept in their bitter position, and when the tears had dried up, they embraced and kissed each other softly as a souvenir of their innocent love when they exchanged pleasant glances, whisked away letters, blew flying kisses, and thought about each other almost 24 hours a day; when a smile, a soft word appeared the most valuable thing in the world. When the shattered glass pieces of their dream palace pinched their young bodies with desire and lust, their fatigued and defeated selves ran to take shelter in each other's flesh with a beastly urge. They made love as many times as their bodies allowed. It went on for a week in the damp and dank light in the initiation cellar.

"Want to sap all juice of each other before seeking greener pastures!" Rizwan winked at Sarkia.

She in turn pouted her lips and gave a lusty pinch into the groins of her paramour, "Hope it will not be the case with us!"

As it happens in the free-wheeling corridors of a sex bazaar, the parasitic undergrowth of desire, love, lust, survival, pleasures, and pains get embaled in a wenchy heap covered with a slutty, stained rag. Time being a great healer Ramesh made love to her aunt, saying it was the price she had to pay for getting them this nice job. Rizwan enjoyed with Sarla prattling she was the most beautiful among all the women he had slept with. Even old Imarti Lal encroached in sometimes mischievously. Ramesh and Rizwan both enjoyed with the new ones. Sarika too engaged with new customers sometimes. Imarti Lal would pay both Sarla and Sarika to arouse him.

In those days sex trade faced little hindrance except for the bitter pill of social ostracism. But who cared—those who poked their disgusting noses at them, their own linen lay scattered on brothel floors. There was no scarecrow of the police. Police? Yes they troubled them sometimes but it was basically meant to increase the local police's share in profits. And the trade and its profits just boomed unprecedentedly. Deeply foraging into the society from their pathetic positions at the social fringe, forgotten in their native lands, they facelessly encroached into the estranged morals. After a decade and half's struggle Sarika ran a posh brothel in the red light district of GB Road in Delhi. Imarti Lal died at the cusp of his glory. His frail heart overcome and over-shoved by deeply rumbling pangs of hunger, alcohol satiated, and over-fed on performance-enhancing drugs as he desperately tried to make up for the money paid to a foreigner lady of the trade in a cheap guesthouse in Paharganj.

"Tried to drink from a dead, dry well and thirsted himself to death," his 42-year-old brothel-owner wife just evinced the littlest of interest in the tragedy and gave a rare cold sigh.

Her face tried to contort and put up a wifely show of sorrow. The heavy mask of cheap cosmetics got a strain, opening a few lines and cracks to allow reality sneak out a bit. In quick desperation she overpowered the urge to be a moaning wife. With pangs of jealousy she stared at the far fresher face of a decade younger Sarla. "Perhaps they do not nibble at her face, as they have done on me over the years," she felt the unavoidable feminine pang of jealousy. It was instinctive female reaction, otherwise they shared a cordial relationship, almost that of a mother and daughter. As a rule, Sarika treated her girls very well.

They moved through the first half of the nineties smoothly. In the drunken haze of loose morals, wanton gestures, lewd stares, illicit relationships, and rawest humour that gripped the naked flesh on GB Road, Rizwan and Sarika's brothel dangerously came close to being the best in the business. Even after 'standard deductions' their girls and pimps were left with decent money. He moved in a car now; was treated with respect in society for money gets you respect and more importantly he maintained a second rung of high society girls, educated, smart and sophisticated, to cater to top-class clients. It included a failed heroine, some struggling models, a couple of ladies from the theatre scene in Delhi, three college girls, and two over-flying airhostesses. Here, costliest deals were struck in the lobbies of posh hotels.

You cannot hope to rise forever. Fortunes fluctuate. His rival brothel owners got him murdered. Profits were going too far and deep one-sidedly. Throat slit, his rotting body was fished out of the dark polluted waters of Yamuna. With him died the pale glow of the hopelessly burning candle of Sarika's life. In the buzzing merciless dehumanised sex bazaar one still catches at the strands of love and relationships, even if these are available in strained, grotesque form. In her case it meant Rizwan. She was now cast into the open sea of loneliness, her anchor gone; life became purposeless. She just could not come out of the pit this time.

As if nursing some inexplicable hate towards the brothel owner, a new arrival sighed, "Now she'll go mad. I saw it. She depended too much on him. He meant everything to her."

Sarika just sulked silently, never wept, stopped painting her face to pretend youth and went further and further into the pit of doom. Sarla did her best. She was more of a manager of affairs and allowed only 'important for the trade people' to touch her. She was no longer just a body of flesh rolling in stained bed sheets. There is a thread of relation management between a brothel and the clientele. The chance arrivals of some frustrated outstation male, with almost finished pockets cannot put a brothel on a speedy track of prosperity. Well-pampered regulars having fat pockets do the job. With Rizwan it was gone, and so did their dark prestige and prosperity.

Moreover, the second half of the decade arrived with all the wrong messages for sex trade. An idealist horde of Bharatiya Nari Sudhar Sabha was frequently making acrimonious inroads into the sex-workers' dungeons along the ill-famed road in the national capital. Most of the times they preached safe sex and sex-workers' rights. The utmost un-conservative sex trade was deaf to the clarion call. Their preaching was sometimes interlaced with talks of rehabilitation and alternative professions. They distributed some sewing machines and parroted many a word before the girls regarding the necessity to get education. How can a huge ship carrying socio-economic filth be stopped from drifting into the abyss by such light, flippant anchorage. Subdued by such a mighty clean voice from the first-rate society, sex-workers too felt duty bound to do something for society. Rubbing shoulders with such clean folks, who were there for higher purposes, Sarla after a long time realised she too was a human being like anyone else. She had come to feel like a totally different species, something grotesquely dehumanised and caricatured. AIDS was becoming a huge scarecrow. Hellish talk of the afflictions born of the deadly virus was sending goose-bumps down the spine of even the most confident and regular brothel hunters.

Feeling like a normal human being in the company of activists, much obliged Sarla presented their leader a fat cheque meant to help them in their charity work. It was her moment of glory when she presented the cheque to the cleanest *khadi*-clad gentleman she had ever met so closely. It was a momentary flash of dignity, pride, cleanliness, and being human like anyone else around. Driven by its pleasant repercussions she even arranged a supper for the workers, which they were forced to accept, not being able to say no and make the inherent repulsion evident to stand as a contradiction to what they preached. Stretching each and every sinew of her stigmatised self to make the function as socially clean as possible, she had chicken soup, chicken biryani, fish cuisines in the non-veg section and sweets, *parathas*, coffee, chocolates, kulfi in the veg section, completely forgetting in her zeal that these clean idealists are not supposed to touch meat. With some hesitant mouthfuls they formalised the occasion by taking some items from the cleaner section. Their embarrassed looks dividing the chasm more and more. Eating with prostitutes! Even the hardened idealist in the leader could not ignore the buzzing scarecrow: AIDS...HIV...these heavy words struck at his rattled senses. During those days the disease was more maligned than the causes. There were huge misconceptions including the one that one can get it even while eating with the afflicted person.

The sex industry got a mighty shove by the rumours and talks of a pandemic. A team sponsored by United Nations Funds for Women went scurrying. They spread hair-raising information about the most lethal disease, dumped condoms at every nook corner to save the clean world from these live-forms of death.

"HIV is a virus that causes AIDS...spreads through unprotected sex...females are 2.5 times more susceptible to the disease...no vaccine to secure life...drug abuse...sharing needles...etc...etc..."

Sarla's courage gave in. She was hesitating in going to be tested at the first referral unit-cum-antenatal clinic sponsored by AIDS Prevention Society and a foreign NGO. Many in the locality had been tested positive. Red alert had been blown in the red light district. Prevalence rate was dangerous. Her head was dizzy with fear. When life is at risk, all other tensions of this world do not mean anything. All we want is just life, nothing else. Spectres of death in all its wanton forms loomed in her head. A group of work-broken farmers, their faces weather beaten, lustfully came begging at their doorstep. They had sold the harvest in the grain market and had plenty of money in their pockets. She knew they had money but turned them away. She had decided to take all her crew to the clinic.

"The sluts, the whores...even they have the choice of choosing by looks!" one rowdy farmer spat.

The results came. They felt like celebrating. Only the latest arrival—who had been least in the trade—was tested positive. The poor girl fainted after hearing the sure-shot chimes of death right in her ears.

"Strange...but it's just luck...ours! Just lucky so far not to have a virus-ridden customer. This poor one unlucky to have one," one was heard sighing in a mixed cauldron of emotions.

Ramesh? Haven't we forgotten him? Well, nothing to tell much either. The glory of his days ended before it could really start. He had spent most of the days as majority of the inside men of the trade do. He never showed the promise to rise high in the profession. Just remained there like a pet dog. He and Sarla had come too far from each other, even though they shared the same place. Pathetic in shape, decimated physically, tobacco chewing and drinking, their relationship had come to be that of almost mere acquaintances since long.

The unfortunate new girl continuously mourned her fate, while her colleagues consoled her with some unease from a distance. A thick wall now separated them. Circumstances had forced her into that ghetto just three months back. From a village in Uttar Pradesh, she had gone intimate with at least a dozen boys and men by the time she turned sixteen. However, the pining won't go away. Her helpless nymphomania was well diagnosed by a widow from the village who led the double life of a nurse (in the eyes of the villagers) and a lady of trade in the city. No need to elaborate further how the poor girl's journey was facilitated to this end.

"Oh the filthy scum...only he has given it to me! All my lovers in the village and customers here were in pink of health," she arrived at her desperate conclusions. "It can only be he. He injected me with foul grease!" she ran towards to the top-storey cubicle assigned to Ramesh. She came out dragging the weakling. "A dying proof of what can this disease do. Oh, only if I had the guts to refuse this skeleton!" she roared and could not control the fits again and fainted.

Fully convinced of the truth of her charges, other girls felt relieved for they felt a strange repugnance to him and could not remember having done it with him.

"So the dog sometimes went outside. Oh we hardly thought him to be capable of walking even. Got his blood spoilt with some sick bitch and then fouled this young filly!" one was heard commenting.

"What is this noise about?" the lady of the house muttered in a strangely resigned tone.

Each passing day brought new strands of grey hair, more wrinkles, and further debilitation of her brain resulting in lesser control on what she said, heard, and did.

A shocked Sarla dropped back into her chair. Reminisces of that night more than two decades back flashed across her memory vividly. A terrible pang of pity, even for herself, gripped her. She silently cried and sobbed watching his weak body cowered in a corner. He appeared so poor and helpless. Later they took him to the clinic. Yes, he was positive! HIV-positive people are the unfortunate lepers of the new age. The information of every new case shook the still remaining frail foundations of their loose self.

The grief-stricken girl almost went insane. She thought of committing suicide. But her boiling guts, vigour, and anguish blunted her instinct to do so. She was burning with anger and agony. "The bitch in me will kill as many dogs as possible before I die," she was rapidly losing control of her senses and ran away from the brothel.

"Throw the sick dog out," most of the girls were adamant.

Just then a spent middle-aged man barged in. "Will have to use a condom," the lady of the house announced even before he could say anything.

"Why that would be even worse than masturbation. Scared of AIDS, eh! Why worry about your wretched life if I do not care about mine that is far better," he was fully drunk.

They threw him out. The business was suffering. The crowd in the ill-famed quarters had distinctly thinned of late. Delhi was a bustling metropolis crazily spellbound by the Western values for inspiration. To have a sexually consenting girl or boyfriend was becoming the norm. It too must have hit the industry.

There was no need to throw the sick man out. The pandemic was in its initial stage. Overzealous support organisations, government agencies, and NGOs condescendingly accepted the slowly emerging cases to test the efficacy of their drugs and management of the patients. The world was lost in the myth of this new challenge to the medical science and everybody appeared puzzled and scared. The man with imperilled longevity and suffering with almost every step was picked by understanding volunteers to the newly created AIDS patient ward of a charitable hospital. There he got sweet–sour company of fellow sufferers and consoling sympathising doctors. When they spoke to him in a normal, unchanging, un-mocking tone, the old man in this middle-aged dying body looked at them with the bright eyes of a child. And there he lived believing in the generosity of God and success of doctors. Ignorant of the biology of his disease that was eating his immunity like termite eat dead wood, he had every right to believe in curability till his senses were struck too weak to think and feel anymore.

With some little moisture in her eyes, Sarla wrote him letters, and sent him gifts sometimes. She still occasionally remembered those old times. She was now being helplessly carried by the current of sex trade in the endless sea of life. Some inner glow was still burning in a clean corner of her conscience many layers below the frivolous make-up of a wench. Subconsciously driven by this semblance of truth she started to spend much of her time in serving the old lady of the house who was rapidly losing and surrendering to premature ageing. She had virtually no control over her thoughts, words and memories. Their business went downhill. Girls arrived hesitantly and surefooted left quickly for greener pastures. From the past savings they had enough to survive. Sarla had attended school till the eighth standard and then had eloped. She now scribbled words with the mammoth efforts but with the eagerness of a child.

Their house was losing its sheen. What else can happen to a whore house where instead of cheap, sleazy sex magazines and books, you have works on AIDS comprising all the information and prevention of the deadly virus and the disease; the owner of the house ill; and the second in command going out of the ways and means of a paid woman?

She took the old patient to a neurologist. Pondering over the brain scan, he evaluated:

"Don't call her a bit mad! Please! She is mentally ill. It is an illness like any other, with the difference that in her case it affects her brain. We call it dementia," he tried to explain.

He prescribed anti-dementia drugs; requested the far younger looking woman to make the mentally ill lady take care of her needs daily so that it might muscle up her neurons. Even their conversation became an exercise module in which Sarla repeatedly put questions, providing multiple clues while the invalid fidgeted with every movement and word she spoke. Her sympathetic touches, drugs, and exercises showed few distinct results and it was proven that the old lady was not completely mad after all. Struggling with her jumbled thoughts, memories, and activities, she raked up some clues to her identity.

"Who are you and why do you constantly nag me?!" she would grind her teeth one moment. Later, staring in the kind eyes of Sarla she would suddenly remember her as the eloped girl who had been helplessly tossed at her threshold. "O the poor girl! So they won't let you remain in your village!" she would hold her against her bosom, totally oblivious to the story further on.

Sarla was now in the whore house to help her see such moments, haphazardly, disarranged, but at least belonging to the old lady's life. On very rare occasions when Sarika called her by name, she thought she had been rewarded. Why was she so sincerely serving the old lady? Well, some basic things are too deep to be ruffled by the superfluous rut of life however sleazy it might be. These may lie dormant but spring forth whenever chance is ripe. Sarla too possessed such natural lotus that sprouted forth through the muddy waters of prostitution. She accepted whatever ray of light was filtering through the gutted by-lane of the sex bazaar.

Despite her best efforts, the old lady forgot her name completely, lost her ability to speak in a couple of years, and then further survived for another two like in a coma. They were not serving as a brothel now. She decided to serve till her death. Problems galore, as they naturally should when you live mis-fittedly in a sex bazaar, not leading a life like those around you. But once the body has been cut, bruised, making one less than average afraid of situations, then it becomes immune to further cuts. She thus braved these challenges, like a lady of her trade should. She knew that the good thing she was doing should not turn her into a cowering female, so her tongue snapped like a rattle snake to ward off any endeavour to take advantage of their changed situation for profit.

As was inevitable, the old lady died leaving her almost all alone in the bustling whore house. Her mourning tears for the diseased, whom she had literally served like her mother, further polished that goodness under her stigmatised skin. Around this time elections for Delhi Assembly were announced. The Election Commission ordered that even the sex workers are to be registered as voters for the upcoming elections. The Electoral Registration Officer of the Paharganj area accompanied by a much amused staff and committed social activists toured the area. For a fortnight she toiled with the field staff to get the sex workers enrolled as voters.

The process however faced a nagging problem. Most of the brothel owners had no lease agreement with the girls. Some had not even the ownership proof of the place. So they were apprehensive of getting their girls' voter identity card, giving the place as their address. Sarla decided to get as many girls enlisted on her address as possible. She held the papers of ownership, inheriting from the old lady. However, missionary zeal was met with an opposition and boycott. She was living like an outcaste now and she and others knew that their ways had parted on the ill-famed road. They warned her of dire consequences if she did not move out of the place—not because of the fear that she had a choice now and break free of the shackles, but because she could decide not to be a whore now. In her early forties now, she sold the property and moved out of the filth with a decent purse and walked in a restrained, shy, unresolved manner. It was like walking on an alien planet. It was like she was learning to walk as a woman with a new identity. Almost three decades of fleecing, flattering coquetry had seeped into her skin and she knew the challenge of forcing herself to change her ways of dressing, looking, gestures, and words to fit in the clean society outside.

Hiring a room in a respectable neighbourhood she optimistically looked at the new dawn from her balcony. She was pondering over her future. But fatigue and drudgery of three decades yawned within and she went inside to lie restfully on her clean bed again.

"It's another start for me. But this time I won't slip!" a wave of determination swathed her in a fold of contended sleep...after so many nights. After three decades in fact.

Lost in Red Mist

❄ ❄ ❄

Kashmir, the paradise on earth; the jewel of the Himalayas; the abode of large glaciers (Siachen, Baltora, Biafo, Hisper); the proud beholder of mammoth peaks (K2, Gasherbrum); the conglomerate of mountainous, fearless details with its successive waves of Pir Panjal, Zaskar, Ladhak, and Karakoram ranges running from N-W to S-E; the carrier of the throbbing arteries of Indus, Jhelum, Chenab, lakes and rivulets; and ending at the knot of Pamir, the roof overlooking the rugged plateaus of Central Asia. The valley of Kashmir lying between Pir Panjal and Zaskar—the heart of Kashmir—palpitates with murmuring ingression of the Jhelum blithely cutting across the valley. With passionate honesty, nature smiles on beautiful female faces. There is magnetic ambience that finds the soul scampering away on a spiritual sojourn. Mystically glorious chime of brooks sing songs of holistic wellness. There are little lilting paradises scattered in solitary groves.

Here the rich forests nurture tropical evergreens like siso, mahua, neem, and khair in the south; leading to lush green Himalayan temperate forests like pine, oak, chir, conifers, silver fir, blue pine, and deodar in the north. What is the exact shape and size of Kashmir? History is muddled, so even more muddled are the interpretations. As per our claim it appears the most beatifically set and balanced crown on Hindustan. Like a triumphant headgear its proudly uplifted N-W fold meets the Pamir knot; pleasantly topographic handshake with Afghanistan through 40 Km wide Vakhan corridor; Vakhan buffer separating it from Tajikistan, hesitantly eyeing imperialist China in north; and recalcitrant Tibet in the east with its distinct socio-cultural and physiographic entity. Multiple forces worked greedily, laid grabbing hands on its horns; shook it and took away chunks—chunks of strategic location in its northern wastelands and strips and pieces on religious ground along the west. Result! See the map of this disputed territory in foreign news channels. A torn topography: older sedimentary and granitic rocks, highly folded, faulted, fossilised glaciers, deposits of boulder clay, U-shaped hanging valleys, river terraces, and average mountain heights around 3000 meters. Torn languages as well: Urdu, Kashmiri, Dogri, Ladhaki, and Gujri. Facing such a paradox of 'who is right; who is wrong?' has no meaning in the hotchpotch manmade clatter. Still there is a floral synergy; there is an inexplicable musical note that plays in the background of gun-smoke and blasts. But then suddenly a disturbing glint punctuates the demure sentence of silence. And it becomes uncharacteristically noisy and cacophonous. In the protectively caring cradle of nature the kids of freedom try to hold onto dying dreams. It's not a matter of who is to be blamed. More important is who is suffering on account of wayward obsessions.

China took the stony wastes for geostrategic and warlike motives. But the war between the famed rivals has torn living tissues, hearts, limbs, cultures, and religions. Meanwhile nature flows still with some inaudible message as breaching torrents of Kishanganga, Jhelum, and Chenab cut through Pir Panjal ranges to irrigate and fulfil human needs all across Kashmir and beyond like a mother beyond this game. In self-sustaining free spirits, time, and topography carved out passes like Banihal through granite, gneiss, and schist to allow the lugubrious, slow-paced caravan passage to the heart of paradise. The mountain soils in their shallow and silty loams to dark and rich un-decomposed organic matter provide just enough for need, far away from greed. In exotically versatile spirits people cultivate Ladhak gram, paddy wheat, maize, barley, and potatoes. In solitary confines they lead almost an unknown life surviving on little occupations like crafting papier mache, Kashmir handicrafts, wood carving, and carpet and shawl making. Beyond the pale of fortuitous circumstances there are so many little worlds hidden in the majestic mist of lofty valleys.

Nature must have had a grand purpose in demarcating the western boundary along N-S line defined by Jhelum. Its embracing curves around the feeble, imperceptible, loose line of symbolism defining a distinct socio-cultural and physiological entity to the east. But then the partition turned it into a bloodied, iron-grilled, and barbed one. The frontier moved and ended in a bloodied LoC to the eastern side. In the north it lost its bloody colour in the vast, uninhabited northern wastes. In south Jammu, Rajouri, Poonch, Baramula, and Kupwara slowly humanity bleeds across both slopes of the Poonch-Riasi hills. Here the clinkers and epiphytes tighten their survival grips around the trees at the sudden shudder of unnaturally banging noise. Wild olives are not wild; they get trampled suddenly by an encroaching human foot. Pine, cedar, silver fir, spruce, laurel, juniper, and bamboo suddenly come out of their ancient silence and helplessly watch the blasting fury, the man-made fury, the war of religions. Chilgoza and cypress on steep limestone slopes hold to their grip more tightly as the game of one-upmanship is suddenly bulleted through the greenery where no human foot had trodden possibly for decades. In the highest alpine forests, dense green scrub buried under snow suddenly comes to life as humans pursue each other in blind desperation. Silver fir, pine, and birch lying in pleasant hibernation like skeletons under snow break their snowy slumber and brace up fearfully as fearsomely hard-hitting mandarins arrive. Surrounding mountain ranges in the valley echo with hate and its carrier weapons. River terraces, snows, glacier, and flowers have taken a backseat. Something more important has taken the front-seat.

In the University of Kashmir and Sher-e-Kashmir University of Agricultural Sciences and Technology in Srinagar some mightier lessons are discussed among the teachers and students. Simple knowledge is no longer relevant. Hazratbal mosque engraved carpentry sells more than any other florid design born of artistic creativity. Srinagar in the bosom of the valley on river Jhelum and connected to Leh through Zoji pass is a sickened heart. Beats with fervid, panicked beats. It's under attack. It shakes. Life still tries its best to take a foothold as people try to carve out a living through growing saffron (kesar), mushroom, zira and honey in the valley, and apple, almond, walnut, and cashews on the hills around. While they look around with suspicion and grudges at the uniformed soldiers they continue working at wood carving, woollen textile, silk weaving, carpet making and many other handicrafts. Gulmarg 'the meadow of flowers' is no longer the Gulmarg known to the outside world. It was defined by the tourists' exclamations, so without them it is just any other place. Anantnag at the foot of Pir Panjal on the right bank of Jhelum is looking insecurely at the arrival of a new heavily weaponised military unit. Of course there had been many strikes at military pickets by the secessionists. Across the fractured line of the tissues of the same limb puss oozes out. There are wounds at all levels, to all sides.

Staring down at this blooded line from the eastern side, the peaks of Pir Panjal range shake with pangs of agony, for beyond lay the heart of the vale of Kashmir, the glittering symbol of Kashmiriyat in it sheenful socio-cultural and environmental connotations. Pleasant pensiveness of this cradle of heaven on earth has been lost and dusted. The uneasiness prevailing between 1947 and 1989 that had not been able to tarnish the slumberous charm of the paradise—including the jolts of 1948, 1961, 1965 and 1971, for these had just predominantly geographic connotations—was suddenly kicked in its belly by the *Jihadi* version of the issue. It 1989 the volcano erupted in the flowery valleys. Long-drawn-out follies (despite best efforts to integrate the state in all forms) and single-minded, devastating proxy warfare of Pakistan were the ammunitions. There were genuine causes of grudge on this side and Pakistan threw oil in the slowly smouldering fire. Richly beautiful peaks, pastures, and wooded slopes of Pir Panjal became the blooded battle ground of insurgents, rebels, militants (with local and PoK bases) and the counter-insurgency measures of India. In place of glow-worms in autumnal dales, rockets and shells flashed. Gunpowder pungency hit the nostrils as the sharp odour prevailed over the intoxicating smell of apple orchards and wild flowers. Love was replaced by hate. Humanity huddled on the highest peaks of mountains. Below violence and intimidation did the nasty rounds. Ecstatic exuberance of sweetly pining solitude was overtaken by a mad raze of one-upmanship. The springs lot their lively, vibrant colours; summers lost their cool, breezy airy openness; autumns lost their surrendering, windfalling siesta; and winters lost their frozen moments of love in the snow.

Isolated from Delhi! The only surface link between New Delhi and Srinagar, National Highway 1A cut through the Pir Panjal's eastern margins, passing through the Banihal Tunnel (2813 meters) acting as the gateway to the valley of Kashmir. These were late nineties of the last century. The famed Kashmiri scenic beauty and panorama along the LoC in Poonch Rajouri sector covered by Pir Panjal had been shot in full blossom by unbridled violence. Incessant clatter of guns along the LoC from both sides echoed among distant peaks. It had become natural and normal like the chirp of a bird. There were also those fierce encounters between militants and security forces in tiny hamlets, forests, and craggy cliffs.

The last major township to the west in Poonch district, Surankote appeared famished of its pastoral charms after almost a decade of insurgency. Neighbouring Hill Kaka tract was awash with militants, their local commanders even boasted of running an Islamic State there. Indian government literally out-swarmed the area with military, but still infiltration continued given the harsh terrain. Casualties on both sides ensued but the worst sufferers were the self-sufficient pastoral people of the Gujjar Muslim community. Cradled in the high altitude climate they roamed the pastured hill slopes. Survival meant migration to upper reaches to escape the rising temperatures in summers leaving behind their shelters empty for the season. There high on the slopes their cattle and sheep nibbled at grass in the green *chiragas* (pastures) while the still higher peaks—snow left just on their crown heads—appeared lost in misty blue. During the days when there was no LoC, people from as far as Mirpur (now in PoK) travelled to this part during seasonal shifting. In the little circumference of their self-sustaining endeavours they formed a world that was just driven by simple need, unstigmatised by any materialistic greed. The pastures were lush green. Time moved on with gracefully languorous strides. Alas, these grazing lands were now being trampled under the beastly man-made hoofs. In the vilified air of suspicion desperate soldiers saw connivance at every nook corner. These proud hilly people in turn hated them as occupiers, for the larger issues of sovereignty, nationhood, nation state, and theocracy had no meaning for them. Beyond the clutches of the larger world, they had led isolated lives following their unique customs. Then militants arrived. They claimed to be freedom fighters, the ones who were waging holy war, and asked for unquestioned requisition of food, shelter, and even sex. Any question and they were termed as traitors to the religion. It was a struggle for freedom they said. But to these nomadic Gujjar Muslims freedom meant only moving with their animals to their highland *chiragas*. They were not much concerned about facts and figures of a larger life beyond this.

Having spent his entire fifty years in these remote Pir Panjal mountains of Surankote, Muhammad Aslam Khan scratched his beard in trepidation. In Marrah (a forward hamlet in Surankote) a gentle gale tugged at his beard to make him realise the disciplined periodicity of his earlier migrations. His world started and ended between *dhoks*, temporary shelters in higher pastures, and his permanent stone, wood, and mud cabins in Marrah. Journeys among these meant life. It was late spring time. Snow had thawed in higher reaches. Blades had grown. Their scent pricked his nostrils as he greedily ogled into the hazy heights. All through the spring he had suffocated his urge to escape into the thawing pastures. However, all the paths leading out of the hamlet had military outposts. How he wished to run unchecked into the far flung hamlets on this and the other side to meet his acquaintances and relatives. He had no photograph of theirs, so despite his best efforts only a misty semblance of their visage and gilded name entered his brain. His closest friend Haji Makhan came to meet him the other day. Coming from Telikatha in Kulali belt this mighty mountaineer and scaler of peaks appeared sagged and worn out.

"At every step you have to show this chit!" he held out a dog-eared piece of card paper that authenticated his identity. "I could have even twice scaled the Tatakutti hills"—Pir Panjal's highest peak—"during this time."

Their friendship had blossomed in mountains. "Last year we somehow managed. But this year it seems almost impossible," his host agreed and nodded into the mountains.

"From our side too we cannot move out. Delhi army is swarming like ants along the surrounding ridges. Still the *Jihadis* succeed in piercing. The terrain does the plainers in. If a goat can sneak in through the densely forested hillside so can the fighters. The army-men just spray around their bullets during nights while they safely land in," Haji Makhan sighed and added another talk about the long-running saga basically of agonies.

Bashir, his nephew, got a few of them into the village two nights back. "*Lashkar-e-Taiba* commander," he had pointed at the fiercely big fellow. The man in turn said that the area was under their control and they would liberate the whole land from here onwards.

"The earlier they do it, the better it would be. Before summers! So that we can go to the *chiragas* freely!" Aslam had a glint of hope in eyes.

During winters about 200 militants had hibernated in an almost inaccessible but strategically important ridge. Many of these were mercenaries. Afghans comprised a good percentage of the lot. Their requisitions devotedly maintained by sympathetic nomads along hidden goat tracks and short-cuts along the historical Mughal road on which the soldiers patrolled while lost in a strange silence cutting across air laden with uncertainty and death. This rugged, dangerous and famished link (short-cut) to the valley had been abandoned after the wars. With hair-raising, pinpointing precision it cut through the daunting peaks of Pir Panjal. In just 84 kilometres of arduous journey it reached Anantnag at the other end of Pir Panjal. People now took two day long tiresome route through Jammu to reach the cradle of their heart—Srinagar.

"That is alright. But every minute of the night I felt an army bullet piercing my chest. Even more pinching was the lustfully shooting eye of that Afghan. Just ate my granddaughter Noor through his eyes. Hadn't that AK-47 been by his side I'd have slapped him hard to teach him manners of the land. The rascal....Then during the winters I've lost almost a quarter of my flock. I have given him several beatings but the lad is just helpless. His back just a pathetic path between my bleating sheep and the *jihadis*' big mouths. Yesterday the Major summoned him for interrogation. Bashir stood stonily while I pleaded, 'If militants succeed in infiltrating then Sahib what is the fault of we poor villagers?' I almost wept, 'We are the helpers of army. My maternal uncle was a legendary informer in Poonch's Chaneri village. Local commander even awarded him during the war in 1965. He also ran a network of information through his nomads in the 1971 war. Whenever he sat for *namaj*, Haji Pir mountain loomed large in his memories, for he had grown up as a child on its motherly slopes. We captured it in 1965, but it was handed back to Pakistan. Do you know the fate of this man? His house was destroyed in shelling from across the border and just from his identity, a few years ago, the militants killed the old man. Then there is my cousin in the Sekhlu village'....hee hee I would have eaten his brain with patriotic stuff. He was bored, the officer. 'OK OK,' the officer cut me short. I had to make Pakistan a villain and Bashir was lucky to give me company back home."

Now the question of reaching the *chiragas* rose. Makhan ruled out the possibility of large-scale herd movement from his side. "May be from your side it's possible. I will just go with you to breathe in the pure air over there. Here it's just gun-smoke. In my absence Ramzan, my younger brother, will take care of the family."

With mellowed, lacklustre steps they were walking along a path passing by an apple orchard. The Major, officer in charge of the nearest military post, gave them a stern lecture. "Swines...traitors...seeking pretexts to go up there and replenish the terrorists' supplies!" he pointed to a bluish ridge dimly visible across the misty clouds high up in the mountains.

Many of them had run from places just near the LoC after Pakistani shelling destroyed their houses. They looked apprehensive as if scared of another onslaught even here. Their dreams razed down in the forward hamlets of Poonch.

"They got compensation for their destroyed houses and now get wages," he pointed out the Gujjar labourers.

"Like caged wild animals they would escape helter-skelter into the west if there is ceasefire along the LoC and would go further," Haji thought nurturing a natural, faded, vague pang of sympathy for Pakistan. This sympathy was born of just one fact: They were people like themselves—the land of Islam. While these gun-totting Hindus were the ones who were fighting against Islam. Their helpless loneliness in counterinsurgency operations evoked, on rarest of occasion, some traces of pity for these professionally bound humans risking their lives for the causes he could not understand. It happened sometimes.

"Sahib, *saar* please remember that we Gujjars gave the initial information about Pakistan's designs during all the wars..." Aslam tried.

"And now provide help to the terrorists!" he heard the Major telling him curtly. "Listen *miyanji*, those *chiragas* of yours are like buzzing beehives of terrorists armed with full ammunition. Till we clear the area, you better stop bleating!"

"*Saar*, how will we survive?" entreaties are to be repeated, so Aslam tried again.

"Government is thinking of some relief and rehabilitation. Rupees you will get. Tart notes...for doing nothing!" the Major rapped the folded newspaper on the wooden bench.

At Poonch, the district headquarters, a virtually non-existent administration was scratching its bald head to chalk out some relief dispensation. Faarukh Abdullah had been ensconced in the hot seat.

"You have your own CM! He will ensure that all your miseries are done away with and you get a nice compensation!" putting all hope on Sheikh junior's burly shoulders, he tore open a letter and was lost in more important matters.

Two soldiers entered the tightly secured premises. Old Gulam Mohammad walked by their side, distinctly carrying his frail pride through quick agile steps. His son Irfan was missing for the last five years. He had been a primary school teacher. Being educated among the simple Gujri- and Pahadi-speaking people meant a status symbol. He looked at problems with a different perspective than others around. But then a fellow teacher from Manjakote near the LoC in Rajouri arrived in his life and those long talks turned him into somewhat peculiarly serious reflections. They then twice visited Pakistan legally—once through the Wagah route and second time by the Uri route—to meet their divided families across the border. The second time they did not return. Rumours had various shades. Some said he had gone to Arab, others said he was fighting in the valley after getting trained in Pakistan; still others suggested Nepal and Bangladesh. A faded dark headcloth folded around his head, an open unbuttoned woollen sleeveless sheepskin jacket over his long flying dark-grey *kurta* and loose pyjama, Gulam Muhammad's tall sinewy figure approached with typical nomadic dignity. His clean-shaved upper lip and well-manicured silvery strands of beard bordering his sagging jaw-line twitched with apprehension and fear.

"Your elder son has probably been paid with a bullet for his traitorship, now we hear the younger one is also..."

"No *saar*, he is just a poor innocent shepherd," Gulam's face betrayed his Gujjar pride.

"Well old man, keep him controlled otherwise you might lose him as well!" the stout Major shouted. "Do not forget we have our informer nomads who tell us about what is cooking in your Pak-poisoned brains!"

Sweet–sour engagements in any society are inevitable. These mundane skirmishes had their inconsequential existence in this simple mountainous society as well. However these harmless flints of sparks could be misused to build up a huge fire in the hayrack of hate, violence and distrust. Just as among the locals there were those who had picked up guns, there were some who had grudges against them born of neighbourly fight over cattle, pastures, and prestige. These things are inevitable among humans who stay in neighbourhoods. The army drew informers from the latter. A couple of months ago two such alleged informers, two sweet-faced minors, had been killed. "Killed as revenge by the *jihadis*," was the common refrain.

To take the chain further, the two victims had their family, friends and well-wishers to whom the *jihadis* became just plain murderers. During the mourning period, the local armymen sympathised with them and a few youths from the positive corners were enlisted as special police officers (SPOs). "Iron cuts iron!" the top brass on the Indian side must have thought. There were four SPOs from this hamlet. During the upcoming summers it was expected they will function as expert guides in the treacherous mountains in army's war against the terrorists. It was the army's strategy of erecting a strong local bulwark against terrorists along the 740 kilometres of LoC zigzagging across Poonch, Rajouri, Pulwama and other districts. The army detachments in this area included many Sikh troops and due to linguistic affinities between Gujri and Punjabi there were at least sweet-sour verbal pot-shots with the troops. Then there were locals who in lieu of pittance of an allowance provided facilities (like conscripting horses, mules, and ponies for transporting man and material for the pickets on stiff cliff faces) many times worth their wages. At least their identities had not been lost. Walking on razor edge they had to somehow support their families and even nurtured some feeble traces of pride to align with the side that was at least numerically superior in the warfare. Those fleeced by the other side led a faceless life, where martyrdom was the only destination for some future fulfilment of the dream.

Muhammad Aslam Khan's problems increased further. Theirs was a big family and he was the patriarch. He was respected for his mature understanding ways. During the decade of militancy he had seen much change. Lifelong his ancestors had scaled the highlands for greener pastures. But when the military and secessionists fouled the virgin blades even before their goats could nibble these, they were forced to register themselves to avail passes for movements to pastures from the revenue authorities. When the bureaucracy comes to plague a place it has its own clean, bloodless form of pillaging. Rules, regulations, renewals meant some folded, crumpled, dog-eared ten, or twenty rupees bills in the *sarkari babus'* pocket. The prices of their livestock products like wool and mutton had toppled down with increased violence. While the guns rattled, it was the fight against poverty that was acquiring even nastier forms. In that little world even small-small pleasures were rapidly becoming rarities. With consummate advocacy larger players had toppled the tiny stage basking in peace and tranquillity. People's psyches carried a plethora of pains.

His younger sister Begum Khatun lived at Chaneri near LoC. During these ten years innumerable wrinkles had come to mark her once beautiful, spotlessly apple-coloured face as the guns rattled from both sides and her face contorted with fear. During this violent decade her two kid daughters, just four and six years old respectively when the violence started on a fiercer note, had blossomed like undaunted flowers amongst terror and mayhem. Finding it an area of most suitable incursions the local army command decided to fence it from this side. Their forward hamlet was left in a lurch between the LoC to the west and the barbed wire fence to the east. Now her eleven-year-old son, whom she wanted to get educated, travelled a couple of kilometres along the fence to reach the road to his primary school. Her husband grew mountain paddy and maize. The crop was but trampled down many times as encounters raged between the interests on this side and those on the opposite.

"Both sides are responsible for the desecration of our crops. The *jihadis* because they take shelter in it; the army because they force us to cut out even prematurely if it creates inconvenience. The place from where we hoped to earn a living, we saw them dragging out the bodies of four boys and two soldiers," she wept before her brother as those rusty red-painted iron posts with V-shaped upper ends with lethal grey silvery barbed wires haunted her conscience.

The fence ran right across their maize fields taking a strategic and safe turn to provide safety to the soldiers during the gunfire. To its eastern side along the footpath gun-totting soldiers in camouflage fatigues patrolled in hair trigger alarm. She often fought with them wordy duels for last night's forays into the breasts of her crop, and swore in alien language so that they could not understand. Those sturdy young soldiers just laughed her away:

"At least you are sleeping with your beautiful daughter's auntie! We are fighting for life here," they mused, staring at those chiselled Kashmiri features.

"Then a week ago there was a bombardment from both sides. Fools on both sides...are too far from each other to taste each other's blood. Their combined rockets just fall on our poor heads. The roof of our house was shattered killing the children's father. Why did not Allah take our lives as well! Just like sheep and goats we too should have accompanied him to the other safer world!" she was choked with irrepressible sorrow. "India's or Pakistan's bomb we do not know."

With a cold and dejected sigh Aslam looked at the girls and the boy. "Things here also are the same! But we will try to help you in these troubled times," he looked older than he really was as he spoke in utter dejection.

****

Talks of village defence committees (VDCs) did slumberous rounds from different sections of the forward districts in Pir Panjals. In strife torn Mahore (Resai), Kalakote (Rjouri) and Surankote (Poonch) the military command charted out an effective strategy to raise efficient bulwarks against militancy in the far flung hilly hamlets of these areas. Whatever might have been the extent of Indian military's frustrated high-handedness in tackling the infiltrators and their local support bases, the shadowy faceless network of the militancy had sown seeds of dissension against the 'freedom fighters'. After all there were forced and intimidated requisitions of food, shelter and sex; targeted killings of Hindus, Sikhs and moderate Muslims; enforced migration of minority to the south of Chenab; and polarisation of society. In fact the *jihadis* let loose a long trail of distrust and fear as after infiltration and strengthening their pockets of support they sneaked into the interior areas for the final kill. However, the people then did not know the larger concept of a pan-Islamic theocratic state. Their distinct lifestyle ensconced in a unique self-sustaining culture cast a distrustful eye over anybody bumping into it. The sheer number of Indian troops in their intimidating convoys, patrols, pickets, and eagle emplacements had created a cloud of fear and suspicion. The militants, meanwhile, lesser in number, had their romanticised share in the cycle of violence. As time passed both sides appeared culpable for their woes to these simple hilly people whose language, culture, and nomadic economy unitised them into a distinct entity.

There were some struggling sinews of minority in these border belts of fire. The easy-going nomadic society had been polarised by religious extremists and the equally harsh measures to suppress the uprising. Initially it was the minority that accepted the military offer to save their home and hearth. The AK 47 (the pen of *jihadis* to write a chapter on freedom) is a mighty big thing. It started pouring metallic venom that was impassive to the wounded agonies of even local Muslims. There were instances of the supposed freedom fighters killing the families of Gujjar Muslims on suspicions of army informers. Revengefully the latter enlisted with the VDCs and it perpetuated the fiery circle further on. When the militants massacred the members of the minority community, the Gujjars shook their heads in disapproval, some denied cooperation, and some even raised voice against the *jihadi* culture openly. Result? Their names also entered the target list. Much to their chagrin they soon realised that the *jihadis* conscripted more pride and matter than swarming (most of the time innocuously tut-tutting to feigned harshness) Indian forces. This dismay slowly spread from the Pir Panjal heights to the richly wooded Kalidhar ranges to the west.

Oh what a dreamy world it was: cradled in temperate forest mountains; pine trees hemming the ridges; walnut trees almost plugging the gullies and hollows; rice and maize standing in sloppy fields; and tin roofed mud, stone, brick, and wood dwellings standing so comfortably composed like these were just harmless part of the nature around. Then everything was savagely deformed. They just anxiously gauzed the relativities between the two warring sides. These poor people were definitely at the receiving end. Paramilitary and military units billeted in their hamlets, these simple people tried to mind their own business. It but was simply not possible. The world around them had changed. It was no longer that small world. It was rashly ignorant of their plight. There were curbs on their movement. Army patrols shoot at any sound in the dark. Army engineers were building bridges and culverts to strengthen the shackles against the terrorists. Rumours multiplied dangerously. Every happening or mishap acquired a religious colour. The extremists pulled their attention and demanded full cooperation and support. It was all getting muddled up.

There was deadly shadow network of *Lashkar e Hizb mujhadins* that had swarmed this rough terrain. In some pockets—which they proudly called as liberated zones inside Indian Territory, proclaiming these as conclaves of Azad Kashmir or Gulam Kashmir—they called their ruthless shots. The religious zealots had mighty guns in their hands to enforce a medieval system of beliefs. Diktats like mandatory *burqa*, ban on worshipping *sufi* saints, and prohibition of Indian styled clothing raised their dictatorial head. Community and clan leaders very soon found that the scale of their sins was swinging from one side to other. Still the army has to work under certain discipline however tough the situation gets because they are answerable. Militants on the other hand can go overboard and take their zealotry to any level, driven by the brainwashed frenzy. The scale even tilted against the militants as the young fire-born souls carried their enthusiasm to the extreme. When there is fire it burns all those around. Even though there were a large number of local supporters among the cadre and a far larger number of inactive (temporary or chance supporters and sympathisers) there were some who cast looks of aspersion at both sides, and a still smaller section that had suffered at the hands of the militants. This last one became the support base of the VDCs. Those who had lost their whole families at the hands of militants became pioneers in enlisting youths for the VDCs.

"Let us get these old .303 rifles. A weapon is a good thing to possess. The wolves are fighting. Whose teeth will come to bite our lambskin we cannot be sure. To defend ourselves from the warring wolves we must not waste this opportunity to get weapons even if it is no match to the devastating assault power of their weapons!" seemed to be the initial refrain of majority of the VDC members.

Thus, squeezed between counter militancy measures lost in bureaucratic apathy on the east and blood thirsty fusillade (the religious avalanche not knowing any limits to violence in its overzealous craze to kill and get killed) and the extremist launch pad on the west, bloody contours of innocent locals suffering were emerging. The VDC members became sinners against Islam for accepting these almost archaic old weapons from the infidels. In reality it was just a fearful reaction to get some means of support to life in a bloody environment sanctioned by the larger force and hence deemed legal. What if it rattled just a single shot at a time and there being even danger of the rifle getting locked at the crucial moment of life and death while the opponents hurled bullets in hundreds without any risk of weapon failure. So it happened tragically in a remote hamlet of Kalakote area in Rajouri district. Paradise safe in mountains, nearest motorable road 10 kilometres away from which a treacherous footpath led its journey to completion among this little group of humans, the middle aged and youth of this hamlet showed almost a childlike fascination for the gun that had just a marginal edge over a plain stick in fight. Before that they had just yielded the sheep-herding sticks. A gun was but a gun irrespective of the make and lethality. They loved it like a toy. Half a company of Bihar regiment was making its way on horses and ponies last autumn. The conduit was an SPO from this hamlet. He was a fully bearded Gujjar carrying a checked shawl and leather jacket in his bag. They camped for a fortnight there. It was a festive environment. Men in woollen caps, turbans and headclothes, *kurta-pyjamas* and woollen open breasted jackets flurried around the weapons. They enlisted 20 men. The behaviour of the young Captain was extremely praiseworthy. These simple nomadic people went out of their way to show respect to the soldiers. In winters they drove away four militants coming to feast and hibernate. During the start of summers they but had to pay the penalty for going overboard in getting enlisted. The militants massacred 28 villagers. Bloodied font of the news was too big to be missed by all those families who had any reason to suppose they had arisen *jihadis'* suspicions born of any of their inadvertent action. Result!? Around 1000 death-fearing nomads from the surrounding area fled to the south of Chenab.

****

The graph of terrorism and counter-terrorism had fluctuatingly ascended during the decade. The quake's tremors bore consequences for each individual, each family, each hamlet and the society as a whole in its myriad specific and hydra-headed manifestations. Aslam had four sons and a youngest daughter. Sajjad, Khalid, Abdul, Tauseef, and Busra in that order. The first three married adding grandsons and granddaughters to his flock. The youngest two were on the conjugal threshold. As per their customs their matrimony seemed to have been delayed a bit. However, there was no stigma emanating from the fact because the prevailing uncontrollable circumstances appeared to put everything on hold. "Times will normalise soon. Then all delayed things will be put in order!" seemed a pleasantly expectant refrain.

The pastoral economy had been brutally beheaded in full blossom. Such a large family could no longer be supported while lying idle helplessly gazing dreamily into the pastures where if somehow they tried to reach the consequences could rattle off in a most unexpected and chaotic spurt. Sajjad and Khalid formed a wood cutters' party from the area and were slogging it out in the plains of north India. Their indefatigable lung power that helped them in scaling most treacherous hills now found an outlet in this axe-work as they cut and chopped down woods of any type. Their thickly accented Hindi—a virtual linguistic filigree laced with Hindustani, Urdu, Kashmiri, and Gojri words—provided a very amusing, somewhat shy, and reluctant means of conversation with Punjabis, Haryanvis, Biharis, and others. Their hard, slim, lithe, steady bodies lost in a wonderwork of axe-manship as if they forced themselves into oblivion far away from the tragedies back home.

The third son Abdul whiled away his time as a grocery store assistant at Surankote township. Tauseef and Busra precariously walked on the path of youthfulness (that is heavenly during normal times) but made now a motley mixture of blunder, ecstasy, and risk bordering life and death. Pari Jan, their mother, was continuously fretting and fuming since the arrival of Abdul's sister. Her often used tormenting tool against the family patriarch was the marriage of their unmarried son and daughter. Now the frustrated pungency increased manifold in her verbal punches.

"God forbid if this young filly commits a sin! Oh you children's father, are you dead not to see such a ripe apple in your orchard. There is a time for everything. Deal with it before it falls or rots. She is a wild river.

Will get into trouble. Curse on these Indian soldiers. They just stare at her like hell. Tauseef! As a mother I can feel what is going in him. Do you think his sinful escapades with his sisters-in-law are enough? He is walking a tightrope. Seems completely lost. Either the *jihadis* will pick him up or the soldiers will fleece him," she was continuously holding her brow drawn taught with tension.

Aslam and Makhan cast a worried look at Tauseef as he passed in the company of Asim Khan. The latter was a surrendered militant. Bearing an AK 56 he walked with militant stealth and military arrogance. The locals called him a traitor because his dreams of *azadi* had dashed somehow. Now having renewed the license of his gun he moved with an undaunted difference, fought last assembly elections, but lost by a narrow margin. He was now busy with a pioneer effort of forming VDCs, recruiting SPOs, and creating an intelligence network for the local army command. People just cast aspersion and spat in his direction saying he was getting huge money from the Indians for all this.

That evening Tauseef did not return. "Seems to have landed himself with a job!" Aslam sounded even relived as he lost a game of *chausar* to his guest under oil lamp in the warmth of sheep shed.

They played their hands without vigour and energy. Each giving the other maximum breach points to self-inflict a defeat. The victory felt alien. It just drew a cold sigh. They seemed resigned to the fate's favourable wind, if there was to be any. With fervourous exude of night time spirits an owl hooted. Outside the splendorous rays of the spring moon were bathing *chinars* and deodars with milky comfort. However, agonies in human heart were beyond the reach of nature's comforting hand.

Makhan sighed despondently, "Yours have not yet started...the problems. Ours have boiled up even in the freezing winters. Due to Bashir the army always smells the rat. Crammed in my hole, unable to go to the pastures, hearing soldiers' abuses, I just could not take it anymore. One night I saw him with a sketch map. He was marking hillside bunkers and soldiers' positions. I saw blood in his eyes as he drew those red pencil lines marking escapes and hide routes. I have left everything to Allah's will! And came here for a few days to..." He was choked with some vague fear and stopped, startled as if some soldier's gun was thrust into his ribs.

Aslam's big hairy hand dropped gently with a sympathetic tap on his friend's shoulder.

Next day, while they were smoking hookah under a walnut tree on a little hillside terrace where Aslam stored forage, his wife came running and yelled, "Enough of smoke old man! Run to Surankote and save Tauseef if you can! He has picked up the *kaafir's* gun against the Prophet. Allah save us!" the force of the calamity was too overpowering for her.

How could he avoid her homely diktats? He hated noise. There was enough of it due to the guns rattling around. Next dawn both friends were setting out for the sleepy township so dangerously close to the line of religious fissure.

"Their son is an educated sahib. Jots down the pillaging demands of his mother and sisters," she dropped a crumpled and bunched sheet of paper that she was squeezing in her sweating fist.

Aslam straightened the crumpled piece of paper. From the far away banks of memory, his sister's childish face lurked in his mind and smilingly he put the paper in his pocket.

Even though she was a helpless refugee, still one needs a few things at a new place. She had absolutely no money to pay for anything. From distant hilltops gunfire echoed through the valley. His sister's boy came playing on the footpath straddling the pine tree covered ridge. Looking at him, at his childish unconcerned ways, everything appeared normal. But it was not. Paradisiacal surroundings echoed with a vague warning. Far away walnut trees stood in fear and suspicion. Terror and counter terror vilified the air. Some flowers ensconced on a narrow strip of fertile ledge stood soaked in fear. A gun rattled in the valley. A pigeon that was sitting on a walnut branch and lost in a corpus of soulful thoughts suddenly fluttered among the branches and lost a feather from its plume.

Aslam's ear though drummed with violence, but he was immune to the noxious fumes of gunpowder smoke. If the fresh fragrance of wilderness no longer reached his nose, then gun-smoke did not either. Last autumn his visit to Surankote had been at the cost of his smelling faculty. Coming back from the shop Abdul worked in, he passed the semi-crowded bazaar. A hand grenade was thrown at the square side watch post. Due to the protection provided by the sand bag parapet none of the intended targets was hit but the unfortunate visitor found himself hurled to the ground. Minor splinters had cut his dress. He but found his bleeding nose more disturbing because there was no outer cut. It stopped by the time he received first aid. However he felt a slight pain when he put some pressure on the olfactory area. There was a bit of swelling as well. He did not know that his smelling nerves had been damaged. It was the first Friday of *Ramzan*. A prayer was to be held by the square. The military brought order. The gathering for prayers was handled with shoves and angry words. Aslam, bandaged, his smelling nerves damaged, still stood with unusual calm, mystically rolling beads in his fingers and murmuring Allah's name to restore the heavenly lore of his land. In utter humility and surrender the people bent on their knees, their head touching the ground to feel the solely supreme power of God. His nose so close to the mother earth, he was unaware that the world was odourless to him now. Yet he was as firm a believer as he ever was.

Heavily armed J&K police personnel stood guard over their backs. Most of them were Muslim and appeared lost in a strange no man's land. While bending Aslam felt pain under the top point of his nose, a tiny drop of blood trickled down his nose and kissed the soil of his famed land. The land tasted a sip of innocent blood. That evening, much to his chagrin, while praying for his family at a Sufi *dargah*—militants had boycotted the worship—he no longer felt the fragrance of incense that gives divine succour to soul at the *dargahs.* Next day his son took him to a doctor who prescribed some cheap anti-inflammatory drugs and read out his verdict:

"You have lost your smelling power *bade miyan.* There is no drug for it. If the damage is temporary, you might regain your smelling faculty after some time. But if the injury is permanent, then..." he tut-tutted to send the message.

It is better to lose smelling power in a grenade blast than to lose limbs or even life. Aslam understood it and knew exactly well how to console him, or even consider himself to be lucky.

This following summer, as he stepped again on the town's soil, he found the whole sleepy town abuzz with strange tension. How strongly he felt the urge to drive his flock of sheep into the misty heights. Far away from all these maddening events and tensions. A prominent field commander of *Hizb-ul-Mujahideen* had engaged the forces in a fierce encounter. Ibrahim Khan the architect of terror for the security forces commanded a brute reputation among the locals. His oeuvre of terror included car-bomb attacks, a hair-raising suicide attack by one of his cadre and several attacks on government offices. Operatives of his cell were spreading far and wide under his astute tutelage. With this open challenge to the army's authority he seemed to have written a distinct chapter in the violent history of the times.

****

Ibrahim Khan and Asim Khan (the latter the famous cog in counter terrorism) came from well-to-do families of the area. Both were fast friends and final year students of the University of Kashmir when mass indoctrination of violence started in 1989. On the campus secession from India seemed more important than curriculum. They had their overzealous conception of violence and Kashmir. Very easily they found an ideological mentor in one of their teachers who from the safety of his chair brainwashed them to believe in violence for Islam's sake. When it came to choosing the fighting groups they chose separate outfits. Why? Because their camaraderie and friendship stood on the foundation of the commitment to excel each other in whatever they did. They were fierce competitors. "Whose cell will excel in inflicting more grievous injuries on the Indians" was the competition now. Asim went for LeT while Ibrahim chose HM. Under the tutelage of Srinagar-based elements they showed enough promise. Crossed the border to kiss the holy land of *jihad* and came back as lethal fighters. Very soon, Ibrahim acquired notoriety for eliminating dissidents, exterminating the moles planted in the organisation and killed a Maulvi with moderate intentions. Asim on the other hand showed his daredevilry on a soft-hearted cog in All Parties Hurriyat Conference, a politician of National Conference and attack on the BSF headquarters. Both vied with each other to fabricate lethal most explosives from commonly gettable chemicals, and in increasing their stockade of weapons and cadre. When they had portrayed enough vengeance at the heart of the valley they were called back to PoK. Muzaffarabad-based central command of Hizb rolled a red carpet for Ibrahim as he teary-eyed met the Chief. Same was the *jihadi* deference shown to Asim by the LeT mentors. Keeping their blood thirsty competition in view they were made respective commanders of insurgent elements in Poonch-Rajouri area to swipe the wild fire across the Pir Panjals. They planned blood-letting meticulously. Riding the wave of extremism they turned the already vilified air into poisonous mass that suffocated dreams, hopes, and aspirations.

The great Mughals used to come on a furlough through the Mughal Road traversing the east–west swipe across the Pir Panjal. While the Mughals came here to assuage their battle-hardened nerves, the militia commanders came to explode the smouldering *jihadi* fire and fury in them. Jahangir, the great lover of nature, had died while enjoying this teeming kiss of nature along the road and had been buried at Chengus. Asim a keen lover of history loved this king for his majestic flirts with nature and luxury. To him he appeared a devotee of the unstigmatised beauty of Kashmir. Paying homage at his grave he vowed to clear the holy land of the infidels. When snow blizzards mercilessly knocked at the peaks and wooded slopes, hibernating with his violence in a dugout on this side of the border, he keenly read Pakistani version of Kashmir history. Here Akbar the great was presented in ordinary terms. He had used this very road, the royal armies from Delhi vanquishing the apple and orchard towns on the way, to conquer Kashmir in 1586. Then the Mughal imperialism consolidated its strength and grandeur along this short-cut. Many *serais* were built along the path. He had spent a night at one such *serai* as a fugitive running away from the security forces. Another such place at Chandimarh had been blown away with grenades by the military killing five members of his cell who had taken shelter there. At Thanamande in Rajouri district there is a little waterfall named Noori Chump named after Jahangir's beloved wife. Once when he had been hit by a bullet in the leg he tore away the bandage and stood under the waterfall yelling "Allah-ho-Akbar" in the biting cold of the night. To him the pride of his religion had come to an end with the demise of the Mughal dynasty.

An extolling emotion stirring the stony fabric of his fundamentalism, he ran his finger across the trail of this road during the times when there was no LoC. The map appeared a strange puzzle under the yellow glow of kerosene lamp. His finger started from Jhelum town in Pakistan, moved upwards and shifted across Pir Panjals to Kotli in PoK and sneaked into Rajouri on the Indian side.

Stopping at Chandimarh he exclaimed, "Here Ramzan Ali, Abdul Dar, Pir, Haseem Bhat, and Hafiz Mughal got martyrhood!" And they chorused a prayer.

Moving his finger back to Thenamandi he seemed lost in the misty moonlit nights of royal past, "Here queen Noor bathed and I washed my blood from the infidels' bullet!...Then after *azadi* we will be sweeping over unobstructed!"

He swiped across the Pir Panjals. Pir Panjals—their friend as well as foe. Foe for separating the valley from the land of Islam; friend for providing shelter in their guerrilla warfare against India.

"In order to separate the soul from the body Indians now make us travel more than two days to reach the Valley," he drew an aspersion-sod finger over NH 1A's circuitous route. "The Valley is just a stone's throw away across the Pir Panjals and they plod people like they are mules. Once we achieve our goal, from Bafliaz on this side to Sophian on the other, Islam's welcoming banner will greet us into *jannat* in less than just four hours like it did for the great Mughals during our rule in India!"

"Hizb men have stopped worship at the shrine of *peer baba* at Pir-ki-Gali. The gujjars are angry about it," his lieutenant informed with some concern.

"Peers are too mild blooded. Too far away from the iron-hard core of the religion of the Prophet. Even the *kafirs* and Indian soldiers go there to seek protection from us. It is good!"

He was tipsy having consumed home-brewed potion of *pahari*

herbs even though his *mullah* mentors croaked it was strictly prohibited in Islam. He had picked this habit at the university in the company of Hindu Kashmiris. Snowy isolation in this belt aided and abetted by violence had seen the migration of many families to Gulf countries. His family was one of these because they could just see a dead end here at Bafliaz after he picked up gun against India. After all it was an influential family of clan leaders. Only his old grandfather would not budge saying he would prefer to die in the lap of the mountains he had been born in.

Tipsily he was bragging, "Once the Poshanna—highest point in Pir Panjals—shook under the hoofs of Amirul Beher—title of commander of ocean given to Afghan governor of Akbar named Kasim Khan—as he conquered this piece of *jannat* in 1586. After 400 years it will be Asim Khan who will make this stretch the life line of freedom movement along this route where the huge number of *jihadis* will not allow a single Indian foot!"

Then a worrying furrow surfaced on his brow. The troops of 28 Rashtriya Rifles—a lethal counter-terrorism unit—had raised an effective base at Chandimarg about 12 kilometres from Bafliaz thus plugging a severe breach in security arrangements against the infiltrators. Here the army commanders had been successful in winning the locals' sympathy; conscripted them as disguised military intelligence operatives who spied on both sides of the LoC; and even sneaked a few as moles into the training camps in PoK. Due to this support the local cell of *Tehreek-i-Jihad* had been completely destroyed by the troops.

****

Chowdhary Zafar Khan who once diligently led an affluent family with political connections now lived alone both braving the stigma and gilded respected for being the grandfather of Asim Khan. His favourite grandson lost in gun smoke, and rest of his family now staying in Saudi Arabia, he had renounced all the heritage (sold and now with his sons, brothers, cousins, and grand-cousins-in-a different form) and sustained himself with carpet and mat weaving—an age-old hobby he had picked up from his grandfather Asfaq Khan. In the evenings his grandfatherly tone blared verses from the mosque's public announce system. On important Hindu festivals he gifted oranges and dried copra to his neighbour Mr. Lal, the sole Hindu left with that surname in that hamlet, with an assurance, "Nobody will dare to touch you as long as I'm alive!"

When he was not working his eyes gloated childlike onto the worn out pages of religious books. For most of his time the superfine touch of his frail fingers weaved a sweet moments for his old age. His cataract-smoked eyes exuded an aura of dreamy self-reliance untouched by all the turmoil around. While working he would pause and reflect over those happy times when whole tribes of weavers looked at them as esteemed dignitaries worth offering woven presents. So, on weddings and festivals they used to receive exquisite hand-woven mats, carpets, and tapestries. They as beneficent patrons doled out rewards totalling many time the market value of the gifts of love and respect.

He still recalled that ultra-fine silken mat, dreamily woven by the most skilled craftsperson of the whole area as a wedding gift to him. Its lustrous finishing flashed in his memory with astonishing vividness. But the shy supple lady with the perfect sitting posture was seas way in her wrinkled avatar. He went up-hill to collect grass strands, returned with a bundle lugubriously, weaved these into threads and made floor, dining and prayer mats in full sheen and texture. While working on woollen carpets his frail bones felt peculiar warmth. However the fine stages of processing and dyeing required him to hire two assistants and that is how he found company and something to talk about to fellow human beings. These two assistants were orphans left to fend it off of their own. Their parents had died in military firing during a violent agitation. Apart from his upkeep he spent his money to support these two teenagers.

On some fearfully shrouded dark nights Asim Khan paid him visits but the look in the old man's eyes was vaguely sterile—neither hostility nor happiness, some indifference bordering on no urge to be part of an unlikeable world anymore. Some silent melodies kept his soufflés going on somehow. With a defiant energy he was bluntly dismissive of any talk in favour or against the parties involved in the conflict. Age makes one a sage. He seemed calm having accepted all that had befallen him and his family. All he wanted was a peaceful death in the dreamland of his heydays. However, even that sounded too much to ask for. After all, peace was being assaulted with brutal regularity.

****

It was pleasant spring time in 1996. Ibrahim and Asim had been well entrenched in the greasy, murky machinery of militancy. Their Muzaffarabad-based respective commanders had summoned them to discuss and solve a problematic sector along the LoC—Uri sector in Baramula district. To foment troubles the *Tehrik e Mujahiddin* had massacred ten Sikhs, all truck drivers, on Uri-Muzaffarabad road. Sleepy hamlets in the Tangdhar range north of Pir Panjals bore a helpless testimony to what man-made boundaries can do to the socio-ethnic fabric. People living in these nondescript settlements and Tangdhar Teetwaal town had their relatives across the Neelam River forming the LoC in this sector. Virtually every family had relatives on either side of the fearsome line born of the ceasefire between India and Pakistan in 1948. Just like natural landslips and slides on the Uri-Muzaffarabad road these faint memories were sustained by the hopes that a day will come when relatives, brothers and distant cousins will be able to move freely into the welcoming homes on either side. To these simple hardworking Rajput, Pahari and Gujjar Muslims India and Pakistan seemed two heavy mill stones between which their poor, simple lives had come to be crushed. Militant organisations were envious of the relative calm in the area despite their best efforts at raking up fissiparous, rupturing facts and fables piled up during the last five decades.

Then quite inexplicably, given all the flaring up tensions after the winter-time lull, the military commanders on both sides allowed people to stand on their respective shores of the river and shout pleasantries to their acquaintances if they could recognise them. It felt like a refreshing deliverance even though the gesture was ludicrously superfluous. Egged on by festive spirits the people walked, waved and shouted along the shores. Some recognised their acquaintances while majority of them just drew solace from the general mass of relatives from the other side. In between, the river Neelam flowed mournfully. Ever-unspooling echoes of sadness impregnated the air with a sad message about irreconcilable disparities between the two sides.

"Shaukat...! Your cousin here...Shabir Khan...me, me...here don't you recall my brother was married...Hey Asfaq...Abdul, the one to whose son Kabir's daughter was married...Khursheed Bi, daughter in law of... Shabir is dead...Muhammad Rashid has picked up gun to liberate you... Merciful Allah unite us after all...Will Pakistan be able to defeat India?..."

As the commanders of the so-called liberating forces, deep and ebullient emotions were stirring in the hearts of Ibrahim and Asif Khan. They had no relatives to look for on the other side, but the recruits in their respective cells were bleating to draw attention of some known face. Muscles were drawn taut under the thickly bearded square jaw of Ibrahim Khan. Amidst the clattering noise of people's accosts, his wireless set beeped the merciless steel of a message that stabbed his heart.

Acting on some wrong piece of information the Indian troops, believing him to be at home to meet the family, had launched an assault at the big house covered under pines from all sides. Gunshots rattled in the dark. The life-saving instinct in his father found him firing from the pistol left by his son in case an emergency should arise. The family was left with a house devastated, almost every member injured and three dead. Now it was a grievous personal loss beyond the pale of extremism, freedom, and fundamentalism. All reasoning was packed off his brain, leaving him under the cumbersome and fatal yoke of revenge and death. Drawing out his toy of death from under his knee-length over-smock he yelled, "No more diktats from the *kafirs*! Lunge forward and embrace your brothers on the other side!"

The loud burst from his throat was followed by the one from his gun. Writhing in rage he fired at the Indian *jawans* on the other side. Panic exploded. Many plunged into the river. Suspecting betrayal by the Pakistani troops the Indians also fired. Then how could the Pakistani troops restrain fire? The fifteen minutes of uncontrolled fury saw many dying and injured. The indiscriminating hands of death swept soldiers and civilians on both sides. The red waters of the river Neelam moved on to leave the scene of the tragedy to regain its impartiality, neutrality, and colourlessness downstream. Was it a Hindu body or Muslim? Whether it was a nomad, or a Border Range Organisation's Muslim labourer, a freedom fighter, a terrorist, a separatist, or hard core Islamist? In blinded fury Ibrahim shot at anything on the opposite side. He was firing standing at a place and was picked by a gun from the other side and a rattling burst gorged through his left flank just below the ribs, and he fell. As he was required to do, Asim too fired with calculating and discerning fury. It was but motley crowd in front of him. However hard he tried and aimed at the Indian uniform, before he could shoot he would be stalled by some innocent civilian running into the line of fire. By the time of completing his duty of finishing his ammunition he knew he had killed or injured dozens of innocents. In hate, pity and disgust, he fell headlong into the riverside grass.

After that massacre Ibrahim, recovering from his injuries, became a volcano of fire and lava against anything symbolising Indianness. His animosity had crossed the goal of liberating Kashmir. It was now defined by harming Indian interests anyhow, anytime, anywhere. Asim on the other hand, always looking at his blood-stained hands and pungent recollection of the bloodied river, found himself falling deeper into the pit of disillusionment with the chosen path. Those blood-splashed stones haunting him, Asim still crossed over to the eastern side with fellow *jihadi* infiltrators to flare up violence in this relatively calm stretch. After all India had to be stealthily cut at as many places as possible to bleed it to death. However this time he was missing that characteristic verve and enthusiasm for bloodletting. The work assigned to him comprised fanning gun culture in the heights of Shamsabari range separating Tangdhar from Kashmir Valley. In the ensuing inevitable encounters with the Indian troops he led his guerrilla squad well below the capability of his shrewd commandership.

Almost all of them were wiped out by the unsparing fire of a troop party valiantly commanded by a Subedar Major of Mountain Artillery Unit. Both flanks of his thick, hairy arms had been torn by bullets. Staggering across dangerous precipices he somehow managed to sneak into higher snowy heights. There in the misty heights, snow was thawing; water was trickling down with lively mirth; with petite gumption a flock of mountain sparrows darted through the peaceful air; in blissful quietude trees were yawning to welcome the spring sun; in sync with spirituality cool air kissed cliff-sides to literally melt their stony hearts. An ethereal solacing mirage was strewn over the surroundings. He fell headlong into a rill and red water trickled down to tell a little tale of humans' bloody ways. A wandering Sufi mendicant who had taken shelter in a nearby cave tracked his almost frozen body following the bloody trail in the little sinewy water channel. During the next month he recovered and recuperated by the sage's healing herbs and assuaging words. His life had been shaped by the shower of hate. It was now was being reshaped by the shower of love. He felt vulnerable due to his rootlessness. But the heat of his injured reaction would soon be absorbed by the cool waters of this convenient harbour, this real glimpse of Kashmir, unaffected by human frailties and failures. He saw the fascinating glimpses of the Kashmir he had forgotten. He had been lured and enticed by the handlers of death. But through the path of death how can you nurture life? The insatiable desires of his hard-core indoctrination had blinded his eyes to misinterpret malaise as the will of God.

When he tracked down he knew that he will surrender before the military. He did exactly that. The militancy network was critically jolted. There was no dearth of people in the flowery cradle who cursed him as a betrayer. He was talked of as a villain. During his one-year prison term, the military used all means, fairest to the foul-most, to conscript him into counter-insurgency operations. He but stoically spurned all such advances. Smelling the disinfected violent man in him they released him. It was a very tired and broken former evoker of doom and destruction to the Indian troops who fell into the receptive arms of his old grandfather.

****

Judith, an artist foremost and a qualified medical assistant in the field of psychology, felt the confines of her mundane circumstances, happenings and life over all in well to do France. She packed off to the scene of tragedy to give full vent to the creative zeal of the social worker in her. It was 1991 when her 24-year-old petite self had landed at Srinagar where the proxy war had left *Kashmiris* traumatised by invisible shell scars on their souls. To the painter in her, whose sensitivity had been nurtured in the relaxing environment of the developed society, it was a buffeting scenario where her soft soul literally shed tears over the man-made tragedy even though the nature tried its best to shine at its best. Working at the Psychiatric Diseases wing of Shere-e-Kashmir Institute of Medical Sciences as a volunteer, she, at the peak of her beauty and youth, started her unique work of art therapy and psychology among the patients born of violence. A local doctor named Zohra gave her ample support as a translator and professional.

Soon the number of patients swelled to nearly hundred. Children, elders, women symbolised the grotesque and disturbing pictures of the mute sufferers of violence. Caught in a swirling avalanche, destiny had scrawled a painful caricature of life for them. A full palette of colours robbed of their lives, they stared abstractedly in stony bleakness. It was a collective loss of *Kashmiriyat* that seemed to be plaguing them through different manifestations of psychiatric illnesses. Many had been killed, orphaned, widowed, and maimed. Scores had been left in a depressive hysterical pit, traumatising scars on their souls gnawing at their existence every moment. In their delirium many showed signs of schizophrenia at the peak of their youth. Their lives daubed in perennial depression they cried, behaved like lunatics, broke things, inflicted serious injuries to themselves, as it appeared the only form of an outpour.

Her calm and gentle face, gently fleecing caring words slowly drew them out of the meaningless pit and they scrawled glaring manifestations of violence on papers. Virtually a flood of pent up, choked emotions was let loose. During the next six years she talked in pleasantly molly-coddling Kashmiri with a heart-warming French accent and came to be titled "Princess of Smiles and Colours." In the beginning of 1997, one more helplessly out of mind patient was dumped in the ward. It was Asim Khan. During the six intolerably harrowing months since his release his condition had grown pathetic like never before. On the one hand the military won't cease from its efforts to enlist him in counter-terrorism by all means and baits, on the other all networks in Muzaffarabad were buzzing with the talk of his betrayal. They called it a defection. Fearing that later or sooner he will succumb to the Indians they planned to exterminate him. After a lethal pre-dawn attack the day saw a brutally shot body of his grandfather. Asim had tried to repulse the attack with the archaic gun provided by the military. However, his bravery was no match for the militants equipped with sophisticated weapons. He too had been shot in both legs. What a terrible life he had led. Shot both by the troops (in arms) and *jihadis* (in legs). His body bore scars from both sides. Whom to call his own? His grandfather's slithered body bearing the fleshy crater marks of AK-46 and AK-56 found him hysterically beating his head. Word spread that the scion of liberation had gone mad.

There he was now lying on bed under the mercy of Judith's art therapy and gentle healing words. She was often moved to tears looking at his sketches and attempts at paining. As a professional she interpreted these scrawlings and prepared his case history. She found these outpours belonging to a man who was once educated and could have gone to excel in any field had the circumstances being normal. The check dam of all his held up emotions was broken in the forms of these sketches. A lot many human lives could have taken a better course had the circumstances been better. Possibly our fate isn't that much in our hands as we suppose. Plum shackles of darkness so many times thrive on the feast of tiny rays of light.

"What paradisiacal emotions were wilted by time! His self has to be drawn out of the stony dead walls!" she sighed.

With her tranquil logic and smiling care she was always there with her rope of professional psychiatry to fetch out a bucketful of normalcy for these injured souls. In the following months her angelic face and softest words found him coming out of the dark and gloomy corner of rootlessness and isolation. And once out of the darkly dismal ditch, his esteemed persona, glittering after the fiery test of tragedies and losses, caught the long-awaiting love buds. He had never felt the power of love of a man for a woman. He was a child of hate lost in the miserable mirage of actions that were shaped basically by unseen forces. His youth had been eaten by the violent pages of extremist indoctrination. In calm beatitude love drops fell on the desert sand of his injured, uprooted heart. Love has its subtle repertoire of emotions that can take even the hardest of a soul into the deepest depths of tranquillity. He was happy that he had found love at last. These sprouts blossomed under the gently acquiescing dew of his heart.

The summers of 1997 portended all the healing and compensating months ahead. Destiny seemed redeeming him after the long-drawn bloody chapter. He could see a life beyond guns and blasts. His soul felt peaceful, colourful music. There was palpable exuberance in his spirit. How nice are the times when a man falls in love and how scary the moments become when a man fills his heart with hate! His happiness knew no bounds that bright sunny day when Judith proposed to him. She the European lady with healing fingers and words! Was life really so kind to him? He just couldn't believe it. It was a dream and he clung to his life-giving dream. However, were the times comfortable with such contradictory outcomes?

No, they weren't. Fatality had a ravenous appetite. The viciously swirling whirlpool of violence had acquired such intensity that once caught in it, it was impossible to get out. To them, the killing forces, he was a traitor to be punished at any cost. This time they aimed the bullet straight at his heart now obliviously sleeping in her breast. In broad daylight she was shot in the hospital premises. Again he went mad, this time but with gun instead of pathetically scrawling pencil. He thus became a famed counter-terrorist.

****

Begum Khatun, Aslam's widowed sister in her late thirties, carried glaring gaping holes on her dishevelled, grizzled pre-greying face. The fact that a Pakistani shell had widowed her, forcing her to become a refugee was enough to convince her that the Pakistani talk of liberation and Islam was a slanderous sham. On account of her personal loss, weighing the both sides' sins on a scale, she found Pakistani culpability in her misfortune outdoing the Indians.

The military wasn't leaving any stone unturned in countering the menace of terrorism. The women had their extra share of suffering in the conflict. The military tried to use this fact of female suffering. Military propagandists gave goose-bump arising speeches and implored the womenfolk to come out of their routine chores to pick up guns and brace up to face any eventuality. In the sleepy hamlets an interesting word was doing rounds among the womenfolk that at Talikata near Surankote even women had picked up guns to defend their peace and security. There had been a thaw in their mute sympathy to the Islamic struggle. They had just come to become the mute providers of entertainment in the form of sex to the battle-hardened co-religionists. Some did it willingly shielding their budding sexuality under the lustrous sun of Islamic revival. The majority however did it unwillingly thinking it to be the only—even though it was vulgar—form of contribution to *jihad*. Once the gate to sex requisition was opened, it carried tales of rape by professional *mujahideens* in its abusive wake. Discontent was brewing up. The cases of repulsing such advances and efforts to protect their honour were becoming more frequent. There were many victims of violence for being the wives of SPOs. So they too formed self-defence committees at their places. The feminine will power was far superior than their wrists. The local army detachments were training them in warfare.

So these women who once nimbly picked apples in orchards were now being trained in operating .303, SLR and even AK 47. Leading a secluded life atop those remote hills, to reach where it required several hours trek from the nearest metal road, they could expect no police or military help if finding such open lawless field for exploitation the militants misused their power. The women were disgusted over the fact that many of the foreign mercenaries were in Kashmir just to taste the famed beauty of the Kashmiri women. These proud Gujjar women who grew up competing shoulder to shoulder in their fight for survival took up weapon training with charming urgency. Sometimes even tales of transgression by the errant army-men also did rounds. So there was no loss in getting arms training. These were violent times and weapons had become as much of a necessity as the staple food. They considered wolves on all sides, so preferred to equip even if it was with archaic weapons. To add more salt to it, everyday tales trickled over from Afghanistan, how Taliban was brutally dragging their womenfolk into the medieval prison of veil and systematic torture. Realising the danger, a local teacher coming from elite background gave a clarion call of Gujjar women's pride and an all women VDC was formed.

Begum Khatun mulled over the news with sweaty palms. She never had any share in deciding her fate. She had done what was expected of her first as a daughter, then as a wife and mother. It was like always being asked to do, just like their meek flock of sheep was herded off to graze for survival. She felt helpless, a mere stone that was being kicked around by situations and bigger players. That was no life. She wanted to live, to shout against her pathetic situation.

Just like a wicker flares up dangerously, energetically before going down into the gloomy oblivion she too looked at the scion of anti-terrorism from her brother's village. Her heart beat like a young girl whenever she saw him. In agreement with the sweet harmony of her heartbeats, she just tried to steal as many glances of him as would help her in passing restless nights, tossing and turning in pining agony. Sardar Bashir, in his early forties, carrying a square-jawed thickly bearded face and grenade scars on his brow drove those dilly-dallying ripples in her heart as he launched the mission to teach weapon handling to the women in the village. Undaunted counter-terror enthusiasm in him was truly heroic given the fact that Ibrahim Khan had gunned down whole of his family. It was a revenge attack as he had helped in eliminating several hard core militants in the area. Seeing the brutal fate, even those related distantly to him (that came to add up to a whole clan) migrated to the south of Chenab in an area where there was heavy deployment of the Indian army.

With a young girl's strands of sunshine and puzzling urgency of overpowering emotions, Begum Khatun was the first one to lay her slender fingers on the cold metal of the gun trigger. Her heart beat violently, full of love for this man and an excitement born of a peculiar feeling of independence. Was it driven as a revenge act for her husband, sympathy for this broken stony man, or her own surrender to the cooing of her heart, one cannot be sure. It was possibly a mixture of all these. There was a fraction of widow, a part of a human being, a fragment of a female desire in her. Beating their blushing blues away, following Begum Khatun's bold and gutsy initiative even other women from the hamlet picket up guns.

"In return of my son's every school month lost I'll kill at least one trouble maker...from this or that side!" she got goose-bumps of excitement.

However, far more effective and pungent was the shock and sympathy arising out of the tragedy faced by Sardar Bashir's family. It was love indeed. She was even apprehensive of the possible fallouts. The feeling was but deeply empowering and she helplessly chose to be taken in its fold. The ridiculously muddled superstructure of bigger clashes across the line of division meanwhile guffawed in trepidation. After all, hate was expected, not love. Love simply wasn't matching with the times. There are times when love gets out-dated. These were simply such times. Unfortunately though.

****

Gulam Mohammad's son Irfan, the onetime teacher who had been missing for the last five years, surfaced in the quagmire of human miseries. He had been arrested three years back without anyone's knowledge. One year of tortured isolation in a military cell was enough to change his loyalty. When he came out of solitary confinement, his educated self had been brainwashed of the fundamentalist filth. He was then planted as a mole in the expanding Students' Islamic Movement of India (SIMI) network in northern Indian plains.

There were reports that SIMI activists from Bihar and Uttar Pradesh were holding secret meetings with Al Mansooriyan militant outfit. Just to show that Irfan was still on *jihadi* side, the military kept on questioning his father now and then, while in reality he was trying to lay bare the extent of SIMI's role as a backbone for Islamic militancy.

The grossly intricate, stealthy network of ISI using local cogs spread out in Nepal was trying to weave a spider snare to catch the beetle. Even in Nepal, the only Hindu theocratic state, there were shadow organisations like Nepal World Islamic Council and Nepali Islamic Yuva Sangh that were giving sleepless nights to the Indian intelligence agencies. Their effort was to take the disgruntled Islamic underground network right to the Bangladesh border; sow the seeds of militancy in northern districts of West Bengal (in Siliguri United Islamic Liberation army) and Assam (Muslim United Liberation Front) and put this as a spice in the dessert of north eastern insurgency (tribal-Christian), thus weaving a lethal shackle of armed revolt across the chest of Hindustan.

Senior operatives of this network poured money via Nepal and Bangladesh to sustain the multiple-bleeding theory of Pakistan. Irfan as the educated mole provided ample clues to monetary transactions and the ways of money laundering to swell up terrorists' funding. It was a long and wavy network taking circuitous route through Arabic and Central Asian countries, and to grease the oil of *jihad* God knows how it surfaced in the local accounts of the persons involved in the network.

After looming between life and death, tracking the dark pathways of this faceless trail, Irfan surfaced in his native hills having completely lost his identity. Now always pretending to be running away from the security forces, people drew their own specific images of his persona. The task he had been assigned here was many times riskier than anything he had done earlier. One night he paid a visit to Aslam's house. All air was thrown in a dizzying fright. Begum Khatun's fingers itched to pull the trigger of her .303 rifle to get her first score. However, her death frozen sister-in-law pulled her away. Being asked for a not so cordial and energetic supper, Irfan sat there like an enigma. When beautiful Busra served him *Dal Ghosht*—mutton cooked with pulses—her beautiful eyes glittered with the risk and pleasant adventure of a storm-tossed canoe. A holder of gun carried such a big aura around him and her young heart was throbbing with precarious agitation.

They were lovers from then onwards and met in the dark under the still darker shades of walnut and pine trees. Society's parameters of success had been etched by gun. Those who lurked under the shadow of death were the heroes by default. By jumping into the fire he had earned his own share of enigmatic heroism. The young girl was in awe of him. She stammered and shivered as he took her in his arms. She was frozen under the tornado shower of unthinkable sensations as he groped his hands all over her body. We just cannot forget certain basic things that we carry with us as human beings, not even under the pal of death and amidst thunder of the gun.

****

Rubeena and Rukiya, daughters of Begum Khatun, were blossoming like undaunted rose in the face of gun-smoke, and clattering and bursting shells. The time, however hard, cannot stop youth's blossom, just like it cannot stop a flower from flaring up with fragrance. Rubeena, 18-year-old, sweetly poised at the cusp of peachy youth, was all starry eyed. Louder the guns boomed, more effervescently it sent sweetly shrivelling, bitter-sweet, and pleasant and frightful shivers down her supple back slenderously hidden beneath her embroidered smock. Well, we ought not to find fault with her, for this is all youth is about!

"What have you been dreaming so pleasantly to be so happy and sweet!?" seemed to be the query of everybody who happened to see her.

Undaunted and unfazed, her marriage having been postponed indefinitely by circumstances, she flirted and darted around like a butterfly over spring-time roses. Like everybody embroiled in the insurgency, she too fancied her little niche in the scheme of smoked up things and situations. Well, the prince of her dreams was not some valiant *jihadi* prowling predatorily in the wooded valleys, ready to shed blood for freedom. It was a handsome man in uniform. Growing up, her sweetest years drenched and drowned in gunfire from both sides, she had caught the fancy of olive green camouflage, epaulettes, and chest ribbons. While large-scale violence clamped down all plightful voices of their communities (Gujjar and Bakerwal) she had reason to inculcate fondness for the man in uniform. Two winters ago, while their father was in Ambala district of Haryana on work, inclement weather, record snowfall and avalanches hit Pir Panjals. The same mountains that had fed them now became carriers of sufferings in isolation. Cowering on the outer edges of the Pir Panjals along the LoC their tribal-cum-nomadic fabric was cut by snow storms and blizzards.

About 20 feet of snow was recorded. Snow the spring and summer time charmer for tourists turns dark in misery. It becomes rigid and un-melting to human sorrows and pain. The systematic disrobement of the Pir Panjal heights by the timber merchants for decades aggravated the natural calamity. Of late, even the militants had come to extract their share in the loot by forming nexus with timber contractors. So the debris and snow wreaked havoc burying cattle and owners. Cut off from the rest of the country no relief could be imagined. The lives trapped in snowy desert just prayed for a helping human hand. Hindu or Muslim it didn't matter. When survival is at stake we behave like just humans, merely like any other animal species around. Theological battles are for leisure times, easy times when we don't have anything more important at stake.

People were thus suffering in these desolate, frozen hills. Snowy blizzards and avalanches turned everything mundane, far less complex, just plain human suffering, spotless white and devoid of any human colouration. In this white solid sea, sorrows swam and melted to again form still bigger flakes of pain.

It was during this period of their almost certain snowy doom that a troop party led by a valiant fresh lieutenant who arrived there having braved militants' bullets during the summers and now coming to tame the diktats of inclement weather. They were rescued and taken to a relief camp.

The rescuer became a hero in her rosy-hued frightened eyes. Heart has its own diktats at that tender age. Emotions are arrogantly flamboyant. The travails of life in the relief camp scampered like shadows of fleeting clouds under sun as she found herself lost in pleasant thoughts about him. They rarely shared words but mostly talked through smiles. A smile can beat thousand words. It can compensate for hundred miseries at least.

Their eyes seemed to utter the coded words of love-lost hearts. She a *Pahari* tribal Muslim girl and he an Indian army officer, and that too a Hindu! Due to this chasm the disciplined soldier knew the limits to the pursuit of his heart. So even after making a short-cut of characteristic bureaucratic wrangling to get their share of relief package, he just restrained himself to a cold distant smile. Meanwhile, the burning love in her sparkling almond-shaped dark eyes just flared up exponentially with each passing hour. There she lay blanketed with the sweet pangs of unrequited love and his cold indifference in their makeshift shelter.

Summers came and they shifted back to their homes along the LoC. Her father came back with pocketful of wages devotedly saved while working in the plains below. His only wish came to centre around Haj pilgrimage. However, given the testing situation around it was a tough nut to crack to proceed out of the violent web. Once again that dreamy prince came to their aid. Again clipping the shrouds of bureaucratic haggling he helped the over-desperate man in boarding his plane from Delhi to kiss the holy land of his faith. Her secret love exploded for him. He saw it clearly but further withdrew into the disciplinary confines of his job and the thick line delineating the separateness of a young Muslim girl of Kashmir and a Hindu soldier fighting the insurgency. While she spent her every second lost in his memory, a bullet that had the young officer's name written on it pierced his chest. He died. During those long nights she shed silent tears for him.

They too had a *Dhok* (temporary shelter) in the heights, but his father having taken to wage earning in the plains they no more visited the place like others did annually while the summers kissed the slopes. Moreover, the haggling over their movement had been growing at an irritating pace. However, during that summer some herders from the hamlet were moving to pastures. In order to escape the agony of the place where the prince of her heart had been killed, she too moved her little flock of sheep and goats in the guarded company of her uncle and his family. She wanted undisturbed time and space to mourn the death of her love. All alone lying in the pastures she stonily ogled into misty blues. In the luxuriously wild summer-time pastures her burning lips pined for a touch.

In soulful silence she recalled his face, his taut military gait, his helplessness in not reciprocating, his gentle eyes, and those handsome features. During nights inside the *Dhok* she cried inaudibly. Silent tears for secret, short-lived love! Gun-smoked time was cutting its crop of little tragedies to grab its quota to complete a chapter in history. Irony is that such unseen pains don't even earn a single line in the fat book of history that gets compiled later.

In youth the body recovers quickly and so does heart. The rivulet of youth is too gurgling to flow mournfully for too long. It's just not in the nature of a youthful river to not make noise against the rocks. It spreads and spends its youthful fury amidst confining rocks. A young heart is helpless after all. Soundlessly grieving, the mountain river of her youth was pouring its water into the reservoir of memories against the check dam of his sudden death. Now here at the new place the forcefully erected dam gave away to the ripples of the wild river in her heart. Life is too strong to be put onto hibernation. It just bursts out of its own. It was the charming Naik of the Infantry Division enlisted as a guard in the troop picket set up in the main street of the village. Manvendra Singh, tall, dark and handsome Punjabi-speaking soldier of the Sikh regiment, clean shaven, and his hair cropped short carried the look of a hero from some Bollywood movie. After the pleasantly evading game of no-no and yes-yes they somehow stole precious moments together. It was the biggest risk she could take almost bordering on the risk of life. It was the true love of the age outpouring from two innocent hearts where some sweet words spoken in soulful proximity outdid the pleasure of spoiling one's clothes in a secret corner. They just talked, hugged, and smiled a lot.

Her younger sister Rukiya, however, knowing the secret as all younger sisters do, gave her reproachful looks. Girls have varying notions of the hero of their hearts. As the sovereign prince of her heart she dreamed of a *jihadi* wreaking death and destruction on the infidels. So a wedge was dangerously building up between the mother and the elder daughter on the one hand and the youngest boy and girl on the other. Like an airy shadow violence was creeping into hearts putting even the closest relatives to doubt each other. A gun in the hands of a *jihadi*. Another in the hands of a soldier. Guns are guns, they just mindlessly blow up flesh and bones. But then they divide hearts as well. They spawn dangerous warps in emotions. That seems even more lethal.

****

Rukiya, recently blossomed and having the recklessness and arrogance of a sturdiest filly, had her own self-possessed stake in the happenings around. Her tart breasts drawn straight with certain arrogance appeared to proclaim: "As a girl what can we contribute to the *jihad*? It is only gifting our virginity to someone who is ready to shed blood for the cause of Islam!" In her dreams she often surrendered to the over-violent ogle of some fierce fighter for the cause of religion.

With confusing combativeness she had flared up at Rubeena, "You will spoil your clothes under that *kafir* soldier! Allah save you sister, you are on the threshold of a sin! At least *Ammi* is better than you, for even though she is helping *kafirs*, but the reborn youth in her has at least fallen for a Muslim!"

Peace was resignedly obsolete. Thrown into a smouldering situation, all of them pitter-pattered in different voices. Invisible walls crept up to compartmentalise even those small hutments. The extended family became a drama of different roles. Although agony was collective, yet its individual consequences brought a chasm among the relatives. As a dithering spring handed over the baton to a curious summer in April, Makhan again paid a visit to his friend's house. The manner of his talking and expressions clearly evinced that he was possessed of bigger worries than he tried to portray. The way he constantly talked of going higher into the pastures, Aslam realised that the unfolding circumstances at home had been too taxing for his friend and he was somehow trying to escape the heat back home.

His nephew Bashir entailed him the next day. The very sight of the youth sent a shiver down the old man's spine. Muttering something he turned his head away. In his old-age defiance he was turning his neck as if that would change the reality.

"Uncle you had no reason to come out of house almost flying like this!" his nephew tried to be as courteous as possible while eyeing Rukiya.

He winked at her and she flushed. He was so straight as if taking it for granted that a girl will only take it positively. It was blunt courage. His manner was raw as if he wasn't bothered of any consequences. It moved her. It was a pleasant disturbance. Her heart beat faster than any other man had caused it to beat. She felt a pang, a pleasant sensation in her stomach. It drifted down, the sensation, and mixed in the agitated folds of her virginity.

"...You swine, fighting for this mother or fatherland of yours is OK. But if you sacrifice the family's honour at its blood-smitten altar to those Afghani hounds then...then..." his uncle could not complete his outpour.

His eyes having sipped her freshly blossomed beauty he was no longer interested in forcing ahead his idea. Imperceptibly smiling at Rukiya he drawled in an emotionless tone: "People are sacrificing their lives for the cause of Islam and ... and you are browbeating over..."

Fledgling shallow waters in the pond of her teenaged self were stormed by his penetrating, prying gaze. "He looks like the man enough to pick up gun against Indians," she evaluated him. With a buoyantly multiplier effect the pores of her skin contorted and goose-bumps surfaced on her fair skin. The air carried the rapturously tender wail of a cuckoo. It blew into the free horizons of her heart.

Rukiya silently sneaked out of the house and walked up to the path amidst pines by which he was supposed to return. Fifteen minutes later he came fretting and fuming after the quarrel. She just pretended to come from the other way. He but was a very experienced hunter and she just an ignorant, excited sparrow.

"Hello girl, I hope you too do not hate my face like my uncle does," he straightway accosted holding her hand.

The electrifying touch was too much and she just shrank pleasantly within herself. Coolly calculating the pleasant and consenting consequences of his boldness he drew her forward and embraced, "The life of a *jihadi* is too short to lose time in such shyness!"

His touch was deliriously desirous. It was just like a gust of air picks out a richly ripe fruit: a deft touch, and a trip, and a resonant fall. He was furnace like hot and groped her with melting fury. There was no way for her except submission to this transcendental allure. Ever frightful joy cascaded down her taut body. She wanted this outpour to be everlasting. Silence expressed its wonder at such sparkle of ecstasy. The stormy river of passion rolled with stones on its bed. She did not resist while he wolfishly lifted her lithe body and sneaked into the safety of a bushy ravine. A very mysterious, mischievous reflectivity was sprawled around in air. Riotous passion dissolved in the fluffy clouds hung with curiosity. She was crying while he hastily prepared to stealthily leave the scene of his hunting. He appeared all too normal, while she on the other hand looked shaken like a wind-lashed flower orchard.

"How will I now face mother and my sister?" she sobbed.

"You should be proud of shedding this tiny bit of blood for the cause of liberation. We, who are always facing death for freedom to all, at least need this much support from beautiful girls like you. I will again come the day after tomorrow and then we will see!" he winked profusely.

Meanwhile his uncle was letting out all his sorrows to his friend.

"...We too sympathised with the cause of the *mujhadeens*. But this monster in our family has crossed all limits. That day I mentioned that Afghan wolfishly eyeing granddaughter Noor. Well our scum has been so taken in by this bearish burly *pathan* that all his senses seems to have gone to *chiragahs* to graze with the lucky sheep there. While I bear witness before the army Major so often to disprove their suspicions constantly cropping up due to his dubious nature...He is an Afghan overlord—a relative of Taliban minister and has been to central Asia. One day to prove the extent of his loyalty he fleeced the poor girl and offered her like a lamb to the wolf. Eh, the scum! And see what strange logic he gave to redeem his sin: 'If not he, who has come to liberate us, some *kafir* soldier would have deflowered her, so why fuss over it so much' he says."

Bashir came next time. Just had a formality of quarrelling and a sham show of breaking the ice with his uncle, winked at Rukiya and waited at the place of their last meeting. She meekly followed him there all the time lost in the grand vision of *jihad* and she a part of the life of a freedom fighter. His talk of holy fight was sure to carry her off her feet. In strangely curious hustle-bustle he groped her body. The extravagant buoyancy of his bloody resolve pacified the last bit of her resistance and again she gave in. With arrogant diligence his words took her in their swirling loop and the girl eloped with him. With this act he had put off all the veil of secrecy from his trove of sympathy and help to the militants hiding in the higher reaches and preparing for a strategic assault across the Pir Panjals. The match had been struck. An explosion awaited Aslam's family.

****

An unwell sheep bleated in the barn. It was a crinkling, sickening sound. It floated and insidiously crept into the fate of this simple *pahari gujjar* Muslim family. It had its members divided in their loyalties towards both sides. After eloping from her home she accompanied her lover on the daylong trek across the mountains to reach the militant hideout. The path stealthily passed along the once Mughal road. Her girlish heart was in awe of his esteemed persona. Whenever she held his hand to balance against a fall it was like he was pulling her to the sacred platform of religious war. She felt lucky and privileged. I'm already playing my part in the war, she thought.

At last they reached the rock cut shelter. There was scared silence around. The cool mountain air was laden with a strange tension. A sudden barrage of contradictory emotions left her numb. Like a helpless lamb she stared at their faces. They were the messiah of freedom, the liberators of Islam. She was scared of them, but then she would have very easily fallen at their feet to proclaim her support for the cause. Despite best of her efforts to overlook the strength and presence of the Indian military, her faith in the *jihadis*' ability to defeat such a big force always lacked firm conviction.

After all they were so many and visible. The *jihadis* on the other hand were so few and invisible. Her doubts drifted a bit as she saw the arms cache of explosives. The harbingers of death to the *kafirs*. There were AK-47s, AK-56s, machine guns, flame throwers, sniper rifles with lethal range, grenade launchers, heavy calibre machine rocket guns, handguns, rifles—all this arsenal of death and destruction having been transported here inside Indian territory. It was a wonderful feat of perseverance and stealth.

The commander of this arms dump was an Afghan warlord cum mercenary having a vast experience in fomenting Islamic militancy in Tajikistan, Uzbekistan and Chechnya. After successfully rubbing shoulders with the *jihadis* in north Caucasus region, operating a lucrative trade in drugs and arms, he considered himself the Messiah of Pan Islamic republic—the ideology psychopathically gutted into his mind by a reputed Islamic school in Saudi Arabia. From that time onwards, firing the cannonade of his ideology, speaking several languages, he had left a trail of extremism and separatism in the region. In Dagestan, commanding a unit of a fundamentalist Muslim organisation's rebel forces he had been seriously wounded. His name was Mohammad Sarwar Azimi, a distant relative of Maulvi Qalamuddin heading the Department for the Prevention of Vice and the Promotion of Virtue in Taliban's tyrannical government. This brutally powerful warlord had blossomed from the prolific seeds of arms culture and opium trade, commandeering ruination, abductions and summary executions entailing the Soviet invasion of 1979, which turned the land into an inferno forcing people to flee from the mayhem and flood the refugee camps in neighbouring Pakistan. With terrorising sweep the homeland had been blood-bathed in atrocities and hostage taking of cadets from rival factions. Unsparing commanders ruled over their territories, perpetrating robberies, beatings, killings, rapes and murders as if these were their lawful taxes. Starting from a religious school in Pakistan, he along with friends Abdul Rasul Sayyaf and Abdul Mohaqiq (who had been killed in the Caucasus region) he had been taking the self-annihilating fire in him to jump into any fray, anywhere with any risk. He was drunk with *sura*, rolled a hand grenade in his fingers, while Ibrahim Khan cleaned his AK-47. With her entry a new energy seeped into the group. All of them wanted to embrace her but then chose to just hold her hand to greet. Their eyes did rest of the job. It was a beginning after all. Fascinated at the sight of this flower in red kerchief they invited her as their first woman *jihadi* in the squad. When you get ready to die for an ideology, fulfilment or non-fulfilment of lesser desires appears the same.

It was one of the most treacherous parts of Pir Panjals here. In the nearby bunkers about 200 *jihadis* were lurking as harbingers of death and destruction. Some very systematically chalked out offensive was on the cards. This summer was definitely auguring a bad omen for the paradise. With competing resurrection of their spirits, they whispered of some unprecedented *jihadi* assault somewhere inside the LoC in North Kashmir. Even their whispers echoed among the cliffs. It felt abstractly monstrous in some mysterious way. With dogmatic certitude they just waited for some trigger from across the border.

****

Suspicion was brewing up in the local terrorist cell about the role of Irfan. Ibrahim Khan had a long call by his satellite phone from the Muzaffarabad based command centre. There was something wrong and it needed attention. They decided to stalk Irfan by poking torturing spikes into his love tale. Everybody knows the hardness of the souls who have taken the path on which death is sure to cross at some or the other time. Surety of death makes one immune to any limitation born of fear or emotions. It leaves a strange plume of sensation, this surety of death for an ideology. In absurdly opulent enthusiasm one seeks heroism in kicking humanity right in its stomach. The soul's salvaging spurts are long dead. One seeks happiness in others' tears. The smile is not relevant; cries of pain satiate the self.

It was happening before Rukiya's eyes. A rifle slung across her frail shoulders, she exuded stony masculinity way beyond her feminine features. She had fleeced the poor girl and her unsuspecting lover into the forest. Busra had no clue to her cousin's real motives and changed identity. Rukiya had been teasing her about the man. It let loose a titillating trail of sensation in Busra's throbbing heart. It is so easy for a conniving mind to fleece a love-blinded heart. She trusted her cousin. She took it to be a part of simple teasing fun as she was led into Rukiya's plan to arrange a meeting in isolation.

The world of blindfolding ideology is a petty world absorbed in its selfishness. It's basically a knife. It cuts throats with airy ease, just like it cuts relations with an unmindful swipe. Rukiya was now a total stranger. She looked as if she had never seen Busra before. She had a more important family now bound by some majestic oath. Busra's all attempts to evoke some emotion in her cousin's eyes failed as they heinously tortured Irfan. But he did not budge. He had seen many such situations in life. So they picked up the soft target. Each cry from Busra, as they burned her breasts with cigarette butts, found Irfan's strength floundering like sand from a fist that was losing its grip. Hate snatches life, love on the other hand sacrifices. He opened his secret. Authoritatively reading out the verdict of his field marshal, Irfan was shot in the head by an eager *jihadi* spirit. As the hefty Afghan raised his pistol to shoot the mole's sweetheart, Rukiya shivered from head to feet. It takes some time to get completely uprooted. She tried to bring herself to intervene, but any of her effort was nullified peremptorily as Bashir held her back. Before fainting she heard another shot. Irfan's death too was faceless like he had lived. Once their bodies were recovered the mourning talks in the nearby hamlets were again hatefully intriguing. Those who believed Irfan to be a *jihadi* condemned the army as the murderer; while those who had some inkling to his dubiousness praised the terrorists. Of course there still many more who talked of scandal. Of love, of relationship, of sin. Anyway it was a little story of invisible, long sorrows. Overall, there was a big story of little sorrows.

****

Rukiya proved to be as supple as a willow switch. Flailing darkness seemed to have taken a firm hold on her young, heaving self. The springs and stars had lost their meaning to her—the wispy gentilities of life that feed youth like dew does a spring rose; the ravishing enchantment of youth that puts smile to lips even without reason. She had dreamless, stony eyes which saw and didn't see at the same time. She took the killings like it was just a matter of snapping a dry twig and overcame the initial shock with awful ease. It even surprised her colleagues. She was a perfect daughter of *jihad*, they said. Their hardly knotted convictions felt the warmth of her proximity. It simply boosted their resolve. A girl cutting away her roots, and thus almost killing herself even before she physically died, was important to them. But the girl being comfortable at the sight of her innocent relative being killed was even more important. It was the true hallmark of a *jihadi*.

Grandly old pines meanwhile reached out to the bluish skies and appeared to seek divine intervention. The air invisibly whispered songs of peace and a common humanity. Primly pleasant sound of water dribbling among pebbled course tried to evoke the innocent child in hardened souls. Weary solitude among spruce and birch hummed with a honeyed silence. Showers fell with pining, wondrous slowness. Beautifully blossomed moments in sunshine and shades mated to surrender their contradictory natures. Big, bold mountains loomed with love, waiting to surrender their existence to the inflamed passion of the breeze cutting across their peaks. Ignited passions of bright sunny days merged into the slowness of twilights. That was Kashmir, invisible, helpless, trying to have its say. Nature but has come to be subservient to the mankind. The beautiful smile was expiring on many a rosy lip. Aspirations helplessly swam in air. We have created hell at places where there could have been paradise as easily as the drift of clouds in an open sky, provided the sweet-singing melodies of the heart aren't smothered by the useless symbology of ideas and ideologies.

Before that final all important assault they decided to eliminate Asim Khan. In the past a dozen efforts at his life had failed. They now had a feminine flirter with the *jihadi* fire of death and adventure. With the suicide belt neatly tied around her slender waist, like a young full of life gazelle, Rukiya proved to be the epitome of the idea of toying with death during the mock exercises to press the all-important final button. The denunciating wrath in her brought many appreciating smiles on the inflamed ruddy lips of the Afghan mercenary. There was a tiniest trace of love in his eyes. But then he just swiped it away to turn his look blood thirsty. Religious war required blood, not love, no fond emotions. They had made love in pale, melancholic moonlight. But was it love-making? The agile brook of desires carried bewailing miseries. She had surrendered to him like the weakest slave giving into the strongest master. But then she flared up so forcibly that he was swept into the self-absorbing fire of her passion. It left him almost shaken. He couldn't but help being possessive about her. These were malignant traces. He hated these emotions. But why did he feel those pangs of jealousy when someone else was being sucked into the smouldering fire of her desire? He had followed the path of death on which life was just an inconsequential shadow. No, it was just impossible to turn around now. He was surprised when he even dreamt of eloping with her to some far place, away from all problems and issues. He forced himself to throw a grenade at any such softer feeling. He would sacrifice for the cause of God. He knew a sacrifice was waiting. And he was ready for it, somewhat even happier than he would have been without any such softer emotion. Ready to slaughter the self as well. That's what his indoctrination had prepared him for. If Allah was merciful enough to give him the opportunity of celebrating another *Eid*, he thought, he will carry his head a bit higher on the auspicious day. He wasn't sure about what was he sacrificing. And if he was, he didn't want to accept it.

At the Rajputana Rifles base camp, on the outskirts of Surankote, a valedictory function had been organised to facilitate those who had come forward as VDC and counter terrorists. Also some charity provisions were to be distributed to the poor. Clad as a poorest of the poor destitute, the female *jihadi* sneaked into the crowd of charity seekers. Her eyes were empty like they no longer saw anything. The face was expressionless as if she was no longer bothered about the best and the worst. Asim sat on the dais along with a Colonel of the Rajputana Rifles and local bureaucrats.

With unmoving air around her she moved ahead when her turn came. Before Tauseef could see her and run to hold her back, she was almost by the table in front of the guests. She looked at her relative, and hesitated for a moment. She but had been religiously brainwashed to the extent of quelling any doubt or fear when face to face with death at the final moments of life. The button was pressed. Ten people including Tauseef, Asim and the Colonel died and many others were injured. Death had taken a liking to poor Aslam's house.

****

Amorously entwined emotions. Delicate majesty of a fresh-springing rose. Love makes, but then it breaks as well. Begum Khatun, fully carried away by the last sparkle of love before the onset of menopause, spent many nights in secret in the arms of SPO Sardar Bashir whenever he came to stay in the hamlet. She carried out the plan in the night so meticulously that not a single soul apart from the couple had the least idea or inkling about the nature of their love escapade. Long chains of silence gripped the scandalous air around their love-making bodies, to save them, to keep their happiness from falling apart. There were but conflicting ironies. Guns ruled and fear seeped into lungs more comfortably than even oxygen. Death was a bigger surety than life. Unchallenged happiness was a rare thing. And mishap carried a weightier guarantee than the most normal routine things of life.

The couple happened to be in bed when the expected happened. Bashir—who had gleaned the facts of his late girlfriend's mother's and sister's anti-*jihadi* liaisons—carried out the eliminating strike at the SPOs house. Right in response to the first strike at the window the naked couple knew they were imperilled. Sardar Bashir had his service machine gun while Begum Khatun had carried her archaic .303 rifle to give her courage and conviction during the night-sashay. Clothes on or off, we have to fight to save the skin. Both naked, they fired back. As the shots rattled exclamatory interjections into darkness, all the women VDC members knew that their male mentor's life was in danger. Duty-bound, they too shot from a safe distance from around the corners of the house. Hoping the shots will scare away the militants. However, the militants were well aware of the innocuous rattles by feminine wrists bearing almost harmless guns and carried on with the seize of the house methodically.

The picket commander of the watch post outside the hamlet informed the administrative base camp of 14 Jat Regiment where his company commander had gone to celebrate the birthday of his Lieutenant Colonel. Nonplussed by the urgency in Subedar's voice, he responded a bit tipsily:

"Do not move from your place! You need not add to the bloodbath. They are both sides of the same coin, let them enjoy their marksmanship, or markswomanship...the bastards love the rattle of gun so much...as if..." and he snapped the call.

When the scared dawn peeped over the ridge, more than the gory deed it was the naked secret of the lovers that became the talk of the day. Most of them saw beyond the bullet-holed bodies of the lovers—a feisty scandalous tale of love. Guns had won, love had lost.

****

The month of May had begun. With melancholic coolness the air seemed to turn hardened, insensitive hearts into softly throbbing, forgiving operators of humanity. With beauty, grace and skill the sunrays melted the frozen peaks. The frigidness in human hearts was but monolithically changeless. Mountain streams gurgled with pleasant melancholy. Teary, dewed moonlight wailed for those times when rapturous romance kissed the knifed stone edges and flowers with equal ease. The nature had lost its grip. It was a human stranglehold drawing its strength from pathetically enlightening dreams. The rumours of valiant *jihadi* deeds in the Kargil sector did rounds to pump up the dreams of freedom. Day in and day out the people gossiped about impending freedom and Pakistani victory.

Still guided by love and misguided by lust for Rukiya, Bashir knew he had one more score to settle in the family and it was with Rubeena, the lover of a *kafir* soldier. Dexterously he planted a mole in the love tale. Nahila, a girl from the neighbourhood, overnight kindled many a friendly feeling for the grieving girl. No sooner had she visited her for a week than she came to know the timings and meeting places of the couple.

It was a fine, hot, suffering saffron evening. In the pine grove the still air hummed with primitive exaltations of tranquillity. The nature is a natural accomplice to love. It was fistful of a cosy world, away from rattling guns and talk of religions. But mankind has turned out to be a plunderer of its own peace. Taking his picket commander in confidence, Shailender Singh sneaked out to steal some humane, relaxing moments with the lady of his heart. Their intimacy had taken the first few steps on the path of love. They were up to hurried, soft kissing whenever they met and held each other tightly looking around for some human eye or a bullet before parting with still more aching heart than before. Every meeting fuelled the fire to meet again. Love seemed to possess so many possibilities in pleasant anticipation.

"A soldier lives by chance, loves by choice!" he was lost in her angelic beauty, "and kills by profession" he muttered softly. "Next time I get leaves, I will take you to my peaceful place. One can move freely in the night. No bullets. No fighting. Away, away from this doomed place. Oh Rubeena, how I wish that India and Pakistan strike peace and leave us soldiers to our own fate. We are so much frustrated that now we feel like totally separate and suffering third party in the conflict..."

Only tragic stories had come to earn a copyright to bloody completion. Dreamy designs and magnetic charms of love stories had no right to meet a happy end. He like his story was not destined to complete his love talk. From a distance Bashir shot him in head with fearsome passion and glee. The killer seemed caught in some inexhaustible and insatiable delirium.

Only love can take something to conclusion. An act of hate is an incomplete sentence having many possible ends, sub-endings rather. It lingers like a ghost and breeds further hate in minds and souls. The effable young soldier was the darling of the whole company. His killing drew away all sense and logic out of his fatigued and frustrated colleagues. They roughshod the whole hamlet and dragged a weeping and wailing Rubeena, rubbing salt on her injuries by calling her an impostor lover who lured away the soldier to get him killed by the terrorists. A horrible fate awaited the poor girl in the interrogation cell.

****

In strained silence the month of May was heating the hay in Pir Panjals. Rumours had twisted all shards of facts. Hundreds, perhaps thousands, it was being said, of *jihadis* and Pakistani soldiers had sneaked deep into the Indian territory and taken hold of strategic heights along the LoC during winters. The whole of the LoC was crumbling under their attack and its repercussions were being felt in the valley. Kargil war (May to July 1999) had broken out. The whole fabric of sanity was cut down. The bitter rivals were fighting; the world community was worried they might annihilate each other with nukes. The spark had begun in the Kargil sector along northern LoC and every second it was feared it would flare up all along the perilous line of control.

Ibrahim Khan opened the front in Poonch.

"Like the legendary Mughal commander we will cut across Pir Panjal along the once Mughal road! *Allah ho Akbar*!" the shouted the clarion call of *jihad*.

Consolidating their rear touching the LoC to maintain supply line with the help of Pakistani army, they annihilated an advance party of 11 Jat Regiment. It was a masterly mixture of hit and run, as well as battle in front-to-front formation. The Indian military lacked troop mobilisation in this belt, most of the replenishments being made for the Kargil and Drass sector.

Before dying a valiant death, the Major leading the party, gave valuable clues to the strength and position of the *mujahideens*. Then the shot rattled like a last stern message. A grenade was thrown at the *jawan* bearing the field telephone backpack.

The main party of the regiment was taken aback by the military perfect assault of the *jihadis*. Its morale was flummoxed when the Lieutenant Colonel leading it was injured by shrapnel. Unmindful of the orders to pull back a few riflemen—not able to control their emotions after seeing their colleagues dead and maimed—remained on the front, advanced thunderously, inflicted some casualties but were wiped out thus adding to the command's frustration.

Cursing and crudely swearing the Colonel from the battalion base called them back. The operation could not be started for a whole week—spent in waiting for reinforcements—during the time the terrorists replenished their men and material reserves from across the LoC. Meantime, the Bofors fired at high slopes from the fire base of the artillery company and air force planes pounded the terrain a few times during the day.

In the sweaty month of June a coherent plan was carried out by the military: 4 Grenadiers linked up with 16 J &K Rifles and moved in dark from one side of the ridge blowing the *jihadi* watch pickets along the way. While 4 Gorkha Regiment linked up with 3 Rajputana Rifles advanced as reinforcements. From the slope that was open and likely to bear most casualties brave platoons of Jat Regiment sneaked ahead, brilliantly led by young freshly commissioned officers.

"*Jat Balwan, Jai Bhagwan!*" they thundered.

"...over and out...*Allah ho Akbar*!"

Sarwar Azimi, the Afghan warlord, adjusted the headgear on his big head. He knew finest and fiercest of hill battles had begun. He had grown up taking Indians to be grass-eating cowards totally lacking killer instinct. But now looking down from the strategically high hideouts, he in heart of hearts was marvelling at the Indian army's capacity to bear losses uncomplainingly, as unmindful of killed and maimed colleagues, columns after columns of reinforcements with their chin up moved upslope to finally overpower the enemy.

Nonetheless, as the rear was still safe, supply to the militants meant Indian casualties were to count even more. The battle was thus prolonged.

It was not before the brave Gorkha Regiment battled ahead on an almost suicidal mission in the rear along the LoC to cut their lifeline that the table was turned against the transgressors. The Indian Army got busy in the killing fields, pulling out weeds from the crop that was sown in 1947.

Once the *mujahideens'* supply lines were cut, they were left stranded in those treacherous heights of Pir Panjals. Death danced on both sides. The circle of confinement went on narrowing and so did the bloodletting. The terrorists battled with dark heroism, totally hypnotised by the ideology of militant Islam. They stood up till their last bullet. The soldiers advanced mechanically with steely patriotism; with each soldier falling, the rank being filled by the backup, without any fear, without any fuss. And hundreds died....

We live in a world of alternative realities. The boundaries transgress and we are caught in deadly pale zones of confrontation. Here the slow grandeur of kaleidoscopic plurality gets lost in the grey shadows of death and destruction. And there are plaintive cries of pain. Of humans. There is blood. Of humans.

****

Direct scars of the strife were now visible on Aslam's face. This internecine conflict had taken away his son, daughter, sister and two nieces. On 14 July the Indian military officially declared the mission accomplished to exterminate the *jihadis*. As a celebratory gesture the local army command allowed the *Gujjars* to move to their pasturage in the higher reaches. "It is but too late now. The summer is at its end!" they refrained. The summer had been too bloody for Aslam. He wanted to leave the place for some time. He still wanted to see the world he had grown up. Possibly it was lying in fragments in the higher reaches. It won't come to them. They will have to search for it and join its broken pieces with the still remaining parts of their spirit to jumble up a little world resembling the past.

He and his friend Haji Makhan decided to go to the *Dhoks* even if it was for less than a month. Having gone a couple of kilometres from the hamlet and moving along the nostalgic goat track Makhan raised his full bearded face upslope and drank in the full vigour of summer's breeze.

"I can smell lush green grass there!"

Aslam looked morosely: "I will have to wait to go that far to be able to see it with my own eyes, for this accursed war has robbed me of my nose's job along with five of my people!"

The Bread of Stones

* * *

God must have been in benign, prodigious spirits when He decided to bless this simple farmer couple in rural Haryana with a child who became talk of the village right from his birth-cry on account of his bulk and weight. In was a culture defined by putting on more and more weight fuelled by copious diet of milk, butter, butter-milk and curd, and digesting the same in competition against the beasts in the fields. The most important cultural items, if we can call 'agriculture' the culture, included the plough, bulls, cart and hookah. In such an agri(cultural) scene, this robust son of the poor, famished farmers could give smirk, solace and consolation to the perpetually toiling parents, that God had showered all blooms and benediction upon them in the form of this exponentially robust boy whom people loved to cuddle, caress, and call Pahalwan.

It was 1950 when God blessed them with this star of their eyes and everyone else around. Looking at him they would forget their hard days and become numb to the bone-breaking drudgery and, like humans usually do, start dreaming of a comforting future during their old age, secured in his mighty arms. The poor farmer's family stretched out its last of the last farthings earned from their small plot of landholding to keep up pace with his furiously increasing diet. By his tenth year people started calling him Bhima for he really looked like the mythical super-heavyweight Pandava. If there is power and those around you smirk at it, making it the first item of congratulatory glances in your persona, you too then, like a fleeced animal, jump for an acrobatic display to win more applauds. He too did the same. The boy would crouch down under a calf, taking his arms around the pair of forelegs, and give a ferocious push to lift the little one on his back. As he grew up fulfilling people's expectations, their hopes also increased in parallel. Such is society after all. It is a playful thing for them to watch someone become increasingly ambitious, venturesome, and adventurous—especially if it does not materialise in monetary gains, in that case they might even start looking down at it, for if money enters the fray it no longer stays a casual time pass and becomes an enviable business.

Since not a single *paisa* was involved in the entertainment, they doled out copious amounts of praise, expecting him to become bold and daring to cross all limits to get crushed one day finally under an unthinkable weight, and become the stuff of local legend that will give them entertaining anecdote to share in *chaupals* sometime in the future.

More the people's expectations, more was the weight on his broadening, bulky back, and still more became the pressure on the resources of his frail father. The prematurely greying man had seen those days when the wrestlers and power jugglers were held in venerable esteem, when wonderstruck Maharajas showered sparkling bounties on their sweating, soil-smeared, muscular frames after witnessing an entertaining, daring show of strength; when the *akhara* was worshipped like a shrine; when in local wrestling duels at fairs people gathered crazily to watch and holler at the brutal show of strength. Apart from the heroic status, object of incessant talk, it fetched rewards as well. However, in post-independent India the returns from the show of strength were getting bleaker. After all, it was a modern India in the making. Show of mind was getting predominance over the show of strength.

He was their only child. Such a huge one. Easily spottable wherever he went. His body was not muscular like stone. It was corpulent, but that sort of flesh which always breaks the shackles of lethargy. He was wonderfully agile for his shaking flesh. The more he tried to tan and harden his body, thicker grew the flesh. The taller he grew, the more became his strength and agility. His critics started calling him a slumberous elephant, but in reality he was agile like a panther. Someone one day shouted from behind the bushes 'elephant's calf' to which one of his admirers might have justifiably added 'but having a tiger's prowess and agility'.

"Studies are for weaklings only! If he torments his brain he will get weak!" his father would easily remark whenever the question of studies arose.

So unsurprisingly he did not know much of letters and books. Despite this his passage through the years was unchecked, his promotion from one standard to another vouchsafed by his brave efforts in the *akhara* of this tiny primary school that complacently saw the students up to the eighth standard before leaving the field open for the studious volunteers to take cudgels at higher studies in towns and cities.

When he was in the sixth standard—here we include this just for chronology's sake—tragedy struck the household. It was a fine evening that seemed all eager to bestow all the prospects of a good supper and rest after daylong ploughing in the fields as his father was returning home. The tiny bells around the bullocks' necks chimed in congratulatory tone for the good acreage covered during the day. He was giving patronising pats at the cattle's haunches. But then pleasant and carefree present is oftentimes ambushed by the advance patrol of future—is the plan predetermined or we just by chance come into the line of fire?—leaving the main body of future to decide and twist our fate. On a path-side tree, a big hive of bumble-bees, of the size of a fat calf, had been robbed of its orderly sense. Some eagle might have tried to sneak out a beakful of honey from some corner. It might have hit at some weak point and a larger section of comb had fallen, letting loose chaos, and gone was that fine thread of responsibility and commitment by the time to maintain normalcy. Big black bumble-bees were swarming furiously to take revenge and fall prey upon anybody who chanced to arrive and fill up the vacancy of 'enemy'. The poor tired farmer fell victim to their unremitting fury. He crouched down and fell at the spot. After heart-rending cries he toppled unconscious to get further stings of mortality. The bullocks also bore the brunt of their fury. Pitifully bitten they ran towards the village. An hour later when the villagers approached the scene of the bees' crime they found his terrifyingly swollen body lying in the sand. If not in life, at least near death he indeed appeared the father of his prodigiously huge son. As the nearest hospital was 20 kilometres away, and no mechanical conveyance at hand, they took him in a cart and beat the bulls back mercilessly to defeat the swift pace of death. The poor farmer died on the way.

He was just eleven when he lost his father. Now was the time to put the stone of responsibility on his bulky childish shoulders in addition to the playful load of entertainment on his back. School was now necessarily a waste of time, for validity of cultural things is relatively defined by the time one has to spend in earning bread and butter. He thus dropped out of the school, like anyone else would have done and in fact scores of others were doing the same, and helped his mother in agricultural chores. It was mere sustainable agriculture on a small plot of land, just to beat the hunger, nothing more. It is a vicious circle among one or the other deprivations, killing of one dream so that others won't grow at all, of becoming a hardworking brute so that no finer thing pinches the hardened physique and roughed soul.

He was moulded unsentimentally as a boy of his bulk is expected to be when buffeted by adversities. But the human soul cannot be a desert beyond the oasis of sentimentality completely. In his simplicity he knew—in vague connotations and feelings—that his father would have drawn maximum solace from the sight of more and more weight on his son's bulk.

So his duties in the fields could not shun his weight-adding worship to his body. He just accepted it as another brick on his back.

A school dropout, a slogger in his fields, performer at fairs and local competitions (whenever time was available) that is how adolescence took shelter in his bulging figure. It was the rattling anonymous pace for survival. The future devoid of all glory now waited as a mundane *akhara* to be treaded sweating and perspiring. He simply followed the rut just like others did, though intermittently encumbering his back and shoulders with unbelievably large weight.

Some sympathiser suggested he should join an *akhara* to try professional wrestling. But quite mysteriously this big strong lad seemed fit for utilising his enormous energy in vertical component more than in any other direction. He could lift huge, unbelievable weight on his back and shoulders. Wrestling, however, is a three-dimensional game of manoeuvrability and force. Everybody expected him to exploit the field in proportion to his weight-lifting capacity. They were not—especially the *guruji*—satisfied with his performance in the field. In one duel, when the rustic, strongly pumped pride of the *akhara* was at stake, this big boy, always in news on account of his mammoth physique, could not uphold the banner and surprisingly hit the dust to everybody's disbelief. It proved decisive.

"You fir-for-nothing big elephant, you slouching sloth! You yourself eat almost half the ration of the whole *akhara*! And let us down like this!" the head *pahalwan* in charge of the *akhara* could not control himself.

Perhaps for the first time in his life, buds of anger sprouted forth inside this calmest sea of eighteen. The head wrestler weighed around one quintal. He just plucked him off the ground and threw him, breaking one of his legs and couple of ribs. It was sacrilegious...unpardonable from all angles. In this mighty game played on the bosom of sand, the guru is even more venerable than Hanuman, the God of wrestlers in northern India. So they condemned him and implicit in this condemnation was the verdict that henceforth nobody would accept him as a pupil wrestler. Led by frustrating, flailing youthful instincts he stopped exercises, increased his gluttony, and worked still harder in fields with lessening returns. Result? The body that could have been sculpted beautifully got puffed up like a balloon. By his twenty-first year he stood six feet four inches around a pulpy weight.

The last vestiges of wrestlership were naturally harvested as his prematurely old mother got him married to a farmer girl. Now in this part of the country, if somebody with power and attitude for wrestling bids adieu to celibacy and ties the knot, putting his *langar* on the door-side wall spike, he just becomes the yoked bullock of the family institution, all his energies being sapped by the constantly demanding role of the family man.

By the age of thirty he led a brood of four kids, a famished wife with spent eyes and a bed-ridden mother. He still ate much and his quarrelling wife cursed him for this.

"You eat 90% of your farm's production!" she often cried with scorn.

When after at least a thousand versions of the same scolding put some weight on his heart, and like a father going to the battle field for survival, he decided to do what deemed fit for him—lifting weights. After some days in the privacy of his cattle house someone was fortunate enough to peep inside and come across this spectacle:

The bulky man caressed the buffalo with his huge hands. The gentle animal acknowledging the gesture raised its tail. The man then bent down and sneaked under the animal's belly supporting it on his back. Resting his palms on the ground, feet planted firmly he heaved gently, softly. His bulk thrust into the protruding mass on him. Another great jerk and his hands were resting on his knees. The animal's spine arched; hoofs barely touching the ground. Giving a huge cry and grunting his teeth, he gave another push and for an instant the onlooker might have doubted his eyes when he saw the four hoofs slightly airborne for the fraction of a second. The animal panicked and kicking its legs threw the man onto the ground, and almost trampling him broke free of its tethering.

From that day onwards the word of his feat again started doing rounds. The man was in streets now showcasing his power-lifts. From his thirtieth year to the fortieth he performed mighty heaves and lifts in the countryside of Haryana, earning mammoth praise and pittance of money, sugar, butter, flour, jiggery, and many other things that bucolic praise could fetch him. With the little money he supported his family and ate almost rest of the offerings, sparing just enough for the children and his accusing wife. He lifted heavy stone-rollers on his shoulders; crouched under a wet sack of sand weighing four quintals and still a man sitting on it and moved ahead; pulled massive wooden beam, with many children riding on it, tied to a thick hemp rope with his teeth. He then claimed the maximum attention he could draw. A photo in a local vernacular paper: a felicitation cheque worth 5000 rupees by a state minister. He had risked his life hundreds of times to reach this level.

Nonetheless, any bull or horse, howsoever hard and sturdy in the heydays, comes across the days of ignominy and neglect. Age was catching up with him, and so was people's expectation. To find no fault with the audience, those who had seen him at the cusp of his abilities, now found little applauding interest in his waning performances. Hence, the quantity of offerings on the linen sheet of his sweat and slogging trickled down rapidly in his forties.

He had three daughters. His son was the youngest. During this period of waning business, with the money he had saved, he married his two elder daughters. The third one, the son and their mother tirelessly worked in the fields to keep the fire going in their fireplace. Now he returned more sullenly and more frequently and earlier from the performing tours.

It was 1995. The third daughter had also blossomed. Sensing the precariousness of youth, his wife continually prodded him to find a match. Out of job he was slouching at home and there was no money. She gave him an ultimatum that the girl had to be married in the upcoming marriage season at any cost. However, before setting out to find a match, he needed the feel of some money with himself to even have the guts to propose because dowry was absolutely mandatory. After much deliberation and no solution in sight, he was thinking of selling the land to save the family's honour at any cost. Then an opportunity glared!

****

In the Buddhist philosophy of interlinking of universal phenomena in a commonly linked cause and effect chain, the phenomena at two places are reciprocally inter-effecting. His individual-level problem and its solution had something to do with the national capital. As the city grew mammoth so did the milk demand, and to meet it illegal dairies boomed. These milk producers—problems or solutions, put anyone before or after at your own convenience—gave rise to an irritation for the urban gentry. It was the problem of stray cattle. These proud beholders of our religiosity now blocked the capital's rapid pace to development. The Municipal Corporation of Delhi (MCD) had some cattle-catching vans, but the city's civic body drew flack for its inability to put a check to the ever-burgeoning problems. These mute and frustrated animals, pushed against the wall for survival in the concrete jungle, started attacking the people. Put into a tight fearsome corner, the people themselves started to chase them away. In one month four people had been gored to death. Their status thus became analogous to man-bovine conflict in the concrete jungle.

The Delhi High Court whiplashed the civic agencies and held them responsible for the incidences. Without mincing any critical remark, it ordered compensation from the MCD coffers, relocation of illegal dairies (most of whom thrived on political patronage), and gave instructions to round up the stray cattle as soon as possible. The MCD in turn reprimanded its Director of Veterinary Services for the cattle menace. Apart from the court's indicting music, delegations from resident's welfare association from different colonies led by their smart, suave retired presidents and secretaries virtually bombarded the agency with their incessant complaints. The posh colonies of south Delhi—whose residents having toiled lifelong for urban advancements and amenities found these characteristics of third-word India quite unbearable—were raising hell of a storm.

Poor cows in posh colonies. Not matching. Religion has its use, but from a safe distance. It was an insult to the retired citizens' right to lead an advanced life in posh surroundings. But then filthy India is too strong and big. It seeps into the islands of peace and prosperity. It was a big problem indeed. They even employed special guards to fight away the pathetic encroachers into the smirking clean neighbourhoods. To fulfil their quota in the problem, these upmarket people left huge piles of garbage on the margins of their localities, where the herds of stray cattle gathered and repeatedly peeked over their boundaries. Further frustrated they installed cattle traps at colony entries, but the problem won't be solved. Cast out from the illegal and legal dairies and *gau dharamshalas*, bee-hiving in hellish stinking environment of Asia's largest fruit and vegetable market at Azadpur and at incalculable small market places and garbage dump-sites, these poor cattle, grossly caricatured in their skeletons, reminded people that India still was a country of masses despite efforts to the contrary by a few selected men of classes.

The High Court bombarded with pleas and litigations from South Delhi colonies had to direct the MCD to announce a scheme of reward to any citizen for catching the stray cattle. The MCD's veterinary officers and inspectors were directed to make arrangements for this. The Deputy Commissioner of South Zone came zealously forward to follow the directive. A lump-sum prize of one thousand rupees per catch was announced in newspapers. However, very few came forward to take up the offer from inside the city to encash the risky reward. After spending some years in human-hugging crowd of indulgent mundane masses, the sight of an animal puts one in perspiration mode. The city seeps into the spirits. It chains the guts. So the Delhi government, MCD and NDMC raked their brains, 'Where could the probable volunteers come from?' The choice was easy: Haryanvis who are born and brought up in the nearest vicinity of lowing and braying cattle and buffaloes. They are more comfortable in the company of quadrupeds than the two-pawed, over-smart animal ruling the earth. So there were quite a few takers for the risky job in the surrounding pockets of Haryana as advertisements appeared in local newspapers. Our out-of-job, 45-year-old man of this type of business also caught hold of the offer. Even if I catch 90 of these it would ensure the marriage of my last daughter, and the dispensation of my responsibility to save the family' honour, he thought.

In the battle for survival, the stray cattle and our Pahalwan were now face to face. Both sides pushed by the larger forces, driving them into the corner of limitations and deprivations. The cattle, once the proud beholders of the emblem of survival and spirituality, carried a much faded respect as their utility had plummeted down dangerously. However, this fact was not sufficient to wipe these out of existence. Even in this majestically shiny cityscape these were needed when young and abandoned later. The male calves were even at greater risk of being let loose and roam ownerless because they were not for milk, and their utility when grown up was just for farming tasks that was not to be here in the cities. So the dairy owners just pushed the males out keeping the female calves with them. Their rival, our Pahalwan, was also almost obsolete on account of the oddity of preferring physical strength over brain. These were smarter times, of brain over the brawn. With education India was taking massive leaps towards development with sharper minds and less show of brute physical strength that could just provide the job of daily wage earning around construction sites.

Most of the stray cattle were just mute and pathetically fragile animals, and just after a frail tip of struggle gave into the bulky man's rope, fist, elbow, and knee work. Still cuts, wounds, sores, and bruises cannot be avoided in a fight between animals and humans. Given his lifetime drudgery in the *akhara* of power game, he performed as he ought to have as per his experience. He did admirably well and within no time became the prized cattle-catcher. After a month in the capital he returned like a soldier on vacation from the battle front; carrying a broken tooth, blooded pupil, swollen lip, and dangerously paining joints on account of his fights in the concrete jungle. However, these things were easily overshadowed and safely bandaged under the note pads of 40,000 rupees under his belt. His ecstatic wife served, solaced, and assuaged him both physically and mentally as to the humble capacity of her weak, work-wreaked body. It was but a half accomplished mission. He needed one more such push, exactly the same in fruits and then he could rest for a bit longer, for the future of his only son should not offer them much problem. In a terribly patriarchal society, the chances of the son of the poorest of the poor are still better than the daughter of a reasonably well-off person. Nevertheless, the son of a poor man meekly saddles himself almost with the same set of problems and solutions as his father.

During this one-week stay at home he was restless; always anxious lest all the cattle are caught in his absence. His tendons, muscles, joints, and ligaments were still protesting when he again set out for the job. As it happens with the two ends of a scale, once evenly balanced, if the weight is decreased in one pan, the other becomes weightier even though no physical weight has been added to it. With each new fight he got more injuries, became less menacing in his approach, and consequently more became the effect of the animals' protests. Like a long-fatigued traveller, he took final steps into the second leg of his journey. After twenty more catches he was having sleepless nights on account of his pains. Some suggested that he must hire some assistant to help him, but he won't share the booty with anybody. All along his life he had worked alone, and he preferred to carry with it even now. More than brute force, now he employed strategies and shrewdness to ensnare the animals, which made it even worse, for it became a game running into days and nights with equal felicity. Using more brain than brawn was not his real self. But the game of survival was forcing him to become smarter in the city. During his initial catches people loved to watch him from a safe distance. He was providing a few street shows as well. They applauded when he, like a heavy grindstone, clasped the animal's neck and forced the rope-end on one of the front hoofs, ran the rope diagonally under the belly to give expertly unbalancing push, and once the cattle was grounded he would just throw his bulk on the terrified body. His huge proportions made him look like any other animal. All hoofs and horns tied, these would be picked by the MCD vans to be transported out of the area of its jurisdiction.

He was in low spirits, bruised, and anxious because the remaining cattle were sturdier, because it is the rule of the jungle, concrete or the green one, the frailest are the one to be wiped out at the earliest. Ironically, the lesser became his odds, the stronger he faced the enemies. In his forty-ninth and fiftieth fight he could have been easily killed. However, drawing out reserves of his strength he turned sure defeat into couple of more thousands for his daughter's marriage to salvage his honour by getting her married at the earliest. Once so near the target, no eventuality and foreboding would fright him away from the grand figure of money sufficient to pay for the dowry of his daughter.

His body was rapidly giving in. He knew any catch could be fatal and the last. The remaining cattle were predominantly bulky bulls. He just could not convince himself to call it quits with immediate effect. It was like leaving the field out of being scared. His brawn was fighting with his brain;

both drawing him in different directions. His brain could not force him to flee with immediate effect. His brawn held him back for some worthy fight, one final soul-satisfying battle. He knew that he was preparing for his final catch and then sweet return to home. He prayed to God—he did it for the first time in his life—to get him face to face against a famished prey. But he knew that none of the frail ones was left. Only hefty beasts were still cocking a spook at the civilized face of urban gentry. The earth is the testing and trying arena of God against our wishes, prayers and dreams. His case was no exception. In proportion to the fervency of his prayer, he came face to face with a bizarre bull that had gored a couple of people to death and injured many others. It was only on account of religious sentiments that it had been given a bit more time to try other means before the final step of shooting it dead. Our Pahalwan, at the lowest ebb of his strength, was against the strongest opponent—one of the few whose attempts at challenging man's authority in the concrete jungle had sparked the *numero uno* animal's anger—the real culprit from among the dozens of previous weakling and innocent ones.

The thought of only one man tackling this monster was a glaring impossibility. However, if one is once at the threshold of a dream's fructification, *possible* and *impossible* lose their meanings. It had even gone beyond the expectation of just 1000 rupees extra. He was fighting it for himself. He believed himself to be the strongest. He had to prove it to leave a local legend so that those who saw it won't forget it till their last breath. Having pity, they doubled the booty on the fearsome creature's head and promised help in man and material.

Well, he nonetheless fought the battle of his life. He at the lowest of his will power, strength and capacity while confronted by the mightiest deed of his life. By this time, he had acquired a bit of local fame. This almost pre-announced fight carried news-worthiness with it. His game of life and death carried circus value. From a safe distance a journalist followed the action on camera to catch the highest point of action. People depending on their bravery quotient chose their safe distances as allowed by their urbanity. What happened for the next one hour, nobody, who witnessed it, will ever forget it till his last moment. The bull went on a rampage. Several times it brought him down on his knees with the huge toss of its horns. He but escaped being trampled to death on account of the still remaining signs of his agility that in the face of death so near worked at full throttle. In frustration, and not without a prick of conscience even at the perilous moment, Pahalwan had to thrust a wood splinter into the bull's eye in order to mellow its lethality and blithe brutality from so near quarters. Both of them were bleeding and panting. The one who lasted more was to win. For dozens of times the bull had escaped the ensnaring loop of his rope. Taking a sharp turn he approached suddenly from the side of the bull's gored eye. It spared him from the rival's peremptory advance. The bull was thus a bit belated in defence. Grabbing it like the last opportunity till eternity, he clung to the left foreleg like lice. Jumping and swinging around wildly, the bull gave ferocious jerks at his neck to kill him with its horns. He had been successful in tying the rope-end to the leg. Taking the other free end in his hand, he jumped into the well of death—dived under the belly to emerge on the other side, taking the rope diagonally across the beast. The people saw the hoofs squelching on his flesh. He but was oblivious to all pain now. He looped the other end around the right hind leg and was dragged by the furiously charging bull for a few paces. When the line was finished, its charge forward became its own undoing. The huge mass toppled down. People looked with horror.

With the spare rope in his hand, the man all bloodied jumped onto the bull and fell between horns. His hands worked till he had tightly tied the rope-end around the horns. The bull had been knotted and embaled. It struggled. The man just remained there on the trophy. Blood copiously oozing from his mouth. All the promised help now arrived. The MCD veterinary surgeon, sure of the safety, injected the bull with heroic fingers. The bull collapsed. The man too. He died. His spine broken. His shattered ribs protruding through his lungs. With full honours he was taken to his native village.

He had gathered 55,000 rupees for his daughter's marriage. And couple of thousand for the last kill to defray the cremation and allied crematoria costs. It was the last kill!

The Platform

* * *

Platforms—they are somebody's destination, someone's starting point. Many people depart, and many arrive. On the parallel rails of departures and arrivals, life chugs ahead with a determined unmindfulness. There is a different type of life at the platforms as well. It is almost a secondary world. Right in the shadows of the bigger world hurtling with an exalted impulse, this secondary world carries limitless desolation. Severely crushed, trampled and trodden under the furtively commuting and journeying larger mainstream world, it's a smaller world on the fringe. It involves beggars, crippled, runaways, petty porters, and nondescript migrant labourers who survive like the wayside thorns and thickets along the rutted path on which there is an incessant stampede of those whose lives are not bracketed inside the gaolic strokes of the term 'platform'. It survives in dreaded anticipation; waiting to grab the fallen crumbs to beat its hunger. Its painful scars lie right there in broad daylight, but are still invisible. To many it doesn't even exist. The adventurous ebullience and pomp and paraphernalia of the bigger world pass over it like clouds ploughing the skies with cotton-soft ease.

The same is the case of the unlived lives on the platforms of Ambala junction. It buzzes with crowds of peasants, railway staff, passengers waiting, walking, deboarding and boarding apart from porters, hawkers and homeless people and beggars. Lost in this jostling crowd are the multitudes of castaways whom the crippling circumstances force to ride the static back of this cemented space along the clattering rails and nettling wheels. It heaves like a sighful wave trying to tug at the sleeves of the bigger world. It pours like a mournful drizzle to wash the sandy screen of human apathy. It shines like remorseful rays to light the darkest corners.

It was mid-November. With pining pioneership the new millennium had just started. More than the sheds—during the day—bright blue apron of the vibrantly lit sky was more comfortable to lie under. So these citizens of the kingdom named 'platform'—mired in pain and penury—now basked in open at the far ends of platforms under the unbiased, indiscriminating and warm beams of the bright father, who seemed chiding the cold breeze naughtily sashaying over the plains after tasting early snowfall in the upper reaches of the Himalayas.

Inshan's hand-pulled cart—on which entailed the fistful of his life (loaded and embaled in fewest of things and circumstances)—was standing at this sunny far end of the platform. The world under the tin sheds appeared unwelcoming, cold, and rebuking. A train was standing by the platform. He looked thoughtfully into the people swarming its doors. There was an ostentatious penchant to grab a bit of space, a bit of foothold, a chit of more life. Then with a shrill toot the hooter went out and with a jerk the train started to move. Slowly...people fought their way rapidly. The last compartment was slowly moving away with introspecting sobriety. The cart-puller's thoughtful gaze was distracted by a heavy footfall from the other direction. Having run along the stones and rails, a young man was now cascading still faster on the smooth tarred platform. The law of relative motions in operation, he ran smartly to emerge victorious in competition against the handle bar of the last carriage coldly running away. Old Inshan was brought out of his reverie. With agility unfaithful to his age, he rose from the rag he was lying on and ran to cross the young man's path shouting:

"O brave son...it's not a suitable place for sprinting and climbing!"

The young man swung around and gnashed angrily, "Enough of it old man...next time you do it I'll break your hand!"

Those who commuted the place were conversant with this old beggary fellow's policing regarding this violation of rule (of boarding a running train). He was a particular eyesore to the adventurous types.

The adventurer just ran ahead. Helplessly, Inshan saw him running to the dangerous end. His dirty, stained, raggish, linen head-cloth draped over his head, standing tip-toe in praying agitation he watched the heroic feat. His hand gripping the door rail and running very fast, the young man launched himself but the spring in his feet was not enough. His knees struck against the foot support. Involuntarily Inshan's eyes closed. He wouldn't open them till the train had chugged away. Fortunately, the man's grip had worked in proportion to the harsh words to the old porter, and hanging on he had somehow sneaked in helped by the passengers on board. There was no commotion of fear around the old onlooker. Hesitatingly the old man opened his eyes and much to his relief saw that the man had been saved. He was all alone in the world, so considered this vagrant fellow as one more belonging to his own family born of *inshaniyat* and thanked God for keeping his blessing eyes over this inexperienced and immature colt, who had just foolishly jumped into the invisible, inexhaustible, and inexplicable snare of accidents stealthily laid by the God of Death.

Thank God, for on this important day in his life no untoward incident had happened! Today he was to be rewarded by the Director of the local railway zone. Yesterday the station master had called him in his cabin and with dignified confidence informed him about it. One day's gap between the announcement and the event only explicitly indicated that it was no pre-arranged and agreed recognition of his services. Still the staff at Ambala had been decent in grasping the opportunity of the Director's visit as a reward function for the poor, homeless man's yeoman service to humanity.

There was nobody from his lineage he could relate to. Before 1947, his poor Hindu family in a downtown quarter of Lahore survived and struggled as daily wage earners, picking up petty jobs thrown into their beggary bowl by the tensioned circumstances of those turbulent times. Then 1947 saw liberation and the massacres. At one of those long blood-hissing nights, when blood came to be strictly grouped as Hindu and Muslim, they somehow managed to board a bleeding train having more dead than alive. And even those on board had little chance of reaching alive to the other side of the border. As expected, before it could cross the newly created border, it was stopped by a blood-thirsty mob at a desolate place and unthinkable hacking of humans happened. It was hideous ecstasy. A savage delirium. He was seven years old and was lucky or unlucky to survive. Later at some station, he was dragged almost dead of fright. They pulled him out all blood stained from the mass of bodies. Blood dripping from the floors, he was thus lucky to come to Amritsar. He saw all his family members being hastily taken away in a truck overloaded with corpses for mass cremation.

From that day the platform became his home and all its allied crowded phenomena the familial things he could relate to. During his juvenile stage, he grew up doing all types of petty jobs, sufferings all types of physical and moral hazards, apart from ever-persistent exploitation that an orphan is destined to come under. Caught in the eternal encagement of circumstances, he worked as a tea-stall helper, table cleaner in station canteens, dishwasher in railway restaurants, balloon vendor, and peanuts hawker. And when his arms were strong enough to pull a handcart, he became a carter to carry all types of provisions on this small two-wheeled appendage to his beast-of-burden-type existence.

He definitely must have been given some name by his family. It but got smudged under blood clots and flesh in that train compartment. Hate doesn't kill just bodies, it butchers names as well. His limbs were intact, but he had lost his name somewhere in the gory stampede. How do you keep your name alive? Only others can help you in this by sweetly or sourly speaking it, either in front of you or in your absence in some context. But a name that is never spoken by anybody evaporates like raindrops in a desert. His name had evaporated. Many a time he would think, who am I, and a blankness struck his like he did not exist at all. He still remembered what his family called him. But just a memory cannot help you in keeping your name alive. You need others to help you keep your name alive, and for that you ought to have a social identity. He hadn't any, so very soon he became nameless. He would have lost his name forever, if not for this wandering mendicant, so prominently bearded and hair braids and all, who gave a warming sermon to tea-shipping passengers waiting for their trains that frigid night. "We should try to become *inshan*, a good human being, who follows *inshaniyat...*" He literally stole the word. Kept it safe in his pocket. Repeated it hundreds of times to stamp his identity. And knowing that a name is no name unless spoken by others, he did all he could to be recognised with that name. So he became Inshan, slowly, over a period of years. That was his achievement. He had earned a name. He was not nameless and faceless like scores of other citizens of the platform.

Time's arms swung silently, straddling the decades of existence. Just survival for the sake of it, like it was the best achievement that could be. It was 40 years ago when he arrived at the Ambala railway station with his pittance of savings on his frail, prematurely withered 20-year-old personage in 1960. His initiation into what was to become the overarching motto of his life happened just after a couple of months after his arrival.

Diwali, the darkest night of *Amavasya*, is followed by the waxing phase of moony nights to reach the milky night's brightest cusp in the rain-washed early winter sky. The moon's unpolluted clarity and cool misty air make the nights smile at their best. During its waning phase after the full dazzle, the moonlight spreads in misty romance over the languorously lying nights. Sometimes during the morning twilight, when there is no mist, it shines like a night sun, casting shadows on earth, beating for some time even the sun's efforts from below the horizon. It was on one such night that a middle-aged man belonging to some other part of the country was cut to pieces by a train. With disastrous discourtesy the time whirred on it axis. An accident. And a sinister silence sprawled over the scene. The sight's horrific details struck him with all the fright possible to a human heart. It was an accident; an unclaimed body; so its removal from the tracks and cremation got mired in the usual hassles that accompany and entail public responsibility. It was broad daylight and the body still lay there. It made the tragedy even more gruesome. A policeman, standing as a sign of the authorities' knowledge of the accident, was trying his level best to get some men and conveyance to take the limbs to the civil hospital for post-mortem.

Coming across the railway policeman's helplessness and gory apathy for the after-death cause of once throbbing life, it was for the first time that Inshan's conscience got those initial pickings, which if welcomed and received cordially blossom into beautiful moral facade.

The wholesale dealer whose packages of provisions were lying in the platform warehouse, having paid him some token money in advance, pulled at his sleeve with the attitude of a master hurrying his slave.

"Oh come on, haven't you ever seen a dead body in your life," he gasped huskily.

"Seen sahib...perhaps seen too many to ...!" from the deep dormitory of memories, cries, and killings flashed.

Solemnly straight-faced, he gently returned the ten rupee note and offered his services for the final journey of the diseased. The tragedy of these crushed limbs connoted the gruesome massacre in that fateful train. While on the way to the hospital, bloody scenes vividly, massively returned to haunt him. The savage behemoth of memories gripped him so tightly that he went numb. For a whole week afterwards he pulled his cart lost in a mysterious feeling. He had refused money for *that* job. It appeared too sinful and against whatever notion he had of dharma. Next month, while he was pulling his cart on the platform, he was beckoned by the same policeman who had asked him to take the unclaimed, unidentified body to the cremation ground. Again he followed the duty, just getting solace from the fact that his soul felt some invisible reward for the kind act. He was getting a sensation that even a 100 rupee note won't give him, offered more as a tip or charity by a wealthy merchant in lieu of littlest of cartage.

It's convenient to fall in the trap of cold apathy because it is easy like just drawing a breath. Goodness is just a one step away. It's another matter that we choose to ignore it. It seems to require a huge effort to take that step. Some people but move out of the rut to pick it up. It gives them a certain satisfaction. He knew the meaning and essence of his name, so just picked up the abandoned speck of goodness. May be to keep his name alive; to prove that he is worth it. We explore meanings in life. He too had found one. His was a small world and he kept that speck of goodness. And held it with marvellous stillness.

As years reaped their share of accidents along the steely furrows, his voluntary acceptance of the job, in a period of time, became a duty in the eyes of others, who expected him to do it without even sparing some praise or appreciation for his unselfishness and without harbouring any reservations for their own apathy. Years rolled in this mundane way, interjected with atrophied chunks of accidents which spattered the earth now and then. He came to be known as the man who carried the dead bodies of train accidents to the civil hospital and even performed the last rites in case there was no claimant for the body.

Now after 40 years, his deeds had accomplished the benchmark of a reward. It was a sort of D-day to him. He drew out his bucket from under the cart and smartly, smugly went out to fetch water from the platform hand-pump. Coming back he freed his old tattered knapsack from its smart knot to the axle of his cart. The cart was his profession, his house, his world. Standing with its hand-bars raised on the peg-support, it served him as a shelter that enclosed his portion of the world. During winters, he put a tarpaulin sheet over the whole of it and sneaked into the tiny interior. A plank supported on bricks at both ends served as his bed.

Irrespective of all caste, class and all other man-made differentials, every person has a special dress to adorn for the special-most occasion. He too had one. Or rather he had a choice to hit the best combination out of various items: different-sized shirt, sweater, trousers, and shoes donated by those daily passengers who donated on some occasions with different moods with the same motive of getting God's blessings in lieu of the charity. Most of these were oversize for him. The shoes, however, should not be too tight or too large; the rest of the mis-fittings can be somehow adapted. These adaptations are what he thought about tidying up. He borrowed hair oil, comb and a piece of looking glass from different beggary neighbours, prompting one of those kind commuters who sometimes spoke to him while coming from or going to office, to say:

"Ho Inshan, are you getting married today?!"

Beaming with shyness he replied, "Yes sahib, it's as important as marriage!"

He had assumed that the function was for him specially. Each particle of his poor existence was agitated with excitement and frightful uncertainty. He was feeling a part of the larger world, not just a faceless speck lying on the platform. The people who mattered knew his name. That was the most important thing to him. He tidied up with a sweeping exuberance. How blissful the feeling! From the dark corner, which sucked all identity and spewed invisibility, he had been put on a shiny stage. He was recognised. They knew him. All the miseries of life didn't matter anymore.

It's very difficult for the world to change suddenly to accommodate such happiness. All these goose-bumps creating sensations were belied very soon as he was made to sit in a last row in the hall. It was some big show for a bigger purpose. He felt being sucked into oblivion again. With joggling force it swept the tiny cottage of his expectations. His felicitation was a mere appendage to the function and that too caused by the generosity of the station master. Still, with a school boy's eagerness and anticipation he saw the proceedings to make the best of the occasion. However, his patience was wearing thin and for a moment he even grew apprehensive that they might just wind it up without even recalling his presence.

Luck but struck for him at last. The station master got up and gave a nice introduction to his deeds of 40 years. It lasted a couple of minutes and during that period people cared to look at him like a fellow human being. He found it too burdensome, the gaze of the gentry from the better world, and stared at the faded leather of his shoes in embarrassment. Walking up to the stage his limbs were trembling. The Director, an enlightened academic man, was impressed by the gilded caption to the long chapter of his unassuming, unknown life. The station master had handed him 1100 rupees to give as a reward to this poor carter in recognition of his services. Deep down in his conscience, however, he felt hurt somehow, in some vague manner. Rolling the notes in his fingers, he was lost in thoughts as this beggary man attired in his best dress approached the stage. He felt that giving just money (without any souvenir) would be trivialising the silent services of this man. So his senses ran to find something to act as a medallion (the real reward) along with the money that would surely get spent. There was nothing but the bouquet presented to him. He picked it up and handed it to the embarrassed and shy person cowering in front of him, patting him, congratulating him for the show of humanity on the inhuman platforms. There was customary round of applause. Inshan just stared mechanically at the objects of his reward. With an overpowering emotion, he hugged tight the flowery recognition of his deeds and stammered:

"Thank you for the flowers sir. But I...I cannot accept money for it seems as if today after years I'm accepting the price for my services to the dead."

Saying this in all humility he put out his hand to give the money back to the chief guest. Dumbstruck by the dazzle of this lotus of goodness in the mud of life on the platform, the Director could not utter a word. He appeared reactionless. He just patted the frail man on his shoulder. Putting the money on the table and embracing the flowers, Inshan saluted in military fashion and moved out.

For many days to come, he ogled with happiness at the withering flowers, drawing more juice of happiness out of those rumpled petals and crumpled stalks...and still more as the de-juiced, crumpled petals lost all moisture and turned to pieces.

So he kept on living and serving in his customary manner without anymore rewards and earning his livelihood by transporting goods on his hand-pulled cart.

A Slippery Edge of Hope

* * *

Simone Clarke from Perth, Australia was an independent research scholar in social anthropology. So apart from enjoying places like any other tourist, she had her professional demands met during her forays into new societies and cultures. Laying bare dust from the issues of race and ethnicity, she looked far more mature and introvert than her blonde figure of 40 years, adored with charming bluish eyes, would have appeared in any other profession.

Our happiness we carry on our face. It is a thing desirable and appreciated, so much so that we sometimes mask even our pains under the make-up smile. There are pains that we prefer to carry hidden. Not for something very important. Just that it is suitable to the image that we carry or want to get. There was an undercurrent of an ever-persistent pain beneath the upper, worldly layer of Simone's countenance. Married twice and single now after the second divorce, she was faced with the imperatives of redefining life altogether. Her two marriages lasting seven years had been spent in, for no major fault of hers, conceiving a child. The doctor's report was merciless nonetheless. It put up a heartless stop to her maternal hopes. The urge to be a mother was so heavy that it had toppled the cart of matrimony, scattering little mundane pleasures of married life. However, such instincts are too lofty to peter out; these turn into even some loftier form of urge. Guided by some new mysterious version, her head held confidently high, she appeared profoundly calm. She could absorb herself more freely in the study of others' sorrows, pains, history and cultures. Undoubtedly, she felt better attuned to her profession than others.

The civilizational superiority vaulting in an arc, triumphantly written in the impressively drawn skyline of her home city, was becoming boring for her. Life was just petering out with ungracious eloquence. If not be a mother, she felt drawn to the prospects of doing something as important as being a mother. She was really hungry for some impressive work. The other night her businessman friend Andrew Watson had spoken in sneering, derogatory tone about the aborigines, her favourite topic of research. As she was drunk, her response to the deliberate misdemeanour was quite unrestrained, and she ended up slapping Mr. Watson's 45-year-old not so impressive face, followed by a rather long recitation of her thesis. The Latin song's bellicosity was, however, superior to hers. People were still dancing, thinking she was yelling an encouraging song at them.

Life just moves on. The moments flow, filling up the vacant dots left by the preceding ones. Andrew had left the place. The seat vacated by him was now occupied by Pratyaksha Mohanty, an Indian student of sociology studying in a college in the city. The words aboriginals, primitive tribes, hill tribes, Risley, Dr. Hutton, Sir Baines which peered through the stormy sea of music and reached her studious ears in a very impressive manner. She was much impressed with Simone's unrelenting passion for the subject. That night helping the drunken anthropologist to reach her rented room, the little bit of conversation was enough to start a friendship. The fire of friendship, after all, merely needs a cosy, sympathetic spark.

"There are still aborigines in India in the most inaccessible and isolated spots," Pratyaksha was telling her on their third meeting next week. "Their primitive state is just charming. A mere look at them from a distance takes you thousands of years back. It seems they have beaten time. It's still. A silence. In staying the same they appear to have beaten all mad race. It's savage. It's beautiful. Shaped by nature they seem inseparable part of the flora and fauna around them. Far away in the safety of the sea lie a group of 573 islands in the Bay of Bengal. About 1200 kilometres from Calcutta and Chennai each. How beautiful the sea, the protector of their primitiveness appears. Even during the storms, the water seems harmless, just shoving naughtily these peals on its bosom!"

The girl was coming to terms with newfound liberty and a few drinks found her completely poetic. "The Andamanese, Jarawas, Onges, Shompens, and Nicobaris. True sons of nature. They are naked. From birth to death they are the same. Like babies forever. They haven't been polluted by the spools of knowledge. We call them primitively backward just because we have run too fast. Too fast in fact to even lose ourselves in the stampede. They don't struggle to come out of their modesty. The government is worried about their extinction. But the militarisation of the islands is far more risky to their survival. They face erosion of identity, displacement and freshly arrived diseases. Mind you, some of these groups are in pitiful dozens only!"

Like a concerned mother Simone gave a worried sigh. Of course she had read about them. But the description was very powerful. She was transported to that distant place; lost in the ringing merriment and cast- and creed-less luxuriance of these naked bodies far away in the lap of the sea. Given the state of her mind, the world had acquired a strange complexity, an overbearing callousness. She could feel its weight. She craved for a far simpler world, a weightless society, a sort for gravity-less air to float aimlessly. She felt like dousing her identity into that unchanged world which was left untouched by the colossal spadework of time over the centuries.

"And how safe they appear in the lap of the sea!" Pratyaksha was rejoicing radiantly.

The reason for the Indian girl's flight of fancy was that she had spent a couple of years in Andaman and Nicobar, where her father was a station commandant at the Car Nicobar Indian Air Force Base. Staying there in her officer's enclave, her girlish drifty young spirits would take her to the remote corners of the islands. She liked the shy, scared, apprehensive aborigines; liked their naked unpretentiousness; was pained at the sophisticated, steely rods penetrating their mysterious kingdom defined by the forces of nature. It was wonderful how a few hundreds of each group could enjoy so blissfully in the alien environment surrounded by snakes, spiders, and scorpions. Not much more was required for Simone to know where her next assignment lay. She needed to be out of the web of her present. She had to dive into the pools of unruffled simplicity. Perhaps that would free her of the major worries of her life—tensions that were stalling her present. She needed a brushstroke to paint everything colourless, to write very simple lines again.

It was really warm and sunny in Australia this December. Sunrays beat down with hideous ease. The call from that ancient, untouched world appeared fiercely urgent. It was a relief to leave the simmering land for some time.

"North India is reeling in mist and cold," the Indian girl gushed with vacillating sensation, as they boarded the plane to Chennai.

Through the entire journey, Simone's heart dived and surfaced excitedly like some love-lorn dolphin in the sea below. Her enticing ogle at the bluish calm waters of the ocean below created a pleasant sensation at a place where a kid might have kicked had she conceived. A woman possesses the basic instincts of a mother. In the womb of her heart, love and care never fall short of seeds to conceive the things that make this world a better place.

"Mother sea is so fertile! So many creatures and beautiful cultures like these Andaman and Nicobar tribals in her womb," she felt envious.

Many times she had asked the stewardess at what time they would be passing over the islands. She was glued to the plane's track on the screen in front. Much to her disappointment, she was told that the islands did not lie on the route.

They spent three days in Chennai with Pratyaksha's old bachelor uncle. The old man's jarring philosophising was tolerable only because of the cushion support provided by the gentle, mild and calmly condescending south Indian version of the winters.

As the ship sailed for its 1200 kilometres journey in the Bay of Bengal, she was struck by the sea's malleable luxuriance. The scholar in her was bristling adventurously at the prospect of studying, analysing and becoming a part of those shy, almost naked bodies protected by the fortress of sea from all sides—away from the ear-splitting noise. As the ship cut across the waves, the sea breeze vouchsafed tranquillity. Sea miles were spread in luxurious austerity. Sea, the untidy chessboard of wavy moves, to change and not to change at the same time. Its faded green ripple carried an enormously elderly aura.

"The waters are the same. The sea hasn't changed. In its cradle they also float unchanged," she thought, smelling the deeply rhythmical sense of infinity sashaying over the waves.

Reaching the Air Force Base, she felt a few knick-knacks of paradoxical feelings. The place was very orderly. However, this type of orderliness, the main-stay of the civilized society, wasn't what she was in pursuance of. She was looking forward to overlap the pleasantly disordered, knotted, ruffled lines of those primitive civilians. Her friend's big, healthy father, his orderly impassiveness curtly signed by a well-trimmed moustache, looked like a beholder of civilizational monotony; as if he was under the charge and duty of destroying all civilian disorder in one swash like the angry sea of the mythical watery deluge of all religions.

However, appearances are just poor carriers of first impressions. It sometimes raises only false alarms. Contrary to the impression he carried, Station Commandant T. Mohanty was a thorough gentleman oozing with magnanimous humility. He knew that the formalities of receiving a guest ought not to blind oneself of the immediate task at hand, i.e., the purpose of visit. So, very promptly with the verve and enthusiasm of a young pilot on his first unaided flight, he made arrangement for the Australian lady's 'mission with the aborigines', as he called it.

Sactius, perhaps the only graduate tribal from the area, working at the Air Force Base, was called for services. This affable, unpretentious man moved with short, quick steps as if pacing up and down to build a bridge between ancient times and the present. Abundant with simplicity, he performed his tasks with an extremely enlivened energy. He was perhaps the only link between the big sophisticated and orderly world of the airmen and the small disorderly world of the *adivasis*. He was aware of it and seemed to cherish the position, all the way eager to stamp his utility in the modern world. He spoke halting Hindi, not so halting decent English and fluent Nicobarese apart from numerous little linguistic sinews that enabled him to get his message conveyed to the remotest 'sons and daughters of nature'.

Sactius was a Jarawa, whose clan's 300 to 400 members resided at Jirkatan. During colonial times, his grandfather had become a favourite of his English teacher, an English Jailor, and let loose an inertia that reached to the third generation in his lineage and the grandson ended up getting educated. From his hard fought information, Simone's anthropologist mind struck on two tribal groups. The first included 103 member Onges residing in Duncan creek. These were nomads and passed their days in gathering food. The other was 105-membered Shompen, primitive mongoloid aborigines, living at unknown place in the Campbell Bay. Apart from these, Sentinelese inhabited the North Sentinel island, Jarawas were found in middle Andaman and Andamanese lived on with primitive means on Strait island. Further, dozen or so villages inhabited by about 20,000 people were a peculiar admixture of civilizational surge and primitive recede. On top were the Indian military detachments. The hundred odd members of the Shompen community attracted her aboriginal fancy the most. Sactius was a bit apprehensive about her chosen group for they were the most isolated, most untouched and most primitive of human beings. However he was supposed to help her and he did the same.

The sea appeared the writer of this primitiveness. The island bound by the sea looked like a big canoe floating with the preserved signs of antiquity. A tiny world beyond the push and pummel of competition; self-regulating and self-perpetuating the little slice of calm here. Their existence defined by the gently swaying waves along the frilled and rugged coastline; coconut trees dotting the mighty father's reach and the mangroves happily and naturally surviving in the intertidal zone. The swaying fringe of the sea seemed to tickle a calmness that clambered into the onlooker's soul.

"The sea is mother, the maker of this island's tribal culture. It protects its isolation like a mother keeps the infant safe in her lap," she thought with a warm, pleasant, maternal sigh.

Mankind has surpassed all animals on earth. He has outgrown the nature and in the process acquired claws, hoofs, and teeth that put anything still part of nature to run for safety. Their learned foot's encroachment into the territory of Shompens was like throwing a stone into the calm waters of a pond. It created a ripple that was heard above the roar of waves. It was like this little world had come out of its slumber. The air gently gliding across coconut trees suddenly scampered to carry forward the urgent message. The world of Shompens jostled like a stone-pelted beehive. The outsiders were met by hostile looks. There was raw and animal fear in those big white eyes. They retreated into the little forest. There was occasional stone throwing also. However, any escalation on the attacking scale was prevented by the two armed young men attached to their party by her friend's father. Pratyaksha had preferred to spend her days at Port Blair. Christmas was about a fortnight away.

They were like unwelcome guests, the host having moved out leaving the house empty. Distances are but bridgeable if at least one end is open to connect with pure, harmless intentions. Simone knew it was a big challenge to allay the raw fear in them. Love but can dispel all doubts. She knew it and was confident of pushing out fear from their naked bodies. Simone carefully chose a spot and pitched their tent. It was about 500 yards from the primitive habitation, if it could be called habitation at all, abandoned presently for the scared souls had retreated into the forest. It was a mere assemblage of grass, tree branches, and wood. A different world, a carrier of a unit of antiquity, a world so different from the world of gleaming, shining skyscrapers she had come from.

There was another anglicised tribal called Hurbartson who joined the group after they had set up the camp.

The smoke of painful memories a bit clouded the sun above her. Simone moved her hand as if to shoo away everything related to that old world. Walking along the beach this sunny forenoon she was mulling the strategy to start first delicate steps on the path to communicate and mix with the Shompens. The line of foam along the coastline made her soul pay obeisance to the sea's protective fencing around these tiny dots of islands, where these little human groups still survived as raw agents of nature; totally untouched by the civilised surge. She looked into the forest where the aborigines had moved into, creating further distance from the world beyond, and a sense of ennobled antiquity seemed to beckon her from that silent world.

A genuine smile can win over all lines of apprehension on a suspecting face. True love can douse the fire of hate in any heart. Peel off the predatory skin of aggression and encroachment from your mannerisms and you become a naked simple human being, as near to nature as an aborigine, even though you might be wearing clothing. She felt all this and planned to show her group's harmlessness. She had watched some documentaries on television in which animal lovers had become friendly even with lions in forests, winning over their trust, breaking that almost unmovable barrier between the man and the animal, and setting up a bond of love. This task was less daunting because these were humans after all, even though in primitive stage. The things that are done with real passion very rarely fail us. Her maternal passion to integrate with their primitiveness, and Sactius and Hurbartson's linguistic abridgement of this communicative predicament found them winning the confidence of these innocent souls, who had never seen totally clad savages from the other world from so close quarters. Their prehistoric nakedness and Palaeolithic struggles for survival struck the social anthropologist in her with awe and reverence.

An old man's curiosity was the first one to be caught in their cordially set up net of friendship. As if to impress them, he stigmatised his nakedness with a scant grassy tuft hiding his modesty in the middle, walked up to half the distance between their abandoned huts and the alien camp. He appeared to be out on some adventure, having convinced himself of the absence of mortal risk in taking a few steps in the outsider's direction. Peeping into the air around the camp, he drank something from a coconut shell and started to chew and suck at handful of nautilus shells as if these were the peanuts of his world. As if to flaunt their cultural advancement, he then started cutting his long hair using a stone ship. Very cautiously, Sactius and Hurbertson started gesturing and speaking words that might be understood by the old Shompen. From a distance, a female figure possessing enormously developed buttocks was anxiously watching. She appeared at the cusp of panic for the old man's sake. Taking many minutes for one step she reached a tiny grass shelter, entered while looking with utmost care in all directions, and came out wearing a skirt of Padanus leaves as if she was afraid of nudity under the prying eyes of the outsiders' covered bodies.

Their boating and fishing foray around the Nicobar group—comprising Bamboka, Chowra, Little Nicobar, Pilo Millow, Tilanchang and Trinket islands—involved their version of the farthest limits of creation. Looking from the little hole of their secluded existence, she peeped insecurely at the bigger world of alien people with alien proportions of clothing, language and gestures. Her body was tattooed with varied patterns, designed with animal leisure during their endlessly free hours. The old man's body too was tattooed with ochre shades. Body-painting appeared more important to them than clothing. Their primitive reddish ochre artistry on the skin is believed to be a protection against abundant evils that stalk the seas and the forests.

The woman was perhaps the old man's daughter, or we aren't sure whether such a relationship was known to them or not. The socialised tribals in the camp went a few tantalising steps forward, speaking all the words they could muster up from the rudimentary verbal kit of these people still surviving in almost Palaeolithic conditions. The old man and the hefty woman appeared visibly impressed with the antics of their civilised brethren from the outside world. Hurbertson took out his shaving kit and started shaving before the curiously bewildered eyes of the primitive mongoloid aborigines. The old man too picked up his stone chip and tried to shave his beard, but having failed to do it, he started cutting the hair around his sagging jaw. Now, the way of doing it was the only thing which distinctly hyphenated the tribal and the outsider. This link—in the form of lather and razor on the one side and stone chip on the other—between the past and the present was caught by their raw instincts. Maybe in their virgin, animalistic instincts, they must have understood that these outsiders were not from some unknown place of the devil spirits they were so scared of. The next hyphen was bestowed by eatables from both sides of the fence, the very next day. The campers ate theirs, the tribal theirs. Cakes, biscuits, canned meat, bread on one side and unsalted, raw fish, dugong, honey, turtles, and brew made of strange roots on the other.

Curiosity took to the foot trails leading to the forest nearby and drew the aborigines one by one, following each other, convinced of the absence of risk. It was like catching their trust with the cord of love. And they trickled out, slowly taking cautious steps, always on their toes to scamper back if there was some danger. It was a shaky bridge made of twigs and branches of feeble trust. And it got consolidated.

It's the same humanity linking the ancient and the modern. Next week Simone was ecstatically fishing in the shallow waters of coral reefs. She joined the womenfolk in holding little nets made of plant fibre and barks; while her male colleagues faltered with bows, arrows, and wooden harpoons. Going into the open sea without rigger canoes was particularly scary, but they bore it man and womanfully because the trace of understanding that emerged on the brightened faces of these isolated beings was the best thing they could aspire for in the universe. The Shompen males seemed more eager to hide their nudity in comparison to the females. Some of them covered their groins with little pieces of animal skin serving as loincloths. They shyly giggled, as if feeling more awkward of their covering. The sound of sea waves chimed like music eulogising this meeting of the ancient and the modern. The two sides mixed through the language of looks, smiles, laughter, gestures, and sounds.

Sailing out in the open sea with these unpretentious human beings, so heartlessly defined backward in terms of the indices of development, she sensed the primordial feel of unstigmatised, unpolluted humanity.

"How sadly we, the monsters of knowledge, have defined their infinitely free and wildly unconstrained existence in terms of the two parameters of relative isolation and backwardness," she grudged within herself. "And this inaccessibility and alienation so paternally vouchsafed by the pride father," she cast a look of genuine gratitude at the gently surfing waters of the Bay of Bengal.

The best of their efforts gave the minimum to survive. It saved them from the worm of greed and planning too much about future. They lived just for a day. It was, from their standards, a bit better catch this day. Sea, the gentle sea, and sometimes the angry one, had been kind. Walking in a file through a mangrove they performed a sort of sea ceremony. They knew the mangrove's utility from their simple experience. The mangrove acted as a natural dyke, allowing breeding, spawning, and hatching for small fish. In a jutting coral rock among the stilted vegetation, they had dug out a little cave. There were strange engravings that would pass as prehistoric painting. An elderly man with a very happy face and watery, pale eyes, wearing a skin-mask and a beaked headgear, made guttural sounds in front of some sacred stones.

She recalled the last time she been to church. She had fervently prayed, hoping things will change to give peace to her mind in the way she wanted. Our expectation from the unknown hasn't changed at all across thousands of years, she thought looking at the aborigine priest. It was the same God for this stone-age tribe, expected to be appeased on a bribe. With a porcupine quill the old man pierced the neck of a pheasant. The bird fluttered for its last moments. With needle-like sharp bones the old priest criss-crossed the dead bird and put it before the sacred stones. It was followed by shouts and strange cries. Faith, even in its most rudimentary form, is the anchor of our existence, she thought. In her life she had swung between belief and non-belief. She wanted to keep her belief now, because she was happy. And there they came back along the lapping waves of the Bay of Bengal, putting little bowls of palm leaves in the water to float, offering flowers to the foamy beach, and sprinkling water over their naked bodies. The ebony hair of a young Shompen caught her attention. The naked youth was handsome in his own ways. Do they fall in love, she wondered. He carried a bow on his shoulder and a grass belt, tucked with four five wooden arrows, around his waist. An Indian military helicopter went overhead, cutting air with a wobbling rumble. Instinctively, the ebony-haired youth drew out his bow. But before he could take out the arrow his eyes met Simone. His fear gave way to a sheepish grin. There were peals of laughter around. The world seemed to have changed for this prehistoric tribe, at long last.

The only bond linking the group that knew too much and spoke more, and the one that knew too little and apparently spoke even lesser than the pets in the bigger world, were few classless, raceless exclamations—a warm smile, an unrestrained laughter, wispily silent but understanding language of the eyes, gestures from full heart, cemented by few words and phrases spoken by the two tribal men who had had a brush against the outside world.

The nagging pain of her soul was gone. She had been sucked back into pre-historic times, away from the present. She never knew the past could give such solace to the self. Amidst their nakedness she was also peeling off layers after layers of frustration, dissatisfaction, loneliness, irritation and anger. These were the trash of the world beyond the sea.

Brilliant sleepy islands, coral reefs, and saltwater crocodiles. (She had stood on the shore with the pores of her skin drawn tight as the Shompens unsuccessfully tried to hunt one.) Luxuriant tropical forests, in which Nicobari Macaque, Imperial pigeon and Narcondum Hornbill hooted, flapped their feathers, flew into the blue skies, painting their freedom on the bluish canvas. It was a small world, yet so substantial; substantial in its beauty, in equal proportion to the immensity of the sea.

The tropical sun kissing her fair skin, the air ruffling her silky hair, she had stood, her hand supported on the sacred stake, in a wood-cleared patch of the forest. There were graves around. With a pinch of irritation, they in the other world, where she came from, derogatorily summarised the culture of such ancient tribes with terms like corpse worshipping cult, ceremonial cannibalism, cannibal practices and animism. She but, as she closed her eyes, could feel some vibes of the primordial religion. Humanism.

At nights the academician, social anthropologist in her kept her awake. By candle light she wrote hungrily and profusely about their survival, diseases, emerging signs of malnutrition, imminent loss of control over natural resources, displacement and ill-suited rehabilitation, and to top it all the erosion of their long-held identity. She felt gloomy and sad about the future, but then the gently lugubrious music of the tides hitting the corals and the lighted portion of the sky by the lighthouse somewhere in the Campbell Bay promptly gave her assurance that these Palaeolithic traits, which have so mischievously side-tracked the modern man's path to culture and civilization, will survive forever because the sea is with them, and these few dozen naked human beings are so comfortable and at peace in their bare skin that to imagine them otherwise would be a sin.

The 70,000 years old primitiveness of their DNA, so paternally protected by the sea since their arrival via Indonesia filled her with primordial awe and raw respect for the forces of nature that shaped human destiny in such fantastic ways. She was in enchanting awe of these human beings, who lived as freely as animals without the chains of modernity, culture, nagging responsibilities, constraining commitments and many other headaches born of the modern-day society.

One night the tiny hamlet was alive with festivity. Their bodies painted with charcoal and vegetable dyes, they danced in a circle around a fire that had been lit after an hour-long struggle with the fire stones. She felt like helping them with a matchbox from her tent, but dropped the idea, considering it an intrusion into their primitiveness. As the fire rose, they jumped and hooted, as if in awe of this strange spirit. They placed the skulls of their ancestors around the fire, dancing in slow, abundant movements, now and then taking out their necklaces of sharp, little bones to touch the skulls, as if seeking blessing to ward off the evil spirits.

The beautiful day of December 25.Christmas. The sun was shining with magnificent eloquence. White fluffy clouds hang in the blue with selfless calm. Sea waves hit the corals with verve and zest. She had always participated in Christmas celebration with a heady ecstasy. Even today she carried the usual festive spirit. She was surprised by her enthusiasm to involve these simple tribals in celebrating her faith. The night was planned. What a Christmas night it would be, she thought deeply inhaling the sea air. Souls' musicality and the sea's at a distance. She felt like embracing the sea, their protector.

Hathu, the man who took first tottering steps towards acquaintance with the aliens and Aatu, his daughter, the big bottomed female who apprehensively arrived at his side that first day, were Simone's favourite in the hamlet. Aatu's one-and-half year old daughter always sowed titillating seeds of flowery hopes in her barren womb. Just a single look at that tiny primitive creature, inexplicably and infinitely fulfilled the thirst of her maternity, completed her. The night was a real beauty, the one that you tend to remember for a long time. The stars shone at their best in the curious sky. With innocent wonderstruck eyes, the child was ogling at the rag-tag Christmas tree so painstakingly prepared by the outsiders. Sactius as Santa was the centre of aboriginal attention. They danced around a bonfire—this string of primitive and cultured humans holding their hands, their feet moving unhurriedly forward and backward, both sides introducing their moves now and then into it, both trying to imitate the other's steps. The gentle cadence of their body movements was in sharp contrast to the robust notes of strange drums made of animal skins. The festivity went on well past midnight, in fact into the wee hours of the next day. Time, but, here was the least botheration. They lacked everything, but not contentment and time.

However, even the immediate future is impregnated with so many uncertainties, haps, and mishaps that many a time our little joys of the present make us heavily indebted to the coming time. Thus, while here on this tiny island, a little group of humans was enjoying perhaps the pleasant most festivity of their lives, thousands of kilometres away, who knows there might have been subsurface undercurrents of chaos waiting to hatch at any moment to give birth to the ugly child of doom and destruction.

Throughout the revelry, Simone's hungry maternity had been copiously satiated by Aatu's little daughter. This little naked black angel kept on looking and smiling at her with her big eyes. Several times it had dozed off to sleep, only to wake up and cry to be taken in the white woman's lap. The ever-increasing curiosity in her eyes that had hitherto seen so little of the same peaceful life made her round face acquire a peculiar expression of understanding that belied her little span of time on this tiny island. Simone couldn't help picking the baby girl many times during their dancing and singing. She danced around the Christmas tree, holding the baby with one hand around her bosom and stretching out the other to hold the tiny hand in a couple's dancing posture. Much to some inner satisfaction to the ever-waiting mother in her, the girl cried every time somewhat apprehensive Aatu took her back.

Time thus dived with its importance into the depths of the sea. It was not before 4 o'clock in the morning before everyone in the tribal hamlet and Simone's camp was fast asleep. Nobody was awake when a tired twilight handed over the baton to a dithering and worried day; worried with its rayed responsibility to see the humanity safely advanced by one more day, by one more step. Another day, thus, dawned. It was none other than the fateful day of December 26, 2004—the day of Asian Tsunami disaster. The day when it appeared as though God had abandoned millions of people around the coastal areas and tiny islands in South and South East Asia to the doomed watery arrows of catastrophe. Dangerously interlocked plates off the coast of Sumatra were readying to trigger a killer quake of magnitude 8.9 and let loose unfamiliar and unknown disaster all across the region.

This geological monstrosity had its focus about 1,000 kilometres south, south east of Port Blair. At 00:58:50 Coordinated Universal Time (06:28 IST), massive geological plates pushing against each other released devastating force that shifted a 1,000 kilometre section along the plate boundary, triggering a massive displacement of water. Starting from the point 3.298° N, 95.779° E, the disaster spread out in all directions in the form of 10 metres sea walls travelling at a speed of 500 Km/hour. Now, who got deluged at what location and at what time is irrelevant. It was mindless act of nature beyond all human comprehension. This silent disaster struck unsuspecting nature and humans. The Tsunami-ravaged sea became a cruel weapon in the hand of death and destruction.

The whole of Car Nicobar group of islands, like so many other places in the region, was suddenly struck and assaulted by monstrously huge walls of water. In just one chaotic moment tiny pearly islands, so safely ensconced in the embroidery of coral reefs and mangroves against the erosion of gently surfing tides on any normal day, were turned into pathetic heaps of muddy debris. The assault was so severe that every type of resistance in the path of massive waves dragging overland was easily ripped apart. Like a massive earth mover, the tidal waves pushed rubble and mud in front of them and then while retreating almost everything was sucked into the sea. Then it rose again. The last remnants of the devastated fronts were thrashed by this heartless assault of nature. Carnage crept miles inland. The horrific tidal waves crashed four five times and left the whole lively places under dozens of feet of water. It was just impossible to believe if anything at all remained unscathed by this Herculean water assault. The same peaceful and protective sea that had cradled the pristine isolation of these islands and their dwellers now became the instrument of annihilation.

Monstrous tidal waves thus triggered an unprecedented and unseen disaster. The primitive instincts of these people might have propped up some inexplicable instrument to save themselves from this watery deluge, if they had been awake at the time while the Tsunami was stealthily moving towards the island. But no, they were caught all asleep. Some mysterious behaviour of the dogs and fowls had given some vague hints of the impending disaster. However, their masters were not awake to interpret their behavioural change. Abnormal noises and hurried scampering, 10-15 minutes before the onslaught, thus went unheeded. All were peacefully asleep when the sea's deadly pout struck the beaches, mangroves, and coral reefs.

The first tidal wave lifted Simone's tiny tent as a prize at it 10 metre cusp. She did not know when and how her sound sleep was broken, and how the slumberous first steps towards one final eternal sleep were taken. The canvas was ripped apart by the surf and foam. Rolling in the mud, clothes ripping apart under the pressure of the water as the returning wave sucked her towards the sea, she could reflect only this much that how could the sea that was a good half kilometre from her tent do this; and the very sea that was the proud protector of these islands' geography and the dwellers' aboriginality.

A horrific catastrophe; a quick, brutal attack of nature. With some unknown contempt, the sea drew back and came hurtling for the second charge. The second wave was even stronger and she was dragged a full mile, as the small bits of her senses, still alive to the fury around, calculated. The sea had exploded suddenly. Her battered body convulsed and struggled instinctively like a tiny insect driven by the danger to its life. As the second seaward sucking started, she found herself clinging to something with all her might. The water ebbed and her jammed senses gained a bit of foothold, showing her pathetic most signs of life. It was a surprise to be still alive, to just know this much that she could feel herself.

The third wall of water struck again dragging her further away from the coast. In between the half cycle of this watery wall's forward aggression, her soft female body got struck into the branches of a palm tree as the watery deluge thundered past. When time explodes, turning death surer than life, ones chance of survival, if one is lucky to have one, is the biggest stroke of luck in a lifetime. She was almost squeezed to death. When the wave sucked inwards, the tree gave away but she clung to the trunk, holding onto her luckiest moment.

The fourth strike found her sticking to a strong bamboo bunch, a mighty old thing by the side a ridge. Providence had struck her to the highest water mark of the tidal waves. She was taking a stock of her remaining senses and trying hard to convince herself that she had survived and would live. Clinging like a badly battered and bruised lizard, she saw the lessening ferocity of the Tsunami swiping its hand of death over the ecology of this island. The island appeared to have been gobbled by the sea. Fearing another strike, she ran with all her might up the elevation. Clothes tattered and mud-soaked bleeding wounds meant nothing to her now. Life is far more precious than mere cuts and wounds. We somehow adjust as long as we are alive.

Dragging her devastated self to as safe a place as she could manage, till the string of her furtively feminine effort broke, she lay down and closed her eyes and ears to the sea's angry rumbling. In the injured vacuum of her inner-self, vast fearsome Tsunamis were still striking at her soul, and no longer able to bear it, she got up like a person coming back to life from death itself. The havoc wreaked around convinced her that her survival was nothing short of a miracle. Sometimes you cannot be happy enough in proportion to your luck. In the face of death and destruction, you still feel a victim, however lucky you might have been.

"Oh *you* sea, why did you take away your offering so mercilessly?!" she shouted at the muddied land around her.

The pain in her visible and invisible wounds was now creeping into the corridors of her senses. She tried to find any vestiges of life in the destroyed and flooded canopy around her, but only the gory spectacle of swashed vegetation caught her eyes. Her first pain was over the almost sure loss of the identity of this Palaeolithic group that had been braving the nature's sweet–sour shoves for thousands of years. The sea had preserved their identity, and in one stroke taken it away. It was sea's absolute right, anyway. It's too big.

"How could their forefathers seafaring in their rag-tag boats reach here far into seclusion from the faraway lands of Asiatic and African mainland? And now their existence eaten away in one single swipe like this? How? Why?" she had her share of unanswerable questions against the chance hand-outs of providence that hammer our existence suddenly, illogically.

The pain of losing her fellow companions stalked her soft sensitive self. She thought about her four fellow campers who had been selflessly helping her in her research. Before she could get into more worrisome aspects of her own precarious position, her dead reverie was broken by a child's cry. Hope darted back like a still bigger tidal wave into her broken self. The social anthropologist in her ran drawn by the sobbing notes of the poor destitute.

She had forgotten her own almost hopeless position. "The name of the Shompens is still alive!" she drew out a moment of happiness out of the death-work strewn around.

She moved unmindful of human or animal bodies coming her way. Life is always better than death. A single person alive is better than hundreds of dead bodies. It helps you to live and survive. It gives you hope. 'Hope' struck her in the form of big, teary eyes of the child as she approached it. She had a co-sharer of luck. Out of the millions of acts of natural calamity, one single smile of fortune and fate flashing like lightning across the darkest of cloud to give her the smile of a lifetime, despite all the reasons to the contrary around. Aatu's girl was lying on a providentially outcropping rock. And below, dozens of feet downwards, the half-drowned lifeless body of the unfortunate mother was lying.

The primal maternal instinct had found the tribal mother safely clutching her child till almost the last onslaught of Tsunami. However, the last punched snatched the child away to the safety of this elevated rock waiting their like a cradle to catch the last Shompen scion; while the unfortunate mother was snatched back to the pool of death. Her big-bottomed, mud-smeared figure was lying as the water was slowly ebbing away to its ultimate reservoir after the terrible avalanche.

"Hope...Hope...Hope..." the famished mother in her was crying.

Primordially hungry maternity in her clutched the tiny life as safely as possible. Now her life became doubly precious, because the fate of this girl, perhaps the sole sinew from the primitive fabric of the Shompens, was linked with hers.

"Perhaps some others are still alive!" hope raised its head as the child came back to life in her arms, after being drawn as near to death as possible.

However, the sheer magnitude of devastation belied all such expectations. She saw destruction wreaked around as far as she could see. Exactly same was the fate of those few hundred (572) emerald islands once safely couched in marvellous isolation. The unique cultures spread over 38 inhabited islands; and dense tropical forests, myriad varieties of flowers, birds and animals strewn splendidly over the rest had been mercilessly trashed. The airbase at Car-Nicobar was gone in a swash. The fate of hundreds of airmen unknown—among them Pratyaksha's father—as death hurriedly wrote its list of mortality. Phoenix dockyard at Port Blair, so proudly built by the Britishers in 1829 and lately upgraded with even more proud by free Indians, was also completely tattered. Like thousands of other lives, the fate of Pratyaksha was also unknown.

In the face of such tragedies even our fundamentals change. She had loved sea, loved it like crazy since her childhood. The surging sea now was the most fearsome thing for Simone. The mother in her took the little child deeper into the island, lest the sea should strike again and snatch the child from the warmth of her bosom overflowing with maternal love for this probably the sole survivor from the family of Shompens.

She was walking along a low ridge that was now drying after being submerged under the watery onslaught. The water to the inner side had not retreated creating a fearsome muddy pool. Her shell-shocked senses were again hurriedly awakened by the raw fury of a crocodile whose jaws were greedily striking at the hard shell of a leather-back turtle. Another game of death; right there in the jaws of death. It sent down a shudder down her spine. Snakes and scorpions, out of their flooded holes, now caught her scared eyes more than once. She would have shrieked loudly if not for the safety and warmth provided by the girl child on her bosom.

Even help needs some *help* during such times. As it happens during such calamities, to get some providential relief means one has to wait by days, not hours. You can show anything except impatience. The only thing that comes handy is *wait*. And a prayer on your lips. She was thus stranded for the next three days on this tiny island totally cut off from the world. Her struggle for survival was overshadowed by her 'motherly struggle' for the child's safety. She had never felt this much of responsibility any time before in life. It was an overpowering emotion. She felt what it means to be a mother. Your baby is a part of your enlarged self, and dearest than anything related to yourself.

Yes, she was mother to her! Tears welled up in her beautiful eyes as the little tribal's lips groped over her shapely breasts, furtively seeking some drops of life. She had to yield to the little one's efforts. Lifting her ruined T-shirt, she offered her uninitiated motherly self to the child. Like a little hungry puppy, it painfully nibbled and smacked her nipples like a hungry colt is unmindful of the cow's pain while it strikes its muzzle forcefully into the udder. It was painfully ecstatic. There was no milk in her bosom; but the nutrient liquid of love and care was sprouting in gusto from her heart. The child nibbled for a long time, possibly imagining that it was drawing something out and slept in the process. The pleasant sensation of being a mother extollingly showered upon each and every ounce of her body and soul. For the rest of the time she contrived many a motherly things from the leaves, strange fruits and barks—tasting everything well in advance herself to feel any harmful effects—to keep the child's wide eyes shining hopefully in her lap.

Meanwhile, rudimentary steps towards the biggest ever relief efforts in Andaman and Nicobar islands had been started. The Crisis Management Group's meeting in Delhi pledged all patent help to the victims. Army troops, ships, helicopters, and naval and air force personnel were making day and night go side by side to provide succour to the victims. Tons and tons of generators, pumps, bleaching powder, food packets, tents, clothing, medicines, and aid and relief workers were being loaded down on the decimated islands. Relief camps were being set up. Sniffer dogs prowled purposefully to locate the buried bodies in sand and muddy rubble.

Helicopters flew very low over formerly habited islands to spot some sole survivor still struggling for life. During nights the sounds of aircrafts plying over made her cry with helplessness. However, every time she cried the child cried even more and she had to stop and smile through her teary eyes to calm down the little thing. Hope in her was ever-persistent in raising its voice at the cusp of eternal optimism. During the day, she knew her sole chance of being spotted by the rescue helicopters lay in running and furtively gesturing along the coastline. To add to her ever-accelerating fear, the islands were being intermittently shaken by many aftershocks of both major and minor types. She knew she had to continue pursuing the chance of life, for herself, and for the girl child equally importantly, or even more so.

Thanks to the unified command of the Army, Air Force and Navy and also the coast guard, on the third day she came across an airdropped food packet of essential rations. She jumped in air like she had come across the biggest treasure in the world. Many a time during those three endless days, life seemed to sing a melody in her ears as a helicopter hovered over the island while she ran and waved furtively beneath; however much to her chagrin it flew away, dithering and uncertain which way to take. She was now getting desperate. All with her hope she was but merely a speck on the ground, and it was too much to ask from fate that she be spotted by some chance helicopter that might come that way.

She knew the fire would be the best means of being spotted, but how to light a fire. Fire so ubiquitous in her world! Life in modern society is so convenient that to think of lighting a fire with stones is almost unthinkable. She had the scion of an old society in her lap. Perhaps to survive now she too would have to act like these primitive savages who had all the time in the world to light fire with stone sparks. She collected stones that she deemed fit to create sparks. Then she was on the mission to collect the driest tufts of branches, twigs and leaves. She then sat on the huge task to create the modern times easiest connivance, fire. Her hands got blisters, the sun changed direction and most of the stones turned to little pebbles by the time some chance spark of her sweating efforts caught an edge of some dry leaf and she fed its warmth like she was feeding life itself.

There was hope, there was fire. It was evening. She had to keep the fire going through the night and raise smoke the next day. She did not sleep lest the fire died, killing her hope as well. Next day, all worn out, her fingers swollen and blood clots evincing the signs of her efforts, she raised smoke like she was fighting for life. This time her efforts did not go in vain. The trail of smoke was spotted by the pilot of a rescue helicopter.

It was a beautifully hopeful forenoon on December 30 when she and the daughterly figure in her arms were dragged up the rescue ladder into the noisy windy machine. They were as helpless and broken as a woman and a child can be in such tragic and testing circumstances of the last four days.

She did not know in which relief camp she was put along with the little tribal girl. Life still was pitiable as can be expected in a relief camp. There was a danger of viral storm letting loose the arrows of mortality upon the survivors, who had lost almost everything in so little time. The incidences of Vibrio cholera, a bacterial infection, put the anthropologist in her on high alert for the safety of the tiny primitive flower from the isolated world, whose underdeveloped immunity to such out-worldly diseases might pluck her away in a stroke. Public health specialists, staff nurses and paramedics were stretching every sinew of their doctoring efforts to prevent the outbreak of such diseases. Simone wanted the primitive flower to be away from the uncertain world of medicines like Cephalexin, Sulphamethaxazone, Roxid, Metrinidazole, and so forth. Nearby, bodies were decomposing due to the tropical conditions in the makeshift morgues; the skins turned reddish black and many a finest physiques erased by the cataclysmic assault of water. Three days at the relief camp were unimaginably long. So on the fourth day, when she managed to board a ship to Chennai with many other survivors, it appeared like a new life and world altogether.

Things were no better on the mainland either. It was a battered world. She was on the verge of breakdown, but those little eyes of *hope* somehow provided her strength. She knew she was up against a long and tiresome struggle to adopt a life that might be doomed otherwise. It's an irony that social and administrative apathy allows thousands of destitute children to die and be exploited without any issues, but there is a cry at the top of the administering voice if somebody tries to salvage a flower from the garbage. She too had to fight. The Australian Embassy provided her much support during the long, tedious struggle to adopt the girl.

Finally, she boarded the flight home with tears in her eyes and 'hope' in her heart. She had named the girl Hope. Out of all the tragic events, she was returning as a more complete human being. Well, that's life—incomplete without hope.

A Nightmare Devouring a Dream

* * *

It was not that late on this Sunday morning as usually it is for the school going children on a holiday. Madhavan was peacefully asleep in his tiny bedstead in the small room of their semi-concrete little house, situated in a little fishing hamlet off the coast, about two kilometres from Velanganni near Nagapattinam in Tamil Nadu.

His sister Jayachitra appeared even more angelic in her sleep. She carried a smile while sleeping, as if an ever-persistent sweet dream safely blanketed her. It was about 8:30 a.m. Their father, a moderately well-off fisherman from the tiny settlement, had left for fishing in his fibre catamaran. Their mother, not expecting the children to wake up for another hour and half, had left for Velanganni about half an hour ago.

Madhavan's house, a little semi-concrete hutment with whitewashed walls and red sloping roof could well have been called a small fisherman's pride. A safe cosy world; an axis of long-cherished dreams; a small world inside the bigger world of the quiet fishing village, the latter still boxed up in the larger world of the houses on the shorefront. At a short distance, light blue waves gently surged and receded. The sea all welcoming and friendly, except on occasions when there were storms.

Life as usual, mundane life dragging with surety, keeping routine, maintaining hope, retaining society yoked in practised roles and responsibilities. Beach sand, mud, masonry, planks, boats, jetties, and beach huts. A fishing world. Sea and fish rule the air. Menfolk going into the sea. Women taking fish to the market. A slightly boasting air sailing over the wealthy fishermen's small villas with their red-tiled roofs, fluted columns, *verandah*, and tiled floor. Golden sand ready to simmer under the sun, like any other day, waiting for the sun to add to its elevation. In the background, the bluish calm of the sea looking meditatively into the Bay of Bengal. A morning as vivacious like any other, so dreamy that a passing angel might have been struck by the majestic calm and languorous beauty of this unit of the world. Specks of grey white clouds in bluish expanses of the sky. Greenish black silhouette of the fishing trawlers moving on the watery bosom. Even the celestial flier may not have an inkling of what lay ahead within a time-span of just fifteen minutes.

It was the fateful morning of December 26, 2004 when a Tsunami wreaked death and destruction across coastal areas in the whole region. When hurtling waves swallowed many a dream. The times when the nature forgot its objectivity to turn furious. Boxing Day Tragedy: a frightful gift of death, doom, and destruction by the sea as it opened its Christmas Box. A black Sunday when white silvery sandy beaches were spattered with calamitous mud wherein rolled the boats, fishing trawlers, and bungalows. The day when cars, buses, and trucks were washed away like toys in a miniaturised play-act of flooding by the children on the beach on normal days. When even mighty bridges and sturdy railway lines collapsed like pack of cards under the monster wave.

So the fate of this little hamlet appeared sealed for the wrong, just at the moment the first tidal wave came silently wreaking havoc like a poisonous snake.

Madhavan's sleep was broken by an angry shake of the tiny house. A boat's bow came in splintering away the feeble resistance of the door, the very same door that their mother closed behind her every night, leaving her two children in the warmly protecting air of the little room. Before he could make out what had happened, water was greedily coming up the little height of his bed. Was it a bad dream? No, it was something worse.

Their house was at the outer fringe of the high-tide mark of the first wave. So giving them first hurried warning, the water swashed back even more dangerously than it had arrived. Elsewhere lower down the coast, the waves swept defenceless people desperately trying to reach higher ground. The things that had been done in years were undone in a momentary swash. In Nagapattinam, Nagore and Velanganni vehicles, boats, humans, animals and houses were converted into a tangled mass of wood, metal, and bodies.

As the next wave came upon their palm-fringed little hamlet, proudly holding its settlement-lore for the sake of these simple fishermen, all structures were razed to the ground. The boat came dangerously smashing in and hit the wall. The evil progeny of the submarine slumping flooded the room in all its muddy flurry.

"The sea has gone mad!" Madavan's death-stricken voice cut across the roaring rage and reached his younger sister's ears.

On many occasions in the crowded bazaars, his mother had left them alone in the past, instructing him to take care of his little sister. Even in the face of this terrible moment, the instruction overcame his danger-struck senses. Jumping into the boat's bow, he dragged Jayachitra safely into his brotherly arms. Just a few seconds later, the house was blown away and the boat was lifted to the level of the top palm branches, whose height once filled him with curiosity, awe and surprise. He was grasping his sister as strongly as he could manage. Luck throws a tiny handful of survival chance in such chaos. Who gets it is beyond the comprehension of any law of determination.

A motley crowd was running futilely away from the sea, unmindful of a costly car turned upside down right in the middle of their path. Nets, masts, fishing trawlers, canoes and mechanised boats lay in a tangled mass. Water muffled the breaking and snapping sounds of the world built with so much of focussed passion. Only the sea roared, subduing all other lesser noises. A young man was running away from the beach with a young girl's body in his supposedly protecting hands. However, the monster was grinning instead of grieving over the massive loss of lives and property around. Plants, wood, and damaged boats lay over dead fish. In just a few minutes it was a changed world; the world which was almost the same with its mundane routines over the years.

We have been running miles ahead of our dreams. As concrete buildings cluttered the seafront, fisherfolk moved within perilous vicinity of even storms, not to mention a Tsunami. The angry sea rebuked: destroyed communities, vandalised beaches, mutilated bodies, and twisted boats. It simply pushed the table, scattering everything like broken crockery. The beachfront engulfed by the disaster, there was only one anatomy recognisable. Disaster's. The massive keel and hull of a ship that moved proudly, smoothly, for fish, money and life, now stuck up, torn and bruised, among coastline rocks. Water is generous to fish and ships. A liveable world to the former, to flap, to swim; a soft road for the latter, to move, to almost run on an even keel. The sea had perhaps momentarily abandoned the customary role. The fish lay dead, hurled inland and left to die muddy death in the world outside. The ship lying on the rocks, tilted to its right on its keel.

A crushed world. Fear hung in the air over the debris. Rumours did perilous rounds. Every now and then people, like tiny insects, began running helter-skelter, away and further away from the sea. The sea that spawned death and destruction. The gigantic seismic waves unleashed by the super-massive undersea earthquake loomed large in panicked air. Buildings, huts, fishermen and tourists became just tiny testimonials to the wanton destructive power of the massive geological plates pushing against each other with demonic pressure.

Fractured images in a broken mirror. Fragments and pieces of broken dreams. Lorries, pushcarts, and pilgrims to the seashore on the full moon day were mercilessly moulded into a muddy slush. The twenty-thirty feet sea wall smacked two kilometres inland, destroying secluded mangrove paradises, people working in salt pans, breakfasters, as well as fishermen out in the sea for catching fish and prawns. Decimated coastal fishing hamlets and battered fishing canoes, torn-apart beach front and an incontrollable mother crying over the shirtless dead body of her daughter of Jayachitra's age, bore mournful testimony to the madness of the killer wave. People were happy in their varied ways, now they cried for the same loss, a monotonous line of loss of relatives, family, and houses.

Hundreds of bodies were lying in the sand. Holding his sister's hand, he passed by the body of Kittoo, her eyes half-closed and her mother, robbed of the diamond of her maternity, crying so loud that Madhavan dragged his sister away from the scene, horribly terrified. The dead little girl had been friendly enough to offer him a lollipop as their mothers introduced them at a local thoroughfare a few months back. He still recalled that particular taste as he moved away. However bitter the life around, a child but has an innocent little world of sweetness. He carried that little world in his mouth. There in the dangerous sea, he saw the coastguard ships braving the unusually ruffled sea. For a moment he was wonderstruck as to why the sea was behaving so madly. The sea appeared playful even. A joyous memory: the boat's rough planking, painted freely, artlessly in red and white; his feet struggling in the bow, stomach taut over the gunwale, his hands holding her sister's as he laughingly dragged her to the edge. A smile on his lips cracking the bloody crust on his lower lip. Pain. Again he was pulled into scary reality.

He thought his parents will return. They will all be together in their sweet home. A child's hope as vast as the sky. And till then it was his duty to take care and protect his little sister like on so many occasions in the past.

The titanic Tsunami caused by the fifth largest earthquake in hundred years occurred on the twenty-sixth—a date that has become synonymous with the destructive face of nature. On 26 December, 2003, it was Bam in Iran that bore the brunt of the raw, unnerving, shaking forces of nature; On 26 January, 2001, there was epical devastation by the Bhuj and Latur earthquake. And now it happened again on the same date—quite unexpectedly since Tsunami is such a rare phenomenon in the South Asian region. It just caught the people on the wrong foot.

All hope seemed to have vanished from the people's Tsunami-tortured faces. Whenever a VIP visited the relief camps, the people folded hands with such desperation and helplessness like they had never done before any of their Gods. There was so much to say for so many losses, for so little of the help that might come their way now. Some even vent out their desperation to the hilt during these rare fleeting moments as the hurried VIP chickened out of the mess lest there might be some mud smeared on his clean shirt.

Holding his hands over his smashed head a man was crying inconsolably. It was the mournful acme of sorrow. Just tears and cries didn't appear sufficient to give expression to the sorrow born of the terrible loss of his little son, daughter and wife. His very purpose in life had been washed away. The four-five years old boy, who had given him so many reasons to start out for work and return home after finishing a bone-breaking schedule, was now lying to be buried hurriedly in line with his eternally asleep sister. The mother's covered body appeared sleeping comfortably under warm clothes like somewhere in North Indian winters at the time.

On every face 'missing' and 'homeless' was written. Explosive tidal waves which had taken many countries in their destructive spectrum now haunted the tormented psyches of these displaced, hungry, and destitute masses. Hospital morgues were choked with unclaimed bodies so there were mass burials. Multihued coastal community that once glittered with the sea's softly gyrating waves now bore horrific testimony to the all-battering sea-surge. Massive relief operations, on the other hand, were turning out to be a small and feeble whiff of desperation. Still people engaged a hopeful talk in the stinking relief camps, narrating the miraculous tale of an infant's survival, written inexplicably on a floating mattress. Kudos to life—one single flicker of life lighting up the endless depths of thousands of lost lives. Well, that's life!

This earthquake off the coast of Sumatra was so powerful that geologists claimed it made the earth wobble on its axis. The evil aftermaths of this emission of energy, caused due to the undersea slippage of the fault-lines, were felt in every nook corner of the earth. Like tiny insects people were scurrying to safety, impassively carrying the leftovers. A battered woman was moving expressionlessly carrying a colour television set on her head. Her little home, fishpond and vegetable garden all lost and other family members still missing. How was the television set saved? It could have been another story of miraculous survival. We cannot expect it to be dry at least. It must have been in water and not in working condition. But after losing your present, you salvage survival crumbs from the past and look into the future with certain shared memories. It was the tiny idiot box that had seen so many moments of their togetherness. She carried the spoilt box of memories on her head, still catching onto the thin strands of hope, to meet her family, to gather the sinews again, to make a nest once more.

Madhavan saw Nikhita. The left side of her face smashed. In place of the childish smile, a purplish scar and reddish right eye gave her a fearsome expression. Seemingly unmindful of her serious, unattended open injury, she was munching a crumb that had luckily fallen in her pleading hands from somewhere. In the face of such calamity, you have to grasp to the streaks of life filtering through the screen from the unknown world. Also you have to be lucky among thousands of hands that try to hold that iota of life. They had played together on many occasions. It was but no occasion to play. Jayachitra smiled at their neighbour carrying a different face now. The girl was too young to feel the pain of loss; she could just sense the dull pain in her head. Nikhita, however, was grown enough to have an idea of the loss, and knew it was not the time to reciprocate a smile. They remained sitting silently. Unable to bear some silent unseen agony, the once agile chirpy girl got up and moved limpingly. He watched her almost lifeless body move away with undecided steps. Where is she going? He thought of following her, but then dropped the idea because she appeared not to even know them.

Whenever something worth eating fell in his hands, he first gave it to sister to eat, happily looked at her as she ate, and with enthusiasm thought of the praise he will get from pa and ma when they will come to know of this. He seemed to forget all the hardships as his present melted to make a happy picture of the future. When they will be together, they will go to the school, their mother will cook, and father will go fishing. His hopeful eyes putting the scattered pieces together.

In what can be termed as the largest ever relief operations during peace time, all three wings of defence forces were notching out every ounce of their professional efforts. However, the extent of the tragedy was such that even the most humane of their efforts appeared lost in the mishandling chaos around. Life had derailed, and so were the common most expectations. The dead bodies had lost reverence and respect, and the scenes like carrying a dead body tied to a wooden stick jolted the last bit of optimism still lurking around. It appeared strikingly unreligious as the dead are given utmost reverence under normal times. Under such disharmonic times, however, all civilized norms get thrown into the dustbin of survival, and humanity sucks out draughts from the same to somehow survive and see another day. Volunteers were dragging dead bodies on all fours to save them from still worse fate of rotting in the open. Relief and rescue personnel worked mechanically; clearing away the rubble and the bodies with the same expression. There was no other way. It was frightening, more so for his sister. You have to be brave, he recalled his father once telling him. Embracing his sister, turning her face the other way, he braved the sight, his breathing heavy and heat beating fast.

Having lost each and everything related to her, an old lady was wailing piteously. Her wide-open, toothless mouth and lost dull eyes drowned in the salty surge of the sea of tears. Her face was questioningly raised to the God's eyes somewhere in the sky. He had seen her earlier. He recalled vividly. No doubt it was she. She had grinned and acknowledged his father's greetings, while he looked happily wearing a bright red shirt, walking with his father on some Sunday, going to the market holding his father's hand. Now her hands hung limply in air; palms wide open having lost each and every belonging linked to the lines on them through the inexplicable and invisible chord of love, relationships, and life's abounding pleasantries.

Badly battered alive bodies were walking upon hundreds of others still buried in the sand. Their vibrant fishing hamlets wiped out of existence. The fishermen robbed of their catamarans and nets looked at the sea as if it was some perennial foe; broken was that sanctimonious bridge that links a fisherman to the sea like a farmer is linked to his plot of land. The army had dispatched various columns to somehow undo the horrendous extent of this catastrophe. The whole of humanity seemed to have been stranded in a tortuous quagmire. It was a struggle to survive, to move in the mud to gather the broken pieces, to find the surviving family members, then walk a bit more to take on what remained of life.

The Coast Guard, Navy, and Air Force were carrying out aerial reconnaissance mission to salvage some pride from the human side in the face of this gruesome attack of nature. Temples, churches, mosques, schools and offices were being converted to makeshift shelters for this badly battered section of the modern humanity.

Bodies in hundreds—naked, half naked, black, brown, some already showing initial signs of purplish decay; others still fresh like they were asleep; children, men, women, old, young, middle aged—were waiting for the final rites. Nobody was bothered about their caste, class, creed, or religion. It was just a gruesome mass of corpses. Manmade differences melt in the face of assault by the larger forces.

Relief workers were frantically digging a big mass grave to provide a quick burial place, where these victims could be laid to rest within the shortest period of time. No ladder was available to carry the bodies to the bottom of the pit, so even the last respect that could have been given to the once-thriving life had to be abandoned. The uncomplaining corpses were thus thrown into the pit. The hands alive and moving being forced to carry out this apparently inhuman burial, almost feeling ashamed and carrying bruises on their conscience. No God-fearing eye could spare even a single look at the jumbled up limbs once the work had been done, so closing their eyes the workers threw earth over these unknown and even casually acquainted faces.

The nearby beach—a little shiny patch of softness to absorb fatigue and tension—had vanished in a deadly jiffy. The beautiful sand-work was unprotestingly swept off as the waves came rising in a flash and then completing the first calamitous cycle, the water subsided as hurriedly as it had surged. Here Madhavan had spent many hours with family and friends on holidays waiting for his father's boat to return from fishing. The seaside hotel, from whose balcony he had panoramic view of the paternal extent of the sea while his father supplied fish to the kitchen, had been ransacked by the mobbish waves. He looked at the rubble. Some happy memory waved at him to bring a smile on his face. He looked more intently into the rubble to rebuild those nice times. Even his childish fancy failed him. That world seemed to have been ripped apart. No, it wouldn't be the same again. He was suddenly scared. 'But I shouldn't get scared because I am elder brother and have to take care of Jayachitra,' he worked up a little resolution.

On Christmas, the visitors had put offerings and money in boxes in the church. The priest was now distributing the same to the needy lined up, of all faiths and beliefs, having lost their colour, mired in the same colour of tragedy, mere battered human beings. The priest distributed the things with a peculiar sense of detachedness as if it didn't matter anything to him anymore. Madhavan held his sister in front of him in the queue. Putting some coins and some candies on their open palms, the priest put his hand on their hands, first on the girl and then her brother. It was the first human touch of sympathy since days, since so long that he hardly remembered the last time he felt the same. He felt like crying out and ask the elderly priest about his parents. But then the queue moved on mechanically and he just stepped ahead. He knew it was futile. How will the priest help him in finding his parents, he calculated the impossibility of the task. But then who will? All he knew was that he has to take care of his sister and continue looking around to catch a fragment of his lost world. But the world had been shattered in a way that all broken pieces appeared the same. These seemed to belong to all and none at the same time.

The gigantic rupture in the earth's womb whiplashing deadly ripples on the open bosom of the sea, which gained horrific momentum over hundreds of kilometres, had broken the languorous calm of that Sunday morning. Hoping to see his father's boat he went to the fishing jetty. It but was decimated, only tiny vestiges remained. Some sullen fishermen were helplessly looking at the angrily lapping watery tongues, more dangerous than fire, hissing against the broken stone and woodwork. Much to the pitiful cry of his tiny heart, a big mechanised fishing vessel had been washed ashore. It was lying on its side like a big whale stranded on sand, like a broken toy on the table. It appeared damn funny to them. They laughed, gesticulating like two little monkeys, pointing towards the funny tragedy. Children can laugh, for the good only, even if there is hardly any reason to.

Children cry as easily as they laugh. He cried. He ran weeping, holding Jayachitra's hand as tightly as he could, lest the chaos snatch her away. She was the only possession he was left with. A trench-like long and deep mass grave was being dug. Coming to its edge, he saw the horrific sight of a girl being carried to the bottom. He cried loudly and ran with his sister, scared that they had gone mad and were burying girls and might snatch his sister to do the same to her.

"Father and mother will get angry at me if I don't take care of her," he was calculating with his innocent mind.

He was now moving towards Velakanni beach hoping to find their mother. On the way he came across the water-work done by the seismic onslaught of the waves. Leftovers were being dragged out of the devastated fishing hutments. Rubble-strewn landscape glittered with Tsunami's calligraphy—mud smeared utensils, battered clothes, smashed trunks, tattered cupboards, broken chairs, unhinged tables, open chests, and dislodged cots. Many a time, they went crashing into battered fishing canoes. The survivors, wailing hysterically, were being led to relief camps and hospitals. Municipal lorries were carrying dozens of bodies to dump them into huge pits and municipal graveyards. Killing the last emotion for the dead, their relatives just handed over the bodies to the relief workers for burial. Most of the bodies had been smashed beyond recognition. There was no need for post-mortem now, so the hospitals were getting rid of corpses as soon as possible.

The huts and semi-concrete houses of Seruthur, a fishermen colony about a kilometre from Velankanni, had been rubbled beyond recognition. Subramaniam uncle, a fast friend of his father, was not at his customary place today to greet him. He just stared at the place where he supposed the house to exist.

A little shrine of the sea goddess, worshiped by the fisherfolk with special protective prayers offering toddy, turmeric water and neem leaves, stood half ravaged. Trail of death and destruction around it still grinned wantonly. He had seen his mother praying. 'God listens to your prayers if you pray with a clean heart,' he remembered her telling him one day. He went up to the broken shrine to pray with a *clean heart*. He wasn't sure whether he will be able to do it with a *clean heart* or not. 'In any case the God couldn't save its own house,' he felt like making fun of God and turn a little joke of it. But then he was scared the God might delay meeting with their parents. Recalling all mannerisms of his mother, he sat down to pray. The agonised air continued to tickle him, the sounds around, and he gave up the effort to muster up a *clean heart*.

Collapsed walls and roofs meekly brandished the signs of destruction at the VIP and official vehicles buzzing around. A fishing trawler had been rammed into a minor bridge. Sacrificed coastal life had been offered at the seismic altar. Boats, electric poles, nets, planks, boards, roof tins, clothes, and ropes were scattered over the grotesque mud. Hopelessly people wandered through the mud and water puddles. Everybody seemed to be hopping around like children, sullen-faced children rather.

Jayakodi, the fisherman uncle who talked to him so lovingly and confidently that the child in him considered the big fisherman as the bravest man in the world, bore the sight of a big mountain collapsing. The big bulky man's spectacularly heart-rending mournful abandonment to the incessant stream of sobs made him more curious than scared. The more the big man tried to control himself, the more uncontrollable became the stream of sorrow shaking his body with piteous convulsions. Bending on his knees, he was holding his boy's lifeless hand against his left eye as if to prevent the stream of sorrow. His wife was wailing by his side, her face convulsing on the boy's chest. He thought the boy was lucky in having his parents by his side. But then the boy will not get up to smile at his parents. He knew death meant the point of no return. They were, he and his sister, but alive and would smile on meeting their parents. Then his heart beat faster. What if, if ma and pa don't smile when we meet them. He was gripped by fear. The scene of him and Jayachitra wailing by their parents unsmiling bodies flashed in his head. He had seen too many dead bodies, so the picture came vivid. He started crying. Seeing him cry, his sister cried even louder. He heard her crying, recalled his responsibility, embraced her, and caressed her to smile again.

Everybody appeared robbed of something most precious in life. Against this background of black-music of death, the sea thundered demonically, forcing the badly pillaged human beings to rush inland and cram the make-shift relief camps. The people were just simply fleeing away from themselves; away from their God-ordained right (or duty) of performing the final rights of the dead bodies coming their way whom they recognised as their direct relatives and dear friends. Their badly smashed selves dithered from taking up this responsibility.

Chinnapillai from a neighbouring colony was bravely putting a flower garland around the twisted neck of his girl wearing a pink frock. His wife's body lay at some distance. Around them dead fish littered the muddied landscape. He had seen thus jolly person. Their small family had been a guest at his house, last year, and had lunch at their place. Yes, he remembered her dress. Pink. Was it the same? He peered into the frock to find out if it was the same. No, he wasn't sure. He was staring at the dead girl, or at her frock rather, when he shifted his look and found the unfortunate father looking at him. He thought he will recognise him, but then found the man was just seeing through him. He was alive, but perhaps he didn't see any longer.

Quite anxious to lay her frail hands upon something useful for the life staring into her feeble old eyes, an old woman, clad in a tattered sari, was furtively roaming around in the Tsunami battlefield. Plastic cans, broken dented utensils, plastic chairs, and a sack of clothes were the things that lay around her waiting to enter some badly contrived shelter. Her once cosy shelter having been blown and scattered away like brittle matchsticks, it was a humungous task, at this stage of life, to make a beginning, to regain a foothold again. The Tsunami had left behind many a dangerous sea resident on the land. Angrily the old woman threw a big stone at a scorpion, as if taking it as the veritable representation of the deadly sea. A boy wailed nearby, fruitlessly pleading that he had been bitten by a snake. In normal times it would have been news, driving people to rush to his help, but not now.

At a short distance, people were running to beg rations from the relief workers. Most of them did not know how the sudden shifting of the sea floor and the consequent vertical displacement of water created disequilibrium in it giving birth to this evil child of death and destruction. Now survival meant with how much strength you could stretch out your begging hands as voluntary organisations came with food and clothes. There were hundreds of hands jostling for littlest of piece. Hands stretched out flatly, tautly on their all five; lines on the palms—the webbing of luck and fate—glaringly evident like death-sentencing signature of the Tsunami.

He, having made his sister stand at a safe distance, tried to fight his way into the faceless behemoth of a beggar, the pity-faced, soulless, multiple-handed creature, jostling, shifting, restless to survive, to grab the morsels of life. He was pinched down in the innards of this ever-hungry creature. Gasping for breath, scared for life, he howled and found himself pushed out. An old woman, beggar before and beggar now, got him up and handed him a handful of plain boiled rice. Smiling through tears, holding the treasure in his cupped palms, he ran to his sister. He held it to her mouth. The little one was hungrier than he expected and ate all of it, like a little puppy gobbling greedily from a bowl. There was rice around her mouth. He wiped these last grains from her face, put these on his palm and ate, closing eyes. He was happy that she was no longer hungry and will not cry for some time now.

The black Sunday had gobbled everything. Temples, churches, mosques, and an odd *gurudwara* had been razed to the ground. The survivors had put red rags as signs of reverence at the former shrines. Here hundreds were trying to sew up their tattered faith and praying for the survival, well-being and finding their near and dear ones. Faith and its symbols had been cut down. It will take some time for it to heal, to grow. Well, all this takes time of course.

One cannot know from where this devastated young couple got dry wood to cremate their four-year-old twins, son and daughter. Two little pyres were burning as the unfortunate young mother buried her face in the sorrowfully heaving bosom of her husband. Though it wasn't cold, he felt a little shiver as the tide of some strange sensation welled up the pores of his skin. He saw the fire. Felt like getting some warmth. He needed some warmth of love. He stood by the pyres, solemnly as if he was a fellow mourner. All he felt was the warmth. Flesh burning. Fire crackling. Then he got scared and ran away to his sister whom he had instructed to stand at a distance.

Some priests were carrying out a religious procession towards the sea for its pacification. One was saying that it was the disaster born of an angry sea God. "No, it's angry Varuna, the water God!" the other countered. Someone was trying to romp in his point that it was a sea goddess who had caused all this.

The twisted time was taking turns to get itself free of the knot it was entangled in. Then some missive triggered a panic wave. An early-morning warning from the Ministry of Home Affairs to the Chief Secretaries of the affected states went around the devastated mobs in rumoured versions. Fearing another sea storm, people abandoned whatever little things they were left with and took to their heels. Horns were blazing. Vehicles and humans competed to beat the swift forces of death chasing them. The

Tsunami *tandava* had been too fearsome to be faced twice in a lifetime. Noise made by the relief planes and helicopters was mistaken as another sea-surge. Many were injured in the stampede. The brother and sister also ran, imitating others. His sister's small legs gave in and she fell. He got her up, tried to lift her in his arms and then run. His mind was up to the task, but his small body wasn't. They both fell and crawled away from the stomping feet to hide by a broken wall.

That fateful day, Fatima's four-year-old son was playing on the beach imminently facing a wall of the sea. He tried to scamper back as the Tsunami struck. She had her infant son in her lap. She also ran towards him to protect him from the perilous wall. Nonetheless, this crippling natural disaster was beyond any of her prayer to the Almighty and snatched away the boy. Tragedies defy all logic, miracles do even more. Clinging to a floating plank, she still clutched the infant and was pushed far out into the mud, and when the sea retreated with even more force, she found the board struck in the branches of a tree. A day later some gutsy fisherman got the mother and child onto the ground. A young mother, she was now feeding coconut milk to her infant daughter. Her dried motherly bosom now spent of its contents, while the heart heaved inside promising recuperation as soon as possible. She was a mother. She had to give life even if she was almost starving. Madhavan had sometimes seen his mother talking to this woman. He ran towards her for support and succour. She did not appear to recognise him. Her glassy eyes just stared into the murky horizon where the sea hissed. Mechanically her hand was raised and she caressed his little head, but then the thought of her own son overcame her like another Tsunami and she started wailing so loudly that he was scared and forced to retreat.

The symptoms of post-traumatic stress infested the foul air inside the relief camp. He had forced his way in, like it was their home. He tried to find some known face. Hundreds of orphaned children were trying to come to terms with this gross reality in feebly-lit makeshift tents. Some were lying with eyes closed but sleep was nowhere near. Some were eating from paper bowls; others were just staring at still others who did the same in return. Doctors and nurses were trying to forestall the battle against impending epidemic. He saw some familiar faces. He had definitely seen them. It was on that fine morning, the weather being exceptionally calm, his father had taken him in the boat. Christian fisherman Miller, Minsha, and Bapsha had greeted so lovingly that his head felt their blessing touch as their fishing boat passed along. He raised his hand towards them. They just looked. Memories had melted in the heat of the tragedy. Possibly they did not even recall him whose son he was. He just allowed his hand to drop down and caressed the little head of his sister.

Collapse of clean water supply had brought the camp to the verge of cholera, typhoid, and other diarrhoeal diseases of poor sanitation. Sickness loomed large in the air.

Still unburied bodies, petrifying, now placed in a nearby camp, turned dogs on the path of scavenging their once masters. A policeman, Sanjeevan, stood guard to chase away the canine onslaught. A month back his father had a row with another fisherman and this policeman had come to their house, had been extremely polite and helped to resolve the matter without aggravating the issue further. He remembered this kind, moustached face very well. He might help even now. He ran and tugged at his baton. The policeman did not remember him, but as a humanistic gesture took him to the stinking corpses so that he could recognise some acquaintance. He carefully left his sister outside and pinching his nose against shirt end to keep the stink away, inspected the corpses with utmost seriousness belying his little years on earth. He did not even know whether he was relieved or sad over not finding his parents there. The air, the stench, the corpses jolted his senses. When he came out, he was older in years in his mind.

Military field hospitals and temporary shelters were being set up to provide basic amenities, drinking water, clothes, and utensils. However, the extent of the damage along the 2000 kilometres southern coastline was so huge that the relief effort proved to be a molehill before the mountainous need.

He had taken up parental responsibility for his sister. Having been almost trampled to the pain of his bones, he grabbed some clothing and toiletries from the military relief site and rolling his sleeves up, sat to the task of bathing her under the tap, like his mother used to do to both of them, carefully recalling each and every nuance of the art. Kamlawati whom he recalled as the condescending elderly lady, who shared some anecdote with his mother in the vegetable market, appeared to recognise him. She sat to the task of bathing both of them. Like tiny puppies finding their mother in a stampede, they felt safest in the world. They had at least a fistful of the lost world. But then life had been jolted so terribly that everybody had lost footing. Before they could even come out of their initial childlike shyness for the casual acquaintance, the chaos grabbed the benefactor, and they lost her face in the unhitched humanity around. They were alone again in the crowd. For a while he considered to search for the old lady instead of his parents, but then looking at the disorder around dropped the idea.

A woman at a specially erected *pandal* was lamenting over her inability to save her elder son. She appeared brutally traumatised by her ordeal to save only one of her sons. The one-and-half-year old squeezed against her bosom, she was haunted by those flashes of memory as the perilously swirling and debris-strewn torrent snatched the other one away. Theirs was a little heaven on the palm-fringed shore before the 30-feet water wall brought overwhelming devastation. Their little hutment was twisted and snapped off its foundations as the Tsunami came crashing. The boy was clinging to her right hand while she grasped the infant with the left. Paddling for life, she knew their fate as combined three had been sealed, so in a stony ennui she allowed the waves to snatch away the boy, somewhere inside her knowing that she could have held onto him for some more time, but that surely would have been the peril of all three. As mother she had to salvage something out of the doom. She cursed herself for allowing him to be offered at the altar of twisted wreck all around. All silent and sullen now, she stared into the distance and safely cradled the baby in her arms, an expression of incalculable guilt written on every pore of her being. Mud-smeared school books, diaries, papers and photographs from some unknown house sprawled around her. She took up a photograph and stared at those unknown faces.

He saw Divakaran, a neighbour of theirs. His father had once a bloody fight with this man and got a bleeding mouth. He had hated him to the core. Even now he stared at him like a foe, least inclined to call out for help. After all, he was a true father's son. He had to prove loyalty to his father. In anger he even felt like throwing a pebble at the enemy but desisted somehow.

Bulldozers and tractors were mechanically laying bare the mud and wreckage to find bodies and bones. Bloated, purpled, and smashed bodies were washed up on the neighbouring beach. Aah, with unstinted brutality natured had devoured live things. The very same ocean that was a source of livelihood had angrily snatched everything from them in one sudden surge.

Nearby, a cement and plaster statue of the local deity had been miraculously left unscathed amidst all the terrible ruination around. The male deity's softly feminine features appeared aloof from the physical world mercilessly swallowed up by the tidal waves. Some people were still standing with bowed heads before this symbol of unflinching faith, praying for the safety of their near and dear ones. A lone coconut frond, survivor, proudly swayed its tattered branches on this serene sunny morning.

At a short distance, people of all religious hues were digging up graves in the *dargah's* graveyard. The mighty sweep of death had removed all post-death distinctions among the corpses.

A boy suddenly went gaga over his find of radio from the wreckage. His shrill, playful cry brought grimace on the faces of gravediggers.

All around fate had been catastrophically locked. The grey crest of seamlessly swelling waves found trees, boats, nets, and concrete from near the shore lying in rice fields two kilometres away.

That was all that remained: The little boy with his younger sister. He had forgotten that he himself was a kid; he just realised that his little sister was too small and needed care. She was sleeping, her head on his lap. He stared into the chaos, to salvage some hope, to grab some more fragments of their past, to build a rope of better hope to reach their parents.

A Hybrid Dream

* * *

He was in the seventh standard in the nondescript village school. One sultry afternoon, the class was yawning over the dead leaves on the sprawling ground surrounded by one-storeyed building around. The air was still, and so was time. The social science teacher was perhaps the only one to hear the sagging voice of a standing student as he tried to go through the chapter as well as the period. He was reading aloud a chapter from the political science book.

"Civil Services!" the burly teacher stomped his stick onto the ground, and many a student came out of the siesta, especially those at the far end of the rows.

The students came to their senses. "It's the highest job in the country!" he informed. "You can become one!" he accusingly pointed towards the one who was reading out the chapter in his moderately shrill voice.

Nobody in the classroom raised a suspicious eyebrow. Why? He after all had been the class topper since they remembered. Shackled by the ignorance and absence of real competition, they thought this 'intelligent one' could outwit anyone with as much ease as he did in class.

That was the first time he heard about the much coveted civil services. Sometimes he had heard his father, a government employee, referring to words like IAS. However, his teacher's proclamation did not leave a significant mark on his student soul. He was just a good student, nice and obedient, who at least would not prioritise wallowing in the pond with buffalos over doing his homework. Only this much! He simply knew that good students sit over their books more than they play errant after the school hours. They work really hard and cram up homework—even sometimes not understanding any bit of it—in order to keep people labelling them as the first student. In fact, they are extra eager to carry that tag at the cost of cut in their childhood fun and floridity.

Without much trouble to his *numero uno* status in the class comprising farmer's children, who cared more for anything else in the world except studies, he cleared matriculation. It was a very good first division and top position in the school with a percentage of 78. He was surprised when most of the villagers said resignedly he is good enough for a top position in the district. But then he will do better at the next level, they concurred. In that small world, they had come to believe in his *numero uno* position at any level, irrespective of the bitter realities of the harsh competition in the larger world.

His teachers liked him, so did most of the people around. The reason? He was thin, docile, slightly better than average looking, and enclosing himself in these boundaries—almost never allowing himself the littlest transgressions like many others of his age—he just crammed what the teachers demanded. Looking at the standard of the rest of the students, even the teachers' demand from him was not that high. They just expected him to stand first in the class, because to them he was an ideal student ready to take up the simple challenges thrown at him in that small almost uncompetitive world.

However, studying non-medical at the senior secondary school at the district city, he found himself continuously slipping down from his former position. It was a bigger and more competitive world. Reason? The unmindful and ever-relaxing science teacher at the village school hadn't taken the trouble to load their (and his) young minds with anything related to science. All they had done was to be asked to read the next chapter by themselves and learn the solutions to the problems all by themselves, no explanation whatsoever. Starting from a scratch and still cramming and not knowing many things, he managed to pass senior secondary with a good first division. He had not scored any position in class and there were many who had scored over him.

Much to his surprise, again those who knew him said the score did not showcase his true potential. Reason? They never found him doing anything un-studently.

"Science is too limiting!" some luminaries came forward with their protective suggestion. "Open him to the vast vistas of arts and humanities where 2+2 is not always equal to 4."

He thus did his graduation from a college where everything went right except for education; a place where only a decent studently behaviour could fetch the honour of a topper.

Again the teachers and fellow students provided him his favourite position. Somehow, he was always far from the real big bad competitive word. So always, some way or the other, came to occupy a position that made him the darling prince of the little dimly lit cave. Beyond was the bigger world with its higher parameters of excellence. Alongside, he had an interview for the NDA, the patriotic National Defence Academy. He had crammed well to clear the written part, but thanks to all his limitations, he was totally out of wits during the four-day gruelling session including psychological and physical tests to access the personality. Returning as a loser and still confounded over the ways of sophistication in the bigger world, they still patted with sympathy, “It’s due to the corruption that prevails in the selection process!” “Army job is just for average students. He’s an excellent student. A cut above the ones who just serve in the army. He is brand cut for the civil services,” others concurred.

His father, who had spent more time in reading books than anything else he had done, was a big fan of his habit of sitting over books for long hours. Similar were the proud sentiments of his grandfather, a former teacher. “Failure does not count much, as far as you are working to the farthest limit of your sincerity,” the wise old man told him many times. Being a good student was more important to them than succeeding every time. So it did not create much ripples when he fell short of good two percentage marks off first division in graduation. People simply had not lost faith in him. He had come to be taken as beyond all such little considerations of just marks and all.

“Forget about your marks! The IAS does not require you to score first division at the graduation level,” the whole lot around him egged on the sulking student. So without knowing much about the nitty-gritty of the toughest battle ahead, over-confident and a bit diffident by now due to excessive confidence put by others and lack of knowledge of the real ground position, he declared from the tiny study room on the upper storey in the village that he will clear the IAS from there itself; without equipping himself with an MA degree or coaching from one of the so many institutions in Delhi.

Optional subjects were to be chosen for the toughest exam in the country. He mulled over his level of calibre and intellect, and Philosophy stood out to be the natural choice as one of the optional subjects. The funny limitation of his perception came to surface an year later when he fell headlong at the first hurdles and lost one precious (out of the four) chance in the bargain. It was simply as good as fighting for just three chances as a general category candidate. They sympathised, “You failure does not mean your unsuitability for the job. It’s just that you missed coaching. That’s it!”

The moment others showed confidence in him and there he was involuntarily being drawn into another misstep. The reason? He thought that there is always one sure way to reach the next sub-target. However, the modern times are such that each and every step needs coolest of a smart calculation, objective deliberations and consultations from as large a group of well-wishers as possible. Cocooned in a lonely world, basking in self-inflicted glory, he rarely consulted anybody to expose any bit of ignorance he was wallowing in. So of course, quite naturally, he did not know the ground realities of the coaching quagmire spread out in Delhi. He simply read an advertisement in a newspaper and like a lamb walked into the den of some academic lion, who easily decided that he should take history as optional for the prelims, simply because the teacher himself specialised in history, apart from his repertoire of most of the subjects falling in the humanities domain.

Later, cramming historical facts in a class of 20 odd students, he and another fellow from Assam were the only two who qualified for the gruesome mains stage. Preparations for the mains involved another optional subject, general studies and essay. The teacher too liked his spirit, but despite best of his intentions the old man could not help him except boosting his already full quota of confidence. Still against all odds, it was a good performance. He just fell a whisker short of qualifying for the interview.

"You have definitely all that needs to be a civil servant. It was just that bloody coaching institute's resources were not enough to guide you properly. Go to such and such institute, they churn out IAS like you have the chaff cut from the cutter," the educated lot from among the little world of farmers suggested.

The coaching was expensive though. Then there was lodging and other little expenses. He was thus furiously drawing into the not-so-deep pockets of his father. His father was retired from the services as he slogged it out for the third time in Delhi. The lump-sum cheques did not stay in the family patriarch's pockets for too long. He remoulded the house; married the eldest daughter who had reached marriageable age long time back; another daughter waiting for marriage; younger son doing graduation; and the pride of the family having a go at the UPSC in Delhi. It was their little world and he the pole star of all their expectations, the panacea for his father's disappointments in his utopian world. The family patriarch sincerely believed the lives of all siblings will change for the better forever if his elder son became an IAS. He was preparing himself to forego thousand other miseries in life so far, only if this success landed up in the family.

It was his third attempt in as many years. This time he stood up to the people's expectations and qualified for the interview for the most coveted job in the country. The surrounding countryside in a diameter of 10–15 kilometres around his village gave a rapturous applaud like a deciding goal had been scored in a football world cup final. It was the last year of the old millennium, and the world in that countryside was famished for such academic glories, so people were very much eager to grab whatever landed up in their poor plates. A good proportion of these illiterate, semi-literate peasants, low clerical job holders, and police and military people believed he had already become a District Collector.

The last but the most crucial hurdle was still upface. The chairperson of his interview board was a former defence secretary, TK Banerjee. The five-member panel was surprised to find so much of confidence in this rustic guy. So in their subtly invasive ways, they tried to gauze the depth of his confidence. It was just a thin layer that he had forced upon himself and like a pack of cards he gave in. The qualities for the coveted post involve maturity of opinion, diplomatic conversation, behavioural sophistication, and so on. So once dislodged from the safe scaffolding of his confidence, he babbled miserably and gave shaking, stuttering one-sided imbalanced views to the burning issues of the day. The result was that again he had taken a longer, tiresome circuit to his failure. All this against some pinching facts: He had scored 53.4% in the written (a very decent score) and just 38% in the interview. But then failure too has bitter-sweet rewards, especially in the UPSC. It carries such a big name that even interview discards are taken with some respect of sorts. He too had many that came his way except the selection. "Don't forget that you are still left with one more chance!" people just won't lose hope in him. Needs are multi-fold in the countryside. People just look with the reverence of a devotee, if there is a chance for somebody to hit big and rid them off the rural miserable shackles. Everybody had his or her share of expectations from the lucky go guy. He was simply supposed to be a panacea for all the maladies.

This time he took a break in the sequence of years after three years of slog out. He tired himself out amongst the big heap of exam material collected over the years. Now it was a multi-pronged strategy keeping in mind all the three stages of the examination. Having crammed syllabus many times, he felt like a master of his subjects. The risk at the prelims stage did not occur to him even once. Life is all about the jolts that we get when we least expect. Shock exploded on the family's head. They had almost mortgaged their well-being against their civil services expectations. Now the full-stop had been slammed against their flowery sentence. It ended up meaning a big tragedy. His father could have literally died of the shock. It was unbelievable. Failure at the first stage and that too in the all crucial last chance! Unbelievable! Too cruel on God's part! The mourning lasted for weeks.

As they say nothing goes waste, the failure this time brought many tragic sufferings and songs from his sensitive heart. Of and on he had been writing poetry during the grind and grill of the exams. The predominant element was of loss, deprivation, failure, tears, and still more. He showed these suffering cooings to his father. His father still wanted to stick to his dream of his son making big. The father's literature-loving soul that considered the artistry of the written world to be the highest in the universe went gaga over these outpours. He declared that India was full of civil servants and every year they churned out more. How many poets and artists it produced? It can be counted on fingers. Poets and writers were thus more esteemed, loftier species. They thus again salvaged their next dream. Perhaps we have to set up and improvise our dreams; otherwise it becomes difficult to survive.

"Your failures have squeezed your soul to draw out creative juices!" his crestfallen frail figure tried to pump courage in his weak body and the son as well.

Poetry is too soft and wispy for the modern time's cackling phonetics. An endangered form, it needs to be supported by the poet's own vocal cords and pockets. The father thus did not dither from contributing a significant amount from his own pockets on the publication of his son's book of verses. Again these disjointed English words created huge ripples in the countryside pond. A book and that too in English! Well that was too much for the simple farmers around who croaked endless accolades like frenzied frogs in monsoon-fed pond. Eulogies did not stop pouring in for months. If we put the economics of the venture out of the way, he got everything out of the investment. Illiterate people just gleamed over the glossy cover page of the thin volume, holding it like a precious diamond carved by somebody whom they always expected to hit the top. Those who could join letters to make words, meaningful or otherwise, termed it as the work of a genius. Hardly anyone could draw out meaning of these utterly subjective and mournfully abstract, reflective outpours. The more they could not understand it, the more he earned laurels! So the next target was well set up for him to become at least a nationally recognised writer.

His fourth and final attempt to breach the impregnable fort of the civil services having been turned a disaster, it was a veritable anti-climax to the historic struggle. The indefatigable academician in him was blown off its feet by the shock waves. He still could not believe that he had fallen at the first hurdle after reaching the interview stage in the previous attempt.

Despite all reasoning, it was inexplicable and not acceptable at all. Still the chapter had to be closed now. Countless times the family was lost in the sea of gloom whenever the thought raised it head. And it did quite often. The more his sulking silhouette found him in a pensive, suffering trance, the more he wrote poems. However, very soon he realised the commercial unreliability of this panacea to his soul, his escape route from the deadly reality that was still too close to his sensitive heart.

"Try more, you have it in you to be a writer!" his father's ever-supporting baritone voice was like silver lining to the darkest cloud he had ever encountered.

Now when the glorious sun of the civil services had set for the first time, the people, at long last, seemed to be getting rid of their obsession of their big dream about him. He even felt that they were ignoring him with his failure. Far from the limelight, and slogging out like a sullen donkey, he wrote a big one, a work of fiction. The typeset itself hurt his father's financial interests still further, but given his taste he bore this literary bruise quite happily. Very soon he realised that finding a publisher is far onerous than writing the best book in the world. Within a couple of years, the enterprising and proud search turned into a desperate scramble.

However, the doors to the civil services had not been tight-bolted completely. Just a couple of lucky days from the final date of submission, some well-wisher told him about his home state PCS examination. Like a weary veteran, he cleared both stages of the written test. Nonetheless, at the interview stage the board's constitutional discretion ensured that nobody got selected except for the ones who managed to walk the political path of seeking blessings. The range of marks from as low as 5/75 to as high as 72/75 did not leave anything in the candidates' hands and made it an all about manoeuvre of those sitting in the corridors of power. This stage was 'make or break'.

The PCS is such a muddy river ridden with mighty crocodiles, putting one at risk—while seeking selection—whichever way one might decide to place an escaping foot to reach the opposite shore. Given his studious ways and almost nil political manoeuvring, he got minimum possible marks in the viva voce despite being one of the toppers in the written examination. People condemned his apolitical approach in not placating the bigwigs at the helm of affairs.

"Seeking political blessings for selection to the PCS is also a part of the examination," they tried to put some smartness into his dull hardworking head.

"From interview to the final selection you require the best of your 99% effort, and 99% of this 99% is political lobbying," a successful candidate from the previous batch tried some prudence with him. "Since they gave you almost fail marks in the interview, you need to work double hard to muster up pass marks on the loyalty chart of those in power!" he was soundly advised.

He did not get his mark-sheet of the failed attempt for the next six months. During this period the newly selected batch was consolidated and cemented into legitimacy. He meanwhile again rummaged through the syllabus because the notification for the next year's examination had already appeared in the newspapers. Then one day his mark-sheet stealthily crept in. Twenty out of seventy-five in the interview. Even twenty-five would have fetched him at least an HCS allied post. Taking lessons, now more than his studies he was thinking about the invisible manoeuvring to pile up his score in the viva voce column. Appeasing the CM was the easiest way out. The literary purpose arose to draw out again from his father's famished pockets who was by now nursing his conscience against him for the old pensioner had been forced to beg a private loan to get his second daughter married a few months ago.

With cooing literary stars in their eyes they self-published a book. It was a political dedication and it worked more than his studies across endless hours into the depth of nights. However, the favour by luck in one compartment was undone by a mis-stroke in another. Before they could join the state assembly was dissolved and elections were announced. When the opposition formed the next government with unbound vigour, it got busy in whitewashing all the rights and wrongs of the past government. The last government had been doling out jobs in thousands. "They are cheating the youth!" the present destiny-makers had shouted from their opposition benches. Now was the time to undo the former's doings. Many recruitments were scrapped and quashed. Like a cowering herd of goats the PCS batch took shelter in the judicial precincts. They pooled money to engage the best lawyers in practice. At considerable costs to their struggling resources they just got dates after dates. Who stands a chance against a belligerent government in such a high-profile case!? Nothing was progressing. Their fates had been sealed in some unknown invisible judicial quagmire. Every new dawn brought new rumours. Everything changed except for their fate. Even standing against the rumours became a gross challenge. It was a terrible vacillation between hope and desperation.

They didn't know that High Court functions as part and parcel of the state government's machinations. This reality was to unfold slowly over the coming months and then years. The government supported some disgruntled unsuccessful candidate in filing writ against the recruitment. The selected candidates were made a party to the case. Like a petty criminal he got his summons for being selected to the PCS. It had started as a tragedy and was now turning farcical. He celebrated his thirtieth birthday as a 'would be junior civil servant' as still the most optimistic of those around him continued to believe in the goal. For months he had been explaining that they were on a constitutional safe-footing. However, as the spool of law kept on upturning the endless thread for months and then years he had to stop this explanation.

"We'll surely be called for the job! But when? Even God does not seem to have a clue to it!" was his favourite refrain now.

Yes, we missed something! During the time he was waiting for his appointment, he was still writing. Nursing his injured conscience, subduing impotent anger, trying to escape the stranglehold of helplessness and consequent depression, he would say, "But I cannot waste any time. I have to utilise every moment!"

As the months piled up into years again people forgot him and his civil-servantship. It had been years now and in between they raked up memories sometimes. The case was as good as forgotten. It was better to forget it. The long wish seemed to have been buried very deep in the ruff and gruff of circumstances.

"Well son, here it might come at last!" his father seemed to say sometimes through the fading zeal of ill health and broken dreams.

Providence had not been kind to the old man. He had numerous memories to feel beaten by the greater forces beyond his control.

The fallen prince of the village was ultimately forced by failing financial resources and creeping requirements to take up the job of a content writer in a company in Noida. Past thirty and as part of the team of fresh graduates, he sometimes wished for the stroke of luck in the form of positive order from the court, or call it the government's nod explicitly or implicitly. He was in a lonely corner suitable to reflect over success and failure. He had a sour trail of experience behind him that allowed him to reflect over things, particularly the topic of success and failure, from different aspects and angles. The perennial query staring the face of humankind, the question of our role in shaping our destiny, or fate's invisible tentacles moulding us like a lump of clay into something predetermined, pricked him in its irritating acrimony.

"Whether we create circumstances; or circumstances create us?" he was mulling over the question, after being tossed by incidental waves and his particular efforts to reach a specific destination, and now churning out mundane words for online marketing portals and websites as a content writer.

A corporate job requires you to be a mini-politician. You have to *manage* the affairs. Just sincere hard work can put you in a tougher situation than the circumstances born of almost no work. Despite his tireless efforts, because he was just master of written words and worked hard, he had a long trail of failures. He now had this hesitatingly vouchsafed assurance that he would get his appointment later or sooner in life. Looking at that *would-be-success* he found himself in a twilight zone where the paradoxes intermingled like day and night; where contradictions seemed mixed up in a vague, mysterious but somehow explicable mixture. He kept his PCS hope alive while busy in the rote rut of churning out as many similar-sounding words as possible from 10 to 5 in the office. The dream drew inspiration from another dream his younger brother had while the initial setbacks to the PCS were shaking the ship of his destiny. His brother dreamt that he, the family prince, was standing in a row of PCS officers and when he saw the profile he could see him as a grey-haired, middle-aged man. Jokingly, they used to say that he will be a PCS officer well past 40 years of age.

His brother, in the eyes of their father had destroyed his career. There were enough chinks in his armour of careership that seemingly bore witness against him during charges and counter-charges.

"Despite being decently talented—he had scored 77% in B.Sc.—you are utterly, callously careless, complacent, uncompetitive that ruined your career even before it started!" the frustrated father voiced his agony, trying to latch onto some hope at the younger son's end, while the elder one seemed to have been taken in by the mundane forces of survival.

His younger brother bore all the best habits of a decent boy, had not picked up any wrong manner, strictly moral in all senses of the term, but surprisingly landed in a cocoon of impassivity after graduation. Right after graduation he had cleared the entrance examination for Masters in Information Technology from a prestigious university, but was lethargic to go for counselling for he simply had not checked about the results. At the turn of the century when the IT sector was a hatchling to become the behemoth that it later became, it would have been a fine start to career in the IT during the boom and bust that followed. He had asked his friends to find out about the results which they never did and he missed the bus. Of nice stature and fine height he was drawn to a career in the army; and appeared nine times for the SSB interview. All retired army officers concurred he had all it requires to be a commissioned army officer. Success however mysteriously eluded.

And here they were, the brothers, in a position to talk about luck, fate, destiny, and hard work. Talks can bury the deepest scars. These can even make life appear purposeful even in the face of endless gloom. These can even raise hope for the future. Talks help life in moving on. Talks are rewards sometime.

S:The mystery defies all explanation. Do we create circumstances that in turn prepare the outcome for us, or are we just poor products of our circumstances?

A:I think it's we who create the circumstances. Good or bad one must have the honesty and guts to own up the bouquets and bricks with equanimity. The logic is as simple as this: you get flowers if you sow them, and prickles if you plant thorny seeds.

The younger brother started from the assumption of himself believing in the doctrine of 'man creates circumstances' because the little negatives of the charges against him regarding career stood self-explained. Everybody knew he had the talent, but just had been strangely complacent, almost criminally negligent—as his father often accused him of—in not using it. These bitter accusations and chidings of the near and dear ones made the point clear that he had almost destroyed his career.

S: No, no it simply can't be that simple. If it was that simple then the world would have been either turned into heaven or burnt in hellish fire. Why? Because we have either good or bad plans. But it's not so. Life as a whole belonging to the whole humanity seems grinding in a paradox. And while it gasps in its multifarious ways we get an open-ended riddle. The very reason that the world is neither heaven not hell proves that we are not the makers of our circumstances in all our sovereignty. There are some factors. Human destiny does not operate on the physical science principle of input of energy and output in some form. Between our endeavours (good, bad, whatever) there is a zone of inexplicable circumstances that most of the time mould our effort, or influence in such a way that the outcome is sometimes good, bad, inexplicably tragic, tragically tormenting or heartfully ecstatic, and so forth.

A: I just give 10% to this so-called unseen hand in moulding our destinies. But for 90% of the rest we are responsible.

S: It's not the question of quantifying it. We can't compartmentalise circumstances and efforts separately, for these operate in a single field, in an inseparable domain. It's just like putting 10% ink in 90% of water. The combination changes the colour. I'm not for the one or the other. I just look at them working concurrently, simultaneously, still retaining their separate identities. It is simply a great mystery. Take for example, how many things are under our control in pursuit of a goal and how many aren't that either help us or let us down. Suppose you are preparing for the civil services. Even the very act of preparation is bound by certain conditions that could have very easily been otherwise. After all not all of us prepare for this examination. A particular set of circumstances guides and motivates us. Who knows a different set of circumstances would have motivated us to become a doctor, an engineer, or not any of these at all, like you have chosen not to be any of these. Even one's birth in a particular set of circumstances is beyond our choosing and is quite inexplicable. Let's come back to the preparations for the civil services. Guided by some chance idea, some intuition, some calculation either in your own mind or some of your peers, you choose 2/3 of syllabus and focus on it, considering it to be most important. Now whether you get topics from this chunk or not isn't in your control. Suppose you get the topics that you had prepared well, what you write during those three hours would be still bound by certain external forces beyond your control. Given the same information level, you might write at different levels of legibility and level of expression. It we move further into the incidental play of circumstances, I'd prefer to call it beautiful or chaotic interplay of incidental hits of various factors. The chance factor predominates visibly, invisibly. It arises at the time of evaluation of the answer sheets. I'm more particularly taking the example of social sciences (for in physical science there is 2 + 2=4, but even without this factual parameter there is great scope for subjectivity), there are chances that the write up might or might not match the evaluator's frequency. His mood—destructive, constructive, positive, negative, happy, sullen, and many other swings—are the externalities that decide your fate.

A: At least in my case I'm thoroughly convinced that I mis-planned or didn't plan my career. That was the blunder I committed in cold blood. Earlier I used to think that it was unfair on their part not to select me in the SSB, but now when I come to recall all those blunders I committed during the interviews my rejection appears credible to me.

S: These were no blunders at that time. These were just limitations bound to you by your circumstances. These might have been blunders in the eyes of the selection panel just as you consider them to be now. Had you known these, you would have definitely avoided them. But you didn't know. Do you think, you are solely and wholly responsible for your blunders that I term as simple limitations imposed on you by the circumstances beyond your control? No, because it was not you who committed these mistakes. It was a young human being—a product of circumstances—styled by your schooling, the environment you lived in, the foundation that these factors have provided you, and these in turn depend on varying circumstances, and this goes on and on linking perhaps all of us on earth in a mysterious shackle of circumstances. A giant rippling wave carrying causes, effects, good and bad in it, crests and troughs of shaping destinies, highs and lows. You were circumcised by your limited, mediocre schooling, carefree rustic society, and family where expectations seem to fulfil the job of career development.

A: It's a horrible theory. By this logic even the most heinous crimes do stand free, for it's not he who commits a crime but the circumstances that made him such stand accused in the dock.

S: Well, in a generalised form, good circumstances and good effort if happen to meet at a good time, at the cusp of productive chance, results are good. And if the reverse or the combination isn't right we see a struggle; as for the crime, hasn't somebody well said, "More than the sinner the sin is abominable!" This sin here is not only a noun; it is a whole phenomenon of negative circumstances linked in an interminable chain of cause and effect across globe or perhaps beyond. So more than the sinner, I pity the circumstances and the pathological agents that create such circumstances.

A: It means you purely support the idea that we are the products of circumstances.

S: Helpless puppets...made to dance on the stage of life! No, no! I didn't say that either. I just realise that there are enough examples to substantiate both assumptions. Quantity-wise one outshines, but quality wise the other inspires further. Furthermore, if the cords of circumstances had been totally under predetermined hands, we would have either reached the goal of universe or God would not have needed to create us at all.

A: But there can be two ways. Either the circumstances are fixed as per a pattern of premeditated destiny, or these occur haphazardly. The latter would rule out the possibility of the existence of God. Well, returning to the question. I think these are just opinions and analyses of success and failure. The victorious, in order to increase the stature and sheen of his achievement, will say that tiresome and unflinching effort definitely fetches good results; we are the makers of our destiny. The failed ones, on the other hand, will try to repaint the black colour on his face, blaming it on the adverse circumstances, luck or bad luck as you have it.

S: No, we just can't confine these two tormenting facts to mere reactions of two particular set of people on the outcomes of their efforts. In that case you forget to mention the people who have experienced both. In fact most of us face the fluctuation of both things in life. It only means these coexist in some mysterious combination. My initial effort to prove the existence of uncontrolled circumstances was just to bring you down from the singular stance of 'man creates circumstances'; it was not even to nullify your hypothesis. It was just to convince you that the thing is open-ended both ways. Both things do intermingle in such a manner to turn it sweet-sour and sour-sweet game that life is.

A: Then what is the way left out for us stuck up between these two incalculably heavy grinding stones?

S: Hope, expectations and desire of some favourable draw in your favour shouldn't hinder your practical, labouring foot on the path of your goal; while the tireless, sweating, heartful slogging on the path of your goal shouldn't make your eyes dreamless of good luck as well.

A: Just like you! Kept on slogging, walling up one breach after another of your limitations and flaws. But this toil didn't stop you from pulling at God's apron whenever you found time for rituals through your hymn-reciting entreaties! Luck! Both ends achieved. Well, maybe you are right. Life is too broad a thing to be underlined by one statement or the other. Maybe both provide us a track of existence on which we can chug ahead. Well, wish you all luck for your final set of circumstances! Wish the circumstances take such a draw in your batch's favour that your earlier result declared by the State Public Service Commission is authenticated by the court!

S: I have done my lot as circumstances allowed me to. With my limitations and capabilities, I've just tried to improve while furtively trying to draw from the pool of my efforts and the binding sinews of circumstances around.

Mr. K arrived on the scene. A silent slogger, he had lugubriously moved ahead on the path of his career without hurrying and without facing any perceptible troubles. In a cool and simply calculating manner he had become a software engineer. A man of moderate and amazingly balanced calibre, most of his finely pulled out cards had fallen in his favour. He had just moved ahead without any dissipation and burning of unnecessary energy.

A: What do you say of him? Did circumstances bless him, or he stoically went on creating them?

S: Oh...my? As many stories as there are people on earth. All with their varying interpretations. Just to keep the sanctity of what we have agreed upon, let's please close the chapter; otherwise it'll boom out of proportions. It has taken a lot of work by our tongues to fish out some meaning of the riddle. Now involve someone else with his own specific story and it will again change colours. The chameleon!

K:A... you have done that course in software science.

A: But who cares for distance courses?

K: I've just got a promotion. Now I'm in a position to recruit you as a paid apprentice in my company. Within a couple of years you will be earning a decent salary...if you work hard!

S: Here he arrives with a load of good circumstances for you.

And they laughed heartily.

That's life is. A string of fragmented dreams, falls, runs, talks, agreements and disagreements. It goes on. Unmindful of victories and failures. In its constant, permanent swipe, it takes away the varied, impermanent dust scattered around. Under the broom we rumble and tumble and make noise. Of agonies more often. Of happiness sometimes.

Broken Smile

* * *

Monsoon was here to foster environmental harmony and rekindle human spirits. All the colours available on a painter's palette were on display on the vast canvas of the sky. The spectacular skylark clouds approached as the harbingers of rain. The sky's apron was dark grey when it was drizzling; it turned silvery grey when gentle showers turned to heavy downpour. Clouds low and high; clouds in different cottony sculpted swathes; in different sizes and shapes. In the mornings when the sun lurked around the horizon these reflected a golden sheen; in the forenoon when the sun was curtained by high veiling of clouds, the lower bluish-grey fabric reflected half the usual brightness. In the afternoon pale grey handed over the baton to most exciting interplay of cloudy colours in the evenings. The atmosphere washed of its linen during the day, now the setting sun virtually changed these vaporous hangings into a vast kaleidoscope of colours. Baleful of clouds and colours in the sky's lap.

He liked this particular interplay of cloudy colours in monsoon skies: scarlet, purple, chocolate, orange, reddish orange, yellowish, and numerous other combinations. He often marvelled at the interplay. He mused about the unknown painter. Nature. He knew it was nature.

He stayed alone and even on nights did not miss the shades of dull white and black. In mid-September the monsoonal sojourn extended into autumnal sultriness of retirement like he felt about himself at this stage of life. And on this full-moon night, fluffy white lumps of milky clouds shone against the background of rain-washed bluish dark sky lit here and there by the brightest stars. The moon shone at the acme of its shape and brightness. He had companions in these beauties of the night. Staring into the distances of the night sky, he felt related to some destiny somewhere at the farthest end of the universe. Gauzy, lacy, transparent fabric of these clouds was drawn like a curtain; and when it passed over the moon, the full-faced beauty smiled through the veil like a shy bride at his excited bachelor self. A sort of lunar rainbow! A silvery hallo around the celestial beauty, fading into yellowish band, followed by a purple one. The night too had colours. He was happy while spending sleepless nights on his solitary terrace. On fluffy, broken cloud pieces, the moon threw yellowish and purplish dye as these fleeted forward driven by easterly monsoon winds. These and other such spectacles were his playmates for old age.

The much-pampered Chau Chun, as big as a leopard cat, fed on his affection and full-cream milk, was snoozing in his lap. It was afternoon. The sun must have been halfway across the perpendicular and the western horizon. A dark sheet of cloud hung horizontally, passing the sun just below its lower ring. Caressing the cat on its sleepy head, he heaved a sigh and looked at the spectacle and stopped for a moment in telling the story to the sleeping cat. A fountain of light burst down like a bright column of stage-light. The easterly breeze carried very low fluffy dark-grey clouds. Against the brighter upper background these appeared smoky puffs of a steam engine. As these passed the bright column of the sun's flashlight their smokiness became prominent. The unmindful pampered cat did not mind interruption in the story. He was telling the stories of his life. The story of a leopard that came his way while he was walking in a mountain forest.

"You go your way and I take care of my path," he confidently instructed the big cat, purporting to brag to the little cat and admonishing the little one not to mess with him.

During his heydays he had the guts to look straight into the eyes of a leopard without showing any signs of fear so that the big cat just moved away. He gave a loud burst of solid laughter as he concluded the story and started another about the bullying monkey whom he had reprimanded like a little child and the monkey had just retreated shamefaced.

He really liked his cat and believed in its ability to sense the paranormal. He was equally fond of its lazy sleepy ways. "If cats do not sleep for so long, their predatory instincts would chuck out at least some of the species!" he proudly explained sometimes to the neighbour.

It was a musty autumnal twilight. A desultory breeze blew across the Doon Valley. Day's white and night's black mixed to produce standard grey of twilight. In the yawning despondency, the thickly wooded Himalayan foothills, tiny ridges, rilled vales—a teasing bonsai of the mighty Himalayas—stood in tired silence. A big, vertical column of cloud stood alone in the sky like a skyscraper. The sun had dived deep beyond the hillocks; and this cloudy tower seemed to stand on its toes to have a look at the day's eye. The upper reaches of the cloudy column still reflected the faint ochre of the downed sun. It thus hovered over the tall strands like a big bulb. But then the sun dived still deeper below the horizon and the fluffy vapours handed over their last sheen to the folds of the autumnal night.

Chau Chun slipped out of his hand and he saw it crossing the compound wall and jumping into the forest's welcoming greenery.

"Haa haa *sala* hunter! Can't help it. Feed him the best *malai* in the world, he but still needs to go on nocturnal forays!" he laughed at the feline creature.

Many times the big cat just slipped out only to come at day-break next day with more love and more pampering at the master's feet.

Situated in a broad bowly depression at the foot of mighty father's Shivalik hills, the little nature's cove had Mussorie facing in the north at the crest of high ranges like a proud queen. Crisscrossing the tiny villages and hamlets the road circuited along the scattered peace of the area. Jakhan, Johri, Sinaula cradled in the lap of this bowl basking in impregnable peace. Along the road there were little general stores, tailor shops, mostly run by womenfolk, surprisingly little doctoring shops of registered unregistered medical practitioners, and PCOs. The rural community as you moved into the forest away from the main Mussorie road looking cosily safe in self-sustaining mode, and what is more important living in peace. Clouds got a full chance to vent out their rainy ecstasy here upon the welcoming canopy of broad-leaved *sal* forests. One would feel blessed by the atmospherics when enclosed by the wispy, dense, foggy strands of stratus and nimbostratus clouds stuck up in a little spur and thereby losing their essence in melting, surrendering abundance.

This little heaven, starting from Rajpur road at Jakhan, didn't give even the littlest clue to the veritable peace and tranquillity lying undisturbed a couple of kilometres into the forest and tiny hamlets. He was moving into this peace. Vehicle noise from the road to Mussorie died after him. He was headed to the forest. He walked with a limp. He had carried a scar on his left leg for the last 20 years, non-healing in nature and asking him to live another day with reinvented determination, take one more step at the cost of more pain. More than the pain in leg, his heart was aching. Chau Chun hadn't returned.

Tiny tidied neat homes, bungalows of retired army officials, local faces showing mild mongoloid features, undisturbed flora and fauna, it was all spread around him with the sense of normalcy like you expect on any day. But Chau Chun was not to be found.

"O Sahab...O Sahab...for God's sake don't walk so much!" he was harked at from behind.

With a resigned sideway glance he looked at the follower and slowed down for the person to catch up with him.

The follower was a very strongly built stocky old man. Now he was a peculiar mass of muscles mired in ageing pulp. From looks and the way he wore his clothing anybody would have dubbed him a lunatic. However, it wasn't really so. The concern that he showed for the limping man belied all such possibilities. He was carrying huge sacks in both hands. His right leg tied in a rag was badly lacerated. With stony nonchalance to his condition he was carrying on his march towards his destination to the next hamlet. He knew the sahib. On more than one occasion he had received some retired ware as a mark of the kind man's large-heartedness.

The old man took a vow to find Chau Chun even if it meant looking every nook corner in the bushes of the forest around. The master but knew that nothing sort of a personal search will satisfy his aching heart.

He walked on calling *Chau Chun, Chau Chun*. He wanted the cat back at any cost. He just couldn't afford to lose this axis of his fatherly affection. The sky will lose its colours if he didn't find his pet, a family member rather. He searched and searched, and returned all tired with the fatigued rays of the sun at the day-end.

It was raining at night and he couldn't sleep. Unable to stop himself he set out in the dark to find the listener to his stories. It was windy and a gust, not showing any respect to the elderly, blew away his umbrella, leaving him open to the storm's fury.

The next day found him sick and the wound still worse. In semi-consciousness he was telling the stories of his youth, when he had been healthy and was not alone because he participated in the mundane mad race. His muffled words. Nobody to hear. Not even Chau Chun.

A Small World around Her Feet

* * *

Her beautiful bluish eyes were sparking with reflections from swift torrents of the Ganges. Standing by the support posts of Ram Jhoola, the huge suspension bridge in Rishikesh, she took a deep view of the spiritual panorama like she had so many times since her arrival, believing the place to provide her spiritual succour, a food for her ruffled soul.

On the steps below an old *Sadhu* was washing brass image of Nag Deva in the sediment laden waters of the Ganges spiritually ebullient in the rainy season. She marvelled at the way his frail fingers, charged with devotional fervour for his beloved god, were busy in creating a shinier visage for the Godly metal. He seemed to be lost in a musical prayer; the rhythmic ripples in the holy mother chanting songs for him. His frail body, long locks of hair and beard all busy in devotional unison. Swiftly flew *Ganga Maiya* with the crop of its erosion work in the Himalayas.

With the enthusiasm of a spiritually spellbound foreigner she took a snap and the flash of light seemed to have disturbed his prayer. He stood erect holding the rag with the help of which he was using the abrasive power of the sediments to make his faith shinier and newer. The talisman of his faith was shining in the sun. The flashlight's noisy whisper distracted his devotional work. In the distance a conch shell blared with devout urgency. He looked at her and a faint smile surfaced on his lips lost in rag tag beard. It then changed to laughter. The bearded laughter was a peculiar one and made her uneasy. People's voice, music in the temples, dull vehicle sounds, incense and spiritual fervour sashaying over the breeze riding Ganges torrents all appeared to have stopped for a moment. She was clad in an Indian way, *kameez* and *salwar*, and looked resplendent with her curves and angelic features. For a fraction of a second he stood like a hypnotised soul.

Uneasily she moved onto the great bridge devotionally named Ram Jhoola. Vidhut followed her like a quadruped and taking a pity on the invalid she stopped. A local guide had translated the invalid's story for 50 rupees. The invalid beggar was born with limbs that just allowed him to crawl on the four. He was born at 'Pili Bheet' she tried to recall the name but missed. He was 20 years of age now and had left home a good seven years back to sustain himself on all fours, while the more important bipeds scampered over him across the narrow swinging bridge that swayed over the majestic sprawl of the Ganges below. He spent his nights in the verandas of *dharamshalas*, making it a point to stick around as long as possible till he was kicked out along with the dogs. When his luck struck best, he even landed with 100 rupees at the end of the day. After hearing his translated story, she had given a nice blue 100 rupee bill as she took a snap, and he had taken it as the modelling fee. After all he was special. As she walked up to him he expected another modelling assignment. But she passed with the best smile ever possible that took him off all his fours.

The devotional world on both sides of the Ganges carried on among the bathing steps, temples, rest houses, *dharamshalas*, ashrams and bazaars buzzing with religious items.

For a whole month the rain Gods had been dripping in their pleasant fury. Even though it was not cold, still after so much of water and dampness it is desirable to have sunrays.

"For the last one month so much water has fallen over us that I feel like a fish permanently relishing the sea!" a saffron clad *babaji*, flaunting his English commented as he looked sideways while crossing her on the bridge.

She was tempted to look back but knew the risks a beautiful white woman carried in this part of the world, and quite contrary to her open nature she did not turn back. Such looks, simply born of curiosity, are misinterpreted very easily as *green signal* for a fling. She thus avoided the trouble.

The incense-drenched world on both sides of the great river appeared slowed down and subdued by the rains. Deep foggy clouds did endless rounds amidst the surrounding little vales and very easily found pretence to unburden themselves of whatever water they carried. From the surrounding ridges, water was perpetually slipping down to copiously feed even the tiniest sub-tributaries of small rivulets further feeding moderately big rainy drainage and the latter finding their way to the big river.

She needed this type of small place solace, far away from New York where the big world had piled up enough restlessness in her to go footloose. A chain smoker she had not smoked even once since she arrived here a week back. It was nothing sort of a miracle and she was looking forward to add many more such soothing miracles.

She loved this seemingly ancient world and more so in this antique shop. It was fragrant with anciently aesthetic fragrance. There were old paintings, saucers, sculptures, brass tortoise, frogs flat on their bellies, dogs, puppies, candle stand, carved silver vessels, a huge cone (God knows for what purpose), lizards, scales, compasses, trays, tumblers, beautiful vases, lamps, chimers, the oldest gramophone she had ever seen, horse riders, Gods and Goddesses, soldiers, crockery, Victorian trinkets, copper bronze and silver coins, a big painting by a Britisher, a Harappa type of violinist sitting on a chair, lamps of various shades, a marble mermaid, horse bust, electroplated punch bowls, an old rusted gypsy pan, old time watches, and so forth. She tried to observe each and everything. It was a pleasant mess. It was more exotic than her city-cramped senses could afford to see, forget about buying. She started taking pictures.

The attendant chided in her broken English, "If all take photos who buy!?"

She was embarrassed and to avoid further embarrassment bought an old replica of a boat. She also wanted to buy the British period copper bugle but found it too big and abandoned the idea.

As she came out she met the gaze of that very same *Sadhu* whom she had seen washing the bronze God in the sandy waters of the river. His face bore a strange look. She got the pin-prick of scare and lowered her eyes to sneak past into the jostling crowd in the narrow bazaar street. She was apprehensive. She knew the risks the foreigners faced in India. But possibly it was incidental and probably the woman in her was exaggerating the risk. She had many muddled thoughts in her mind as she again found herself lost and spread out in the unknown world of agonies and ecstasies.

****

Sitting by a small roadside tea stall the old man in ascetic robes—but real earthly self of worldly needs clearly visible through the charity-expectant look—was asking for a packet of biscuits. With a fistful of coins he had purchased himself tea and retrieved a bit of honour, but to carry his will further, i.e., tea and biscuit both, he still needed the favourite aid of asceticism, i.e., asking for alms.

"Can't see, lost my specks, now who would take mercy on an old man like me?" he pleaded.

Oh thou holy place! So many disbanded, discarded, and obsolete human beings take shelter in your teeming streets laden with religious fervour. Incense, chanting, charities, soul-salvaging rituals, flying locks, saffron robes—it's a world in itself catering to the needs of as many as they dump their poor selves here. In between mother Ganges washed away littler, muck, and sins without any complaints.

Somebody bought him a biscuit packet and the religioner opened his worldly identity. "I'm from Pushkar in Rajasthan."

He was on a month's tour to the orphanage here. However, arriving here he might have calculated his chances better at this place than home because it literally won't even raise any issue in his family if he didn't return at all.

"Let me see if there is a man of God who can get me specks!?" he quaked in pleading fervour, trying to pull the strings of devotee's salvage-seeking spirits.

"You are asking too much *maharaj*! It'll cost about 100 bucks, so you should ask in instalments, collect your money and then buy to see this beautiful world!" a fat gentleman mused.

"There is a place but from where you can get one in charity," another person wrote hastily an address on a chit of paper and the old *sanyasi* proffered a blessing over his head.

This world is a little merry-go-round thing. The very same person who had taken the pains to write the address of a charitable organisation found the old man trying to invoke kindness in devotion-smitten souls walking over Ram Jhoola. "O men and women of God, can't you spare something for my stomach treatment. It pains...day in and out. They say an operation is required. Please-please I die daily of this pain. God will bless you with pleasures unimaginable if you help me relieve from this pain!" the sonorous notes of his pleading voice mixed into the cool breeze blowing over the waters of the kind, cleansing river.

The address giver moved towards him with a meaningful smile. The charity seeker but was unmoved and stood solid with his present version of need. "It's not that I just survive for free. I work as well. I wash brass utensils of that big temple over their!" before the gentleman could start with some lesson in morality and ethics of charity, the old man put up his defence guard.

"You had told me that you'll directly go to the charity shop, get your specks and leave for your home!" the gentleman seemed up for some jest with the old man.

"Yes I'm gathering fare to reach the spot you mentioned. And to get money here you have to have a good reason, so this stomach ailment," the old beggar was trying to salvage some respect.

The gentleman gave him 20 rupees and asked him to take a shared auto to reach the place before it closed for the day. Possibly he wanted to accomplish one pious deed in the day at any cost! He literally shoved him to the auto stand and deliberately hid himself around some corner to see the old man's chain of action.

The old *sanyasi* was suddenly spellbound and looked at her feminine majesty as she passed at a distance unmindful of the gaze that was anchored on her with particular interest. The hiding gentleman could not hold it anymore and came angrily chiding, "Tricky old man, befooling people with need of specks and here you have all eyes for that beautiful white woman!"

****

Vidhut, the invalid from birth, had a sort of office on the Ram Jhoola, crawling on all fours, wearing *chappals* in his hands and another pair tied on both knees of his malformed little stumps of legs. As the devotees came gazing into the majestic torrents of the holy river, he pulled at the strings of their conscience, coming as a means of their salvage, a means of drawing God's blessings by being kind to him. Crawling like this in the spiritual path of the pilgrims he daily earned 80 to 100 rupees. These days he visited his family very rarely.

Pili Bheet in Uttar Pradesh was a totally different place and his parents almost satisfied with God's verdict to have him at the holy site as an instrument of Godly blessings for the luckier chunk of humanity. Yesterday he had a strong sense of purpose in life and rented a room for rupees 400 a month. He felt like respecting himself more, and draw more respect from the *dharamshala* caretaker who had kicked him out the previous day.

Once again her angelic face was gathering all these interesting tit-bits from him through another paid translator, a local street urchin who had picked up smatterings of English to get some pocket money in the bargain. The Ganges was creating stormy ripples below the mighty suspension bridge drawn from corporeal to the incorporeal. A man with puckered face watched with jealousy and interest.

"I have helped him many times, saved him from the policeman who try to drag him off the bridge. They in turn hit me with batons. I still carry the mark!" desperately he tugged at the local interpreter's shirt to translate it for the Madam and get some attention on him for being good to somebody whom she liked to talked to.

"It's a fracture. You must have got it while stealing something," the translating boy just snubbed him in rough Hindi and shoved him away.

Surely, Vidhut was in news among the beggar group on the Jhoola.

"These white people are so strange that she might even adopt you and take you as far as America, the heaven!" one of his fellow beggars was creating the celestial world of luck beyond imagination.

And of course Vidhut hated the particularly interested stare of the old beggar from Rajasthan whenever she passed along. Had he approached her like any other beggar then it would have been normal. But the old *Rajasthani* was particularly drawn to her persona and still did not go for what is expected, i.e., alms or charity, but simply looked from a distance. It convinced him that the old man was drawn to her in a hateful way. And he cursed him for that.

****

If you are a foreigner and happen to be at some pilgrimage place, you are then supposed to enjoy the devotional and spiritual fervour of the place, however tedious the exercise might come to you. The experience is, however, recommended.

After the *Satsang* organised by Swami Ramsukhdev ji Maharaj, in which innumerable chants and hymns and preaching interventions passed over her bent head, she was wearing her shoes crouching on the ground. A truly, we mean really religious persona decked in religiosity for the visual delight of it, priestly hand moved and was placed on her head with all the showers of this and the other world. She was awestruck looking up at his religious make up. It was amazing and impressive from all corners of this world.

"Are you from England?"

"No *Maharaj* I'm from America," she had learnt to address the people attired as such with this word.

"Need a place to stay? You can stay here at the ashram. A very nice room!" he pinched slightly at her arm, straightway driving a strange intimacy.

She got to the immediate fringe of some vaguely lurking danger. The Ashrams vied with each other in having more and more white skins staying there for more impression and more gains in more than one form. It was a big industry to cater to money and carnal desires. She was shocked beyond apprehension and found herself going along with him. Now he was becoming more and more direct.

"This Godman is a ruffian...bastard...Has fun with girls staying at the ashram," again he pinched at her arm mischievously, his voice now shaking with some fearful, natural passion.

She was scared beyond all her limits, even scared to scream loudly, after all these people are revered even more than God. She had seen hundreds falling at their feet since her arrival.

"You know we as humans should love each other. Oh, you don't know how much I have liked you since I saw you. I'm blessed to have your company," he was becoming more direct taking her shell-shocked state to be her consent. Or had she been drawn into some trick of hypnotism?

By now she could feel the pangs of lust effulging from his holy robes. But she was scared even to say something, forget about shouting. Vidhut just lunged forward in his dusted world, straying around like a puppy among the stampede of the bigger world above.

"*Maharaj, maharaj*...this life is wretched...I won't let you go of your holy feet, bless me...I'm a worm and die every minute, please, oh please..." he was squirming like in fits and howling so piteously that even dozens stood around to have a look.

She regained her senses and just took the fraction of a moment to sneak out of the place, but not before looking into those dull dark eyes of the invalid, knowing fully well that he had done it deliberately to help her sneak out of the difficulty.

****

As per the norms of the society set up according to the appearances, we have to call him a lunatic. Her attention was drawn by the oddity of his forlorn situation. He was sitting on a heap of stones and a rimmed paramilitary hat perched safely on a towel wrapped around his 'lost somewhere' brain. To add more to his otherworldly attractiveness, he had wrapped a polythene sheet around him as if to guard his identity about which the bigger world wasn't concerned anymore. Much to her surprise he somewhat positively responded to her accost. Saggy beard around the jaw-line moved to faint vestiges of smile on his face which appeared that of a Sikh. The smile seemed like an iota of appreciation for the swathes of sympathy on her beautiful features. He was eating soybean seeds from a packet. Sandals picket out from somewhere; a little school-boy's tie; a sweater; a bag full of empty bottles and packets—it was all that remained to him in this world. In his pockets he had a torn diary and a pen.

"What is your name...name, name!" she treated him like a fellow human being, emphasising on 'name'.

It was like talking to a stone, to something, to some empty bottle in the garbage pit stinking with all the muck in the world. We are sure he had not been called so particularly for long with such specific attention. He even got scared, getting into that evasive action to avoid a hit on the face. But then the beauty on her face was too assuring. His petrified eyes groped into the depths of her blue eyes. Sanity lurked deep from the unfathomable well of his miseries.

"M...M...Meer Singh!" his eyes closed under the impact of the push he gave to his crippled mind to draw sense for this beautiful creature from the outer world.

The way he had responded he seemed a case of somebody who had lost human sympathy rather than his mind.

She could recall Vibhut so particularly emphasising the place he was born to the translator. People carry the place of their birth even more importantly than even their names.

"Where are you from?" she was trying to make him understand the question more through gestures.

He kept on muttering some name again. Perhaps he was telling the name of the place. Since she was not aware of the local names any guesswork in that direction was of no use. He was trying to say the same word with a huge effort of his salivating mouth. Having failed to go any more, he gestured with his finger towards his head and finally like the dreamy world of an opium-fed man, he circled his finger over his hand to indicate he was mentally crippled. He had conveyed his identity.

"Education, education, studies, studies, books, school, school..." she held onto the iota of sanity that the anchorage of her sympathy had caught onto from across the unknown dark gloomy sea of his oblivion.

"Matric!" the effort found spittle dandling across the tufts of beard on his chin.

Again he circled his finger over the hat. Well, that was his identity now.

Possibly, drinking had something to do with his mental disorder for he picked up an empty cold drink bottle and muttered, "Bad, bad, hicc!!"

His eyes contorted with fear and he was looking now at something behind her back. Scared herself she looked back and was terrified beyond imagination. So it was not incidental. That smile by the riverside when he was washing that idol and that appearance by the trinkets shop, it wasn't just simple coincidence. He but seemed even more scared than she herself was. Realising this, her fear turned more of a curiosity. The man stood there with folded hands. Before she could even react she saw Vidhut crawling up from behind and he straightway lunged into the old *Sadhu's* legs, misbalancing him and toppling him on all fours. He was shouting like anything, raising a scare, drawing people's attention, trying to save the princess from the danger that this old bad man, more beggary than anyone else in the semblance of saffron religiosity, presented. Vidhut was crying as he hit the man and clawed his face. The lunatic man also got up and unnerved by a strange sense started stomping the ground like an angry ape. He too started beating the old man with his hat. It was a real melee and before the people got together to disentangle the three of them, Vidhut had shown enough crawling clawing heroism to thoroughly roughen up the old man who was shaking and crying with convulsive sobs.

"All I wanted was a photo with her, *hai hai* send this rascal to jail, this crawling villain has shaken up my bones, police-police, is there any... is there a God-fearing man to take side of this old *Sadhu* who has been unjustifiably beaten up, *hai hai*, look at this worm who wriggles around the *firangi* woman!" he pointed to Vidhut.

She had already left the scene. People saw them going together. She was walking at a moderate pace and he crawling as fast as he could manage. Many tourists clicked a picture of this beautiful moment. There was mud across the narrow path. She put all her strength to lift his mud-smeared body, getting herself soiled in the effort, and put him to the other side. People applauded.

Somebody cheered, "She might have even fallen in love with him, these are crazy people, white people, expect the most daring from them!"

www.ingramcontent.com/pod-product-compliance
Lightning Source LLC
Chambersburg PA
CBHW062137160726
48282CB00027B/850
* 9 7 8 9 3 8 6 1 4 8 2 6 1 *